International P₁

MW00399773

"If there were more people like Jón Gnarr the world wouldn't be in such a mess."
—OLIVER SACKS

"[*The Pirate*] is a highly readable book, enormously powerful and particularly heartfelt. ... A book not soon forgotten."
—KOLBRÚN BERGTHÓRSDÓTTIR, *Morgunblaðið*

"He's a bit of a genius, that Jón."
—EGILL HELGASON, Icelandic National TV

"The strength of *The Pirate*, the second volume of Jón's memoirs, is its sincerity: the boy's point of view and the narration shaped by his inner voice. This sincerity makes it easy for readers to put themselves in his shoes, even when he breaks into a kindergarten night after night, urinates blind drunk on the floor of a police station, steals from his parents and raves at his teachers. He succeeds remarkably well in describing the thoughts and reasoning of someone at odds with his environment, who in fact is hounded and persecuted."
—FRÍÐA BJÖRK INGVARSDÓTTIR, Víðsjá, National Broadcasting Service

"By turns funny and despairing (Gnarr had ADHD and severe dyslexia as a child), as well as providing a glimpse into Icelandic culture beyond Björk, *The Indian* is entertaining and enlightening."
—CARY DARLING, *Fort Worth Star-Telegram* (Critic's Pick)

"A dark memoir full of black humor that details the author's painful experiences as a child unable to fit in due to struggling with learning and emotional disorders, [*The Indian*] illuminates the struggles that come from being considered broken. Written with cleverly shifting points of view, this haunting narrative invites readers to consider the trauma of an outcast child."
—WORLD LITERATURE TODAY on *The Indian*

"Certainly my favorite mayor. No competition, in fact."
—NOAM CHOMSKY

More International Praise for Jón Gnarr

"Gnarr's finest accomplishment in [*The Indian*], surpassing others in the genre, is the absolute immediacy of the childhood experience…Gnarr returns those emotions—all the emotions of childhood—to their context, adding the suffering of learning them, finding new restrictions, fearing ones you don't know, and we relate to them once again. This is the gift of *The Indian*, the way that it makes the child, our child-self, alive, close to heart and mind, in all his pain and his happiness. *The Indian* is brave in this gift, and dares me to be brave too, enough to find the child of my past and make him present."
— P.T. SMITH, *Three Percent*

"*The Indian* is refreshingly original because it not only speaks to a very specific subset of people who have learned to cope with, or are learning to cope with their learning disabilities, but also anyone who has ever experienced feeling like an outcast or alone in their childhood, aka: Everyone."
— YOUNG ADULTS BOOK CENTRAL

"Let 'normal' people have their 'normal' heroes. The rest of us have Jón Gnarr, and the world's a better place for it."
— MICHAEL SCHAUB, *NPR*, on *The Indian*

"Jón Gnarr is a great man who I believe has helped change our opinion of politicians. By doing it his way he has shown that it is possible to not only channel the will of the people but also to influence it positively."
— YOKO ONO, *on awarding Gnarr the Lennon-Ono Grant for Peace in 2014*

"Jón Gnarr has given the mayor profession a new human earnesty with radical stand-up style, and has chiseled away the stagnancy in that post with explosive humor."
— BJÖRK

"Painful yet intensely beautiful."
— NANCY O'DONNELL, Rochester (NY) *Democrat & Chronicle*, on *The Indian*

THE
PIRATE

—

Jón Gnarr

WRITTEN WITH
HREFNA LIND HEIMISDÓTTIR

TRANSLATED FROM THE ICELANDIC BY
LYTTON SMITH

DEEP VELLUM PUBLISHING
DALLAS, TEXAS

Deep Vellum Publishing
3000 Commerce St., Dallas, Texas 75226
deepvellum.org · @deepvellum

Deep Vellum Publishing is a 501C3
nonprofit literary arts organization founded in 2013.

Copyright © 2009 by Jón Gnarr
Originally published in Icelandic as
Sjóræninginn by Forlgaið in Reykjavík, Iceland, 2009
Written with Hrefna Lind Heimisdóttir
Published by agreement with Forlagið, www.forlagid.is
Translation copyright © 2016 by Lytton Smith
First edition, 2016
All rights reserved.

ISBN: 978-1-941920-20-6 (paperback) · 978-1-941920-21-3 (ebook)
LIBRARY OF CONGRESS CONTROL NUMBER: 2015946456

—

This book has been translated with financial support from:

 MIÐSTÖÐ ÍSLENSKRA BÓKMENNTA
ICELANDIC LITERATURE CENTER

—

Cover design & typesetting by Anna Zylicz · annazylicz.com

Text set in Bembo and Letter Gothic.
Bembo is a typeface modeled on typefaces cut by Francesco Griffo
for Aldo Manuzio's printing of *De Aetna* in 1495 in Venice. Letter Gothic was originally
designed by Roger Roberson for IBM sometime between 1956 and 1962.

Distributed by Consortium Book Sales & Distribution.

Printed in the United States of America on acid-free paper.

CONTENTS

BLACK DEATH

There was a knock on my bedroom door. I looked up. Mom opened the door. She had a downcast expression.

"Come have a chat with me, Jón."

She wasn't angry. I hadn't done anything. I'd even been unusually quiet. But whenever I heard that tone in her voice it meant she blamed me for something, like the time she found cigarettes in my pocket. Her voice sounded dry and windy. This time, though, she clearly wasn't angry. She was almost friendly. She must have some news. I followed her into the kitchen and sat at the kitchen table. What was up? What did she want to tell me? Was she about to tell me I was adopted? That I wasn't my father's son, but the son of the famous Icelandic author Þórbergur Þórðarson? I'd long suspected that. I was so very like Þórbergur. Maybe Dad was always so weird around me because he wasn't my real dad. And maybe he was always so annoyed at Mom because she'd cheated on him. Understandable. Perhaps I had other siblings out there. But maybe it wasn't that at all. Could she be about to tell me they were going on vacation, and they were inviting me along? I never got to go anywhere with them because I was so much trouble. Recently, though, I'd been very calm. Could it be that Mom was rewarding me for being good by inviting me abroad? But where? Mallorca, perhaps.

I'd need to get myself some cool swimming trunks and a necklace with my name on it. I'd go to the beach and have my picture taken with a parrot on my shoulder. Or were we going to London, instead? Mom had visited her friend in London several times. Now, perhaps, I'd get to go along with her. I'd rather go to London than Mallorca because I might get to meet a real punk and go to some gigs. And then I'd be able to buy some proper punk gear. I couldn't imagine punk stuff was easy to find in Mallorca. I waited and waited for Mom to start talking. But she was just silent, friendly but awkward.

"What?" I asked, excited. I almost started laughing in anticipation.

"Grandma's dead."

My dreams of sunny beaches and bustling urban life vanished with the wave of a hand. I wasn't going anywhere. Þórbergur was in all likelihood not my dad. And Grandma was dead.

"Is she?" I asked to say something.

"Yes, she died during the night."

I hadn't thought about Grandma much, or at all, since she went into the nursing home. I hadn't been keen to visit; it seemed distinctly discomforting, going to see her. Not least because she'd become a bit confused by the end. She'd gotten so old that she'd started dying a long time back.

I'd known for a while Grandma would die soon. I knew it would happen. My grandmother was named Guðrún Guðmundsdóttir. She was born on April 1, 1888 at a place called Arnkötludalur, in the Strandir region. I don't know where that is exactly. She had eighteen siblings. All of them were dead. Most of them died soon after being born or when they were still children. That's how life was in the old days. People died all the time. When Grandma was seven, she lost her mother. She was from another world, a shadowy, ancient world where it was always cold and everyone was wet and either hungry or very ill the whole time. So they tended to die sooner or later. The men drowned, one after the other. Those who survived were hunched by life's adversities. Like Grandma. I never knew how she made it through such a miserable life. Maybe it was because she was so good. Maybe it was her faith in God. Maybe she didn't know anything better. Whatever it was, I counted myself lucky to have been born when I was. I was horrified when Grandma told stories about life in the country and about when she was young. She had been dying for a long time. Pitiless old age ferried her away—her spark weakened and flickered. She grew ever more tired, had trouble walking. She started to forget things. Sometimes, she forgot who I was. Sometimes, she thought I was my dad. *It's me, Jónsi*, I'd say again and again to remind her. Sometimes she'd realize, but more often she didn't. She'd keep asking for news about the farms or tell me she'd seen people I knew were long dead. She'd wandered back to a time that seemed to me like seventeen hundred and sour cabbage. It distressed me to see Grandma ebb away like this. Sometimes she got anxious about something she imagined was going to happen. Those times, she'd want me to ride out to some farms to warn people. I felt awkward, not knowing how to respond. I tried explaining that it was just her mental deterioration, but that didn't compute. So I just tried to play along.

"Where are the children?"

"Um, they're outside, playing," I said, encouragingly.

"They're not allowed to go down to the estuary. The current is too strong."

"No, they're nowhere near it, Grandma," I said, still being encouraging.

She was sure the woman sharing her room was plotting to go through her stuff and steal from her. It was very awkward when she talked about that, but also a bit funny. Funny in an absurd, tragic way: the woman who shared the room with her was, in reality, paralyzed—she lay motionless in her bed. But Grandma was blind, so she couldn't see that.

"What are you doing there?!" Grandma hissed.

"I'm not doing anything, Guðrún, dear," the woman wearily answered.

"I can see you! What did you take from the drawer?" The paralyzed woman sighed sadly while I shook and trembled, stifling laughter at life's absurdity.

And now Grandma was dead. I didn't know what to say.

"Don't you find it upsetting?"

"Of course."

But I didn't think it was upsetting. I thought it was just normal. People get old and die. Grandma had looked forward to dying. She wanted to die. So it definitely wasn't upsetting; if she were alive, she'd be very pleased to be dead. It's one thing when people die young or from a terrible disease like my uncle Gulli, who got lung cancer. But even he was fairly old. It was still miserable, though. I was actually almost glad that my grandmother was dead. It was what she wanted. I was more sorry we weren't going abroad together.

Death has three stages. The first is the physical death, which occurs when the heart ceases beating. The second stage is the wake, when friends and relatives see the dead person for the last time. The third and final stage of death is when someone mentions the name of the deceased for the final time.

Funerals are weird rituals. Death unites people. It's like the pain of having lost someone to death stops being rote and distant—suddenly, it's present and for real. People's eyes meet, they cry together, and embrace one another. At a funeral, people reveal sides of themselves they never show anywhere else, except perhaps at home, behind closed doors. They openly weep in front of each other. They give deep hugs, even if they're not the kind of people who usually embrace. At Christmas and birthdays, everyone says hello with a handshake. Not at funerals. Death draws forth the life in people, forcing them to take down their masks and show their true faces. People who haven't spoken in years start talking to one another again—facing death, people often realize that their everyday concerns are inconsequential. Old enemies make truces and new friendships blossom. Death is something we all share. He ambushes us all. Eventually. No matter how rich, beautiful, or strong we are. No one escapes death.

I went to several funerals over the years. Many of Mom and Dad's siblings have died. I preferred being at funerals with Mom's family. Especially once people start drinking toasts: they'd begin to laugh and tell stories about the deceased.

I was never aware of Mom or Dad expressing grief. I'd never seen them cry from grief. Perhaps they'd both seen so much sorrow over the years that they'd stopped being affected by it. Maybe they were just mourning in their own way. Mom would be silent and reflective. She'd sit and listen to the radio, chain-smoking. She was quite the tough cookie. She didn't wear her emotions on her sleeve—she always tried to take life's shocks with equanimity. Dad just got even weirder than normal. He'd seen and experienced so much unpleasant stuff at work for the police. For example, he'd come across dead people who had either killed themselves or been murdered. He was repeatedly the first man on the scene after a terrible accident or fracas. He sometimes told me about it. Once, he told me about a time he went looking for a man who'd been up in the mountains in winter. Because of the roads and the weather, they didn't find him until spring. When Dad found him, finally, ravens had eaten his face. The poor man completely lacked ears, eyes, and a mouth. Dad also told me about a friend of his, another police officer, who was locked in an isolation unit with an insane man. Dad was supposed to relieve him and take the next shift, but when he arrived, the psychotic had beaten his friend and colleague to death. Dad had been struck by the silence that met him when he arrived at work, and felt it was odd. He'd expected to hear the men talking. When he didn't hear anything at all from inside the cell, he called his colleague's name but got no response. When he went into the cell, he found the miserable spectacle of his friend lying dead on the floor, covered in blood, and the psychotic guy sitting motionless on the bed. Dad often told me stories like that from work. I had no idea, though, why he told them to me. They didn't have a moral or message. Dad never felt the need to talk to anyone about the terrible things he'd experienced at work—he simply said that he was always able to forget.

But he never did forget those experiences. Perhaps he believed he'd put them behind him, but no: the events remained vivid for him.

Grandma's funeral was great. It was her farewell ceremony. She was finally dead. I didn't feel the need to cry or to hug anyone. I was distant and distracted. I thought it all just made perfect sense. Grandma hadn't been a bit apprehensive of dying. She'd frequently talked about it with me. She believed in God and believed she was going to meet Jesus when she died. I seriously doubted that. Why would God get involved with a person after death given that he hadn't while they were alive? Wouldn't it make more sense if he was kind to my grandmother while she was living? If Jesus was going to meet her, why not while she was alive? And since God had made Grandma blind, why hadn't Jesus healed her? He could have. The whole time, Jesus could have gone to the Gufudalur region. He could have taken some earth from the ridge, mixed it into a paste with his spit, and rubbed it in Grandma's eyes. I don't understand the purpose of Jesus meeting someone once they're dead. Grandma's hardly going to be blind when she's dead. For me, once you die, you disappear. Like a candle flame that's been put out. You simply no longer exist. There's nothing terrible about it. It doesn't matter. Being dead is no different from not yet existing. There is nothing more mournful about being dead than about not having been alive during the Middle Ages. Grandma's asleep and has no knowledge of herself. I don't believe in God.

I don't know Mom and Dad's families at all well. I recognized Mom's sisters. Dad's family I was even less familiar with than Mom's. His family was also much weirder than hers. Mom's relatives were normal. My dad's family have marked peculiarities. Some of those at the funeral were his siblings. I looked at many of them, but recognized no one. The truth was I had no idea what most of these people were called, and even less what they did. Some were cops or prison guards; others were criminals. I didn't know who was just a friend and who was a relative. There was one man, for instance, who I thought was my father's brother, but who turned out to be just a good friend of his from the Barðaströnd Association. I met these people so rarely, at best once or twice a year. Mom rarely took me to family gatherings when I was little. I was usually stuck in childcare since you couldn't possibly bring me along: I was naughty, a prankster. Mom couldn't even sit down for a cigarette if I was there. She always needed to be running after me; she couldn't let me out of her sight. When I was a kid, I simply did everything I thought of: breaking lots of windows, setting things on fire, climbing on roofs and throwing stuff off them.

All funerals are the same. First, you sing: pitifully sad and annoying songs about flowers. Then the priest talks about the corpse's life, though you know he has no idea what the dead body got up to while it was alive: he's just reading something the deceased's family wrote for him. Still, he talks like he knew the person in question well, telling everyone how entertaining and wonderful the corpse was when it was alive. Ashes to ashes, dust to dust. Then there's a sad song about Jesus that makes lots of people cry. When the coffin is carried out, people stand up and follow it. Some cry a lot, so others put their arms around them and comfort them; everyone follows together at a distance behind the coffin, which gets put inside a hearse that drives to the cemetery for the burial.

Once people are done crying, they have a cigarette and sniff loudly. Some people go to the cemetery, but others go straight to the reception and start drinking toasts. It's always the same. When I die, I'm not going to have any songs. No sad hymns and not any bull about Jesus.

It was fun when we went to parties that involved Mom's family. There was lots of laughing and storytelling. Everyone smoked and drank wine. Dad's family was another matter. Those gatherings were quieter. People were just silent, then perhaps someone in the group would awkwardly say: "Yes, indeed, like you say." If people started talking about anything, the discussions were mainly about jobs, even if there wasn't much to say. The most lively discussions happened about things that had been in the news. That revived everyone. Especially if it meant talking politics. They were all strident in their agreement or disagreement, and many of them got a bit overexcited.

A few days later, a small van came from the old people's home with Grandma's worldly possessions. Everything was put into her old room. A chest of drawers, a rocker, and her personal effects were thrown into two cardboard boxes. When Mom and Dad were out, I snuck into the room and rummaged through the stuff. In the chest of drawers I found a bunch of things. I opened the drawers and grubbed around, examining old photographs and postcards she'd received from people. I didn't know anyone in the pictures. They were old and black-and-white. Everyone looked serious, no one smiled. Judging from the pictures, back in the old days all men wore suits and all women wore the national dress. Grandma had also collected containers. The drawers were full of iron tins that had once held candy, wooden boxes that had held cigars, empty chocolate boxes with pretty pictures on the front. In the tins, my grandmother kept small objects: figures, coins, pictures, letters, and all kinds of crap like keys, broken jewelry, thimbles, and sewing stuff. I recognized some of the tins, remembering them from when Grandma lived with us.

I also found an envelope containing money. A lot of money. To me, at least. I took some and put it in my pocket. Grandma had no need of it anymore—she definitely would have been willing to give it to me. She didn't need the money. I, however, needed it to buy cigarettes and LPs.

The next few weeks, I lived like a king. I bought some records and punk badges from the Thousand and One Nights store. I got a bum to go to the state liquor store for me and buy me a pint-size bottle of Icelandic schnapps: Brennivín. I gave him enough to buy himself a bottle, too. I got plenty of cigarettes. The next weekend, I went on my first bender.

I'd tasted wine before, obviously. I'd often get a swig from older boys in the Scouts, and you could sometimes sponge a gulp of this or that downtown, outside the food court at Hallærisplan. But I'd never before had my own bottle. Most kids drank Brennivín or moonshine. It was easy to get hold of moonshine. The regional officer in my Scouts troop brewed it and sometimes sold it to the oldest boys, though he wouldn't sell it to us younger kids. I'd also tasted Anheuser and Christian Brothers white wine. That was quite good. But you didn't get as drunk on that stuff as on Brennivín. Brennivín was cheap, but it had a disgustingly bad taste. Mom brewed alcohol. Inside the closet were two large cylinders.

In them, Mom brewed rosé and beer, which she put in bottles and capped with a special pressurizing machine, then put in a cold closet. There were cases of beer on the floor and shelves full of unidentified wine with screw caps. At the time, beer was banned in Iceland, and you could only buy it in duty-free or on the black market. Everything that was banned, fishermen smuggled into the country. I'd sometimes managed to sneak bottles from the closet and take sips from them, but I'd never gotten drunk. Possibly what I was sipping hadn't even fermented. It was decidedly repulsive. But now I had a whole pint-size bottle of alcohol.

Alli went into town with me. It was Friday night, and we went to Halló. I was wearing my favorite torn jeans, a leather jacket, and military boots. Under my jacket, I had on my brand new Sid Vicious T-shirt I'd bought with the money I stole from Grandma. I'd hidden the bottle inside the garage then snuck it out with me, making sure no one could see it. Especially not the cops, who would immediately confiscate it. If older kids had caught sight of it, they would have demanded a drink and threatened to tell the cops if they didn't get one. We kept the bottle entirely to ourselves, wandering aimlessly and smoking. Every now and then we'd slip behind some trashcans to swig Brennivín, safely sheltered. The burn was so bad I retched after each swig. The bitter cumin flavor gave way to a strongly alcoholic taste, but I was looking forward to getting drunk and finding out what that sensation felt like. Drunk people seemed to be at ease. They were carefree; they sang and danced with joy. But how much did you have to drink to get loaded? I didn't know. Hopefully, no more than a single bottle. I was scared we'd run out before we got drunk.

The Brennivín made me feel comfortable and gave me confidence. I stopped being shy. I was warming up and I felt amazing. I even stopped kids and talked to them before they spoke to me. If someone called out "fucking punk," I didn't look down like usual, but challenged them back: "Shut your mouth, fucking disco freak! Death before disco." I talked loudly. I liked talking loudly and making myself heard. I had an uncontrollable desire to do something extraordinary, something spectacular. I wanted to sing in a band. I tried to climb the statue of Jón Sigurðsson so that I could get a piggyback ride from him. After I'd fallen down his trouser leg several times, I gave up and ran to the entrance of Parliament, positioned myself there, and sang "Anarchy in the UK" as loud as I could across Austurvöllur, the public square. Someone yelled at me:

"Shut your mouth, stupid punk."

I replied defiantly:

"Shut your own mouth, disco shitfreak!"

I wasn't afraid of anyone. I wasn't afraid of anything. No one could do anything to me. I wasn't ashamed of anything. I was free. Free to do and say what I wanted. When the police arrived to investigate what was going on, Alli and I ran into the Parliament garden and hid behind a bush. Once we were confident no one was chasing us, we sat on the bench and drank the rest of the Brennivín. Alli was in the middle of an unstoppable laughing fit.

"Jeez, listen to that!"

"Just some damn morons!"

The next day I woke up with a horrible taste in my mouth. I lay there in bed. There was a deafening ringing in my ears. It took me a while to figure out where I was. I felt around for my glasses, put them on, and looked about. I was in my room. What had happened? How did I get home? The last thing I remembered was that I had been in town with Alli. We were in the garden behind Parliament...and then someone had pushed me...

My heart jerked, and I jumped up. I experienced a searing headache. It was like ten ten-inch nails were trying to push their way out from inside my skull. When I stumbled to my feet, my eyes swam. I felt sick. I staggered to the toilet. My whole body shuddered and my hands were shaking. I bounced off the doorframe and slammed the door harder than I'd meant to. Then I threw up. I reached down to open the toilet lid. My stomach, thinking for itself, decided to have cramps and seizures. Gushes of puke sprang from me in long, rhythmic streams. What was happening? My hands shook so severely that I couldn't use them. My heart rate was so fast that I could feel it without having to put a hand on my chest—it was like my heart was going to burst out of my body. It was as if my whole body was nothing but pulsating blood. I closed my eyes, and it was like a glacial river ran right through my flesh, like a pillar of ice had been driven deep into my soul.

I was hungover. It was worse than the worst illness. I'd never been so sick before. Headache, stomachache, shivering. A gnawing mental torment. My soul shook. An atomic bomb of anxiety. Another of doubt. What had happened? How had I gotten home? What had I gotten up to? Who pushed me? And Mom and Dad? Did they know? What would they say? Did they think it was all okay?

I stumbled out. Mom was sitting in the kitchen and didn't look up when I arrived. Her invisible stare burned into me. They knew.

"Hey," I said, low and wretched.

I was startled to hear my own voice: a croaking, hoarse whisper. Mom didn't answer; she didn't look up, just continued to play solitaire. Shivering and shaking, I stumbled back into my room, undressed, lay on the bed, and fell asleep.

When I woke up again, it was evening. I felt a little better. My headache was just a memory, and I could think again. How could I lie my way out of this? I would run into Mom sooner or later. What lie should I tell? Most of all, I wanted to ring Alli and ask him what had happened. But I couldn't do that until I'd faced my mother.

I snuck into the bathroom and changed clothes. I smelled disgusting: sour and bitter. I smelled like rotten caraway. I ran a bath and washed myself vigorously with soap. I gulped down water, and brushed my teeth over and over again. Then I put on some patchouli and went back out.

Mom was making food. I sat at the kitchen table like a condemned man waiting for her to start. She didn't speak. She didn't even look at me. Dad wasn't home. That was a relief. I felt it was better to deal with an angry Mom than to listen to Dad nag. Mom slammed the plates on the counter with a vengeance. I tried to be as innocent and normal as I possibly could. Every now and then she stopped, sighed, and took a heavy breath. I looked down and waited. Suddenly, she turned to me.

"You should be ashamed of yourself!" she yelled.

"Yes," I muttered.

"Thirteen years old!"

I nodded my head in agreement, like I knew how ashamed I should be. I did, but not quite. I wasn't sure if she was so mad because I had drunk too much or if I had done something else. I found it hard to remember anything. I was desperately trying to remember something more, but everything was blurry other than some brawl.

"I just don't know what to do with you! You're absolutely intolerable! Fooling about downtown, dead drunk, and brought home by the police!"

By the police? The police had brought me home? Why? Because they knew me, or because I had done something? I had no memory of it.

"How could you do this to your father!"

I kept quiet. There it was. Was she angry because it was embarrassing for Dad? Perhaps, then, I hadn't done anything wrong? Maybe everything just revolved around my dad. I had to call Alli. I looked at her searchingly.

"What?"

"Why do you act like this!?!?"

Why do I act like this? What was I thinking? I'd just wanted to try being drunk. I simply thought it would be fun. I hadn't thought about the consequences—I'd thought it would all be fine. I'd not thought about how I was going to hide it from Mom. Things just happened of their own accord.

"I don't know," I mumbled.

Mom sighed.

"I don't know what the devil to do with you, child!"

Then she slammed the food down on the table and ran into the bedroom. I sat there alone, staring at meatballs. I thought about calling Alli but didn't dare. Mom couldn't hear that.

When Dad came home from work later that evening, he went straight to the television room without talking to me. I wondered if I should just flee to my room or go and talk to him. I didn't know how he would react. Probably he'd just nag. But it was best to clear things up, so I followed him.

"I'm sorry, Dad."

He wasn't pretending to be angry or hurt, as he so often had done before. He actually *was*. He was obviously spooked. He felt terrible, actually terrible. It wasn't just that he was ashamed about facing his police colleagues. A strange feeling filled me. This was real. Although it was bad, it was at the same time somehow also good. I felt bad. I was ashamed, and he was scared. But all the same I felt some strange joy at having a real interaction with my dad. We weren't playing some game. He wasn't holding my hand or looking at me with cow eyes. This wasn't about some paintbrush I had ruined or a meaningless ashtray I had broken or some stupid nonsense about promises. There wasn't going to be an uncomfortable hug. No whispering, no murmured assurance never to do it again. This mattered. This was serious. This was real. And that reality was almost more valuable than all the pain that came with it.

He was silent. Speechless. No nagging. I didn't find him repulsive, like so often before. I waited a while, but when he said nothing, I decided to go to my room. I sat on the bed and thought about it. It was like a new light had been turned on inside me, a light that felt warm and cozy. Dad didn't care about me. But this time it really mattered what I'd done. So I felt fond of him. Perhaps that was the purpose. Maybe the bender was a blessing in disguise. Like a funeral. Could we come together over some kind of self-destructive memory? What would my dad do if I died? How would it feel? He would definitely stop pretending. He would definitely cry. There would be real tears. He would cry over me and not just use me as a shoulder to cry on about something else.

Like at a funeral.

It wasn't until Monday that I could call Alli.

"Hahaha!" he laughed.

"What?"

"Doing all right?" he asked.

"Yes, what?"

"Man, you were insane!"

That sounded exciting. What had I done? I was scared and excited.

"I don't remember," I stammered, albeit with a bit of pride.

"Seriously? You don't remember going into the police station?"

Into the police station? What was I doing there? I avoided cops at all costs. They were all more or less friends with Dad, who might even be there. He was a cop, and he was always at work.

"Last thing I remember is being in the Parliament garden," I said.

"That's it? You don't remember a thing after that?"

"No," I said.

I'd never had a "blackout" before, but I knew what one was. "Blackout" was a milestone—almost like having sex for the first time.

When you'd had a blackout you were so much more grown-up than before.

"You were fiendishly drunk, man!"

"Yeah…"

A lot of fun stuff had happened during the time I couldn't remember. I was loaded. It had been weird to move my head, I was up in the clouds and cracking up, and my sense of balance had all gone to shit. I kept tripping and falling over curbs. Alli had supported me.

"But you're an even bigger idiot than that!"

That bowled me over. What? What had actually happened?

"Just tell me what happened. What happened?"

"You don't remember?" he asked, as though he doubted it was possible.

"No!" I hissed.

"You were so drunk that I was planning to try and get you on a bus and take you home, but you kept giving me the slip and running away…"

"I did?"

I didn't remember doing any of it.

"But you couldn't run away because you'd just fall on your head. I was trying to talk to you but I couldn't understand a word you were saying."

"Then what?" I asked, excited.

"Then you rushed into the police station. I tried to pull you away but I couldn't stop you…"

"I did?" I asked skeptically.

"They thought you were stoned."

"Okay, and so they drove me home?"

Alli was silent.

"You really don't remember anything?"

"No!"

"You took out your cock and pissed all over the floor of the police station!"

Alli burst out laughing.

"That's when I cleared out!"

The world went black. This was awful. Why on earth would I have done that? It was so unlike me. I usually found it almost impossible to pee around others. I couldn't even take a piss in public. But I'd peed not just in the city center, but on the floor of the police station, right by the front desk, in front of all the cops. Had any other kids been there? Any girls?

JOHNNY POTTEN

The risk increases every minute,
Death is on the move.
He sits upon an atomic bomb,
He doesn't pass you by.
Keflavík, Grindavík, Vogar,
Reykjavík, Þorlákshöfn—burn.
Fathers and mothers,
your children will roast.
All the children born today
have less and less to live for.
If you're in your thirties today
your ticket is counterfeit.
You will all, you will all, you will all die.
You will roast, you will burn,
Fathers and mothers, your children will roast.
*—*UTANGARÐSMENN

After seven years in elementary school, I graduated. I hadn't
learned a thing. I couldn't remember being taught anything in particular. Most of my classmates had the sort of knowledge that had
somehow totally escaped me. I had no idea who Jón Sigurdsson
was. I didn't know he was a hero of the independence movement.
I didn't want to know. For me, he was just some statue downtown.
Judging from the pictures, he didn't seem like an especially fun
guy—he had silly hair and sideburns. He was like the annoying
politicians on TV that my Dad liked to watch and argue with.

Mathematics was likewise a closed book to me. I knew plus and minus but little else. I couldn't multiply or divide. I refused to learn the multiplication tables. I wasn't going to use them, ever. I'll confess I once learned, just about, the five times table. But after that I flatly refused to have anything to do with multiplication. I fought with the teachers and Mom and completely refused to learn multiplication. Division was incomprehensible. I couldn't follow it. I started thinking about it and instantly it was like it'd taken on some form then gotten stuck somewhere in the dark corners of my mind, lost forever. I didn't understand a single example.

Einar has a birthday party.
He has half a cake.
Óli, Ása, Garðar, and Bjarni are guests at the birthday party.
How does Einar divide the cake so that everyone has an equal amount?

I don't know! Why only half a cake? Isn't that stupid? Will Ása want the same size slice as the boys? What is she even doing at a boy's birthday party?!? What if Garðar doesn't want cake? There was no reason to learn this.

I often quarrelled with my teacher, Svanhildur, about the importance of knowing math. She repeatedly told me: "You'll never achieve anything in life, Jón, if you don't know math."

I couldn't care less. There was absolutely no purpose for it. I knew tons of adults who'd achieved all kinds of success without being good at math. My dad didn't need math to be a cop. Mom didn't have to know math to cook food at City Hospital.

"What will you do if you need to know the outcome of a mathematical problem?"

"I'll ask someone."

"What if there's no one to ask?"

"Then I'll ring someone who knows."

"But if you're not near a phone?"

"In the future, everyone will have their own phone."

"That's never going to happen!"

I was certain there'd be someone whose advice I could get. I didn't need to worry about it. What I wanted to do in life didn't require math. Mathematics is like catching salmon with your bare hands. Sometimes I went to Elliðaárvogur and tried to catch salmon from under the rocks. No matter how fast I snatched at them, they always eluded my grasp. Same with math. Why couldn't I choose not to learn math? Einar never learned to ride a bike. He didn't want to. No one cared. No one lectured him about the importance of knowing how to ride.

"Einar, you have to learn to ride a bike!"

"But I don't want to."

"But, Einar, you'll never get anywhere in life except by bicycle. What will you do if you find yourself in mortal danger and have to get away lightning quick?"

"Then I'll run."

"But you'll never run as fast as you could cycle!"

Einar had simply decided that in future he wasn't going to ride a bike. He didn't want to. And I didn't want to learn math. That was that. No one could get me to learn it. Not even my mom. I thought it was too much trouble and lacking in goal or purpose.

I had also learned from experience that math tended to get more difficult year on year the more you learned about it. I started by learning how to add. That was easy. Once I knew that, I started learning how to subtract, which is rather more complex and caused me quite a lot of hassle. For example, I had a really hard time learning how you take away a higher number from a lower number, like nine from seven. What about twenty-seven from twenty-nine? I worked damn hard learning how to do that; it cost me a great deal of effort. I was way behind my classmates. I'd barely begun to master minusing when multiplication came along. And then sets and decimal places and division and area. I realized it was all a conspiracy. They were trying to trick me into being someone I wasn't, enticing me to do things I didn't want to do and banning everything I liked. They were trying to change me. The only one who could stop them was me.

I set fire to my report card on school grounds. It wasn't a judgment about me but about someone else. It was a judgment of a person they wanted me to be and confirmation that it hadn't gone well. The report had nothing positive to say about me: just that I was always talking and disturbing others. I got "pass" in most things but "insufficient" in math. I was "good" in English. But I was the best in the class in English. I could speak AND read it. I was just bad at writing it. But that was the only thing they tested. Why is writing more important than talking? I don't know. This report said nothing about me. They didn't know me. They didn't want to know me. They'd never seen me, not properly.

I also set fire to my schoolbooks. I tore them to pieces and threw them into the fire. I felt good seeing them burn. I relished the thought that I would never again have to sit and stare at those sleep-inducing books. I spat on my Danish grammar before I threw it on the fire. A crock of disgusting shit! Danish kids, too, are a bunch of annoying, hippie morons in clogs and overly baggy pants. I knew all the Danish I needed. I'd learned Danish from reading *Donald Duck* in Danish. He was the only Dane I needed to know.

My school bag went in the fire, too. I wasn't going to carry it with me as a reminder. A group of giggling kids had gathered around the flames. I didn't care. I didn't know any of them. I didn't want to know them. I didn't want to know anyone at school, not even my old friends. We had nothing in common anymore. I'd never get where they were going. They saw me as an odd bird they had to pity. But they weren't ever going to get where I was going. When Kári, the principal, came hurrying in my direction, I ran up the school stairs and shouted across the schoolyard:

> *We don't need no education*
> *We don't need no thought control*
> *No dark sarcasm in the classroom*
> *Teachers, leave them kids alone.*

The principal was trampling on the fire.

> *Hey! Teachers! Leave them kids alone.*

Fat Dóri also failed everything. But that wasn't so strange. He'd only just moved to the area. His mother and father were divorced.

His mother had started a relationship with some new guy and had moved abroad with him. Dóri lived with his father, who was never around and didn't care about him. He was almost always home alone. Except those times his grandmother came over and cooked for him. Because Dóri was fat, he was always being teased. He was called Little Blue after the blue elephant on children's television. I was his only friend in school. Our friendship was based on our mutual exclusion. We hung around together after school, found solidarity in each other, and backed each other up in our anti-social sentiments: everyone is an idiot, people are dumbasses, school sucks. We didn't find education worthwhile and made crank calls instead. We called old people and spoke English with them. Dóri was smart. He ripped the phone apart and connected it to a tape player so we could record our calls. I was quick at thinking up some nonsense or other to say to people, so I did the talking. Then we listened to the tapes and laughed ourselves silly. For example, one time I rang and this old woman answered.

"Hello. My name is Johnny Rotten, and I'm a punk rocker. Do you listen to Sex Pistols?"

"Forgive me, I can't understand what you're telling me."

"My name is Johnny Rotten. Do you listen to the Sex Pistols?"

"I simply do not understand you. I'm going to ask my son to talk to you. He speaks English. *[pause]* There's an Englishman on the phone. Would you talk to him?"

A young man comes to the phone.

"Hello."

"*Já, góðan daginn,*" I said, having stopped speaking English right away. "*Er Halldór heima?*"

"No, no one called Halldór lives here."

Then Dóri and I burst out laughing.

After my bonfire, I strolled home victorious. I went into my room. No one was home. Mom and Dad were at work. I had acquired an old turntable from Óli the Stud. I put Utangarðsmenn, the Icelandic punk "Outsiders," on the record player and threw myself on my bed. I had several albums, like *Polar Bear Blues* and *Radioactive*. I'd also broken several of my albums, including *Grease* and ABBA's *Arrival*. Disco shit. Brainless morons listened to *Grease*. ABBA was for aging housewives. Mom liked ABBA. She also really enjoyed Meatloaf. Sometimes, music videos were shown on television, and when Meatloaf sang "Paradise by the Dashboard Light," Mom looked seduced. Then she'd say:

"He's repulsive, but he sings beautifully."

Anyone who knew anything listened to Bubbi Morthens. He was awesome. Beyond that, I didn't know much about music, less than most others. I just enjoyed this and that song. Mainly, I listened to the lyrics. After I listened to songs, I read the lyrics. I was usually more interested in the text than the music itself. It could be difficult; they were often in English. I didn't understand all the words, but was determined to learn them.

Sometimes I went over to Óli the Stud's to listen to albums. He owned punk albums, like the Sex Pistols and Sham 69. He also had headphones, so you could really turn up the volume without it being heard throughout the house. The Sex Pistols were the main punk band. I'd seen pictures of them in the paper. The lead singer was called Johnny Rotten. He had red hair like me.

He didn't try to be cool so much as disgusting. His clothes were torn, and he always grimaced in front of the camera, and when he was standing upright he tried to carry himself like a loser. That was awesome. I sometimes imitated him in the bathroom mirror. I felt a bit like him. Maybe he was like me when he was thirteen years old. Perhaps he'd felt out of place and not like the others. He definitely wasn't good at school. I seriously doubted that Johnny Rotten knew multiplication tables. The most famous song by the Sex Pistols was "Anarchy in the UK." I didn't fully understand the lyrics.

I am an anarchist
I am an antichrist

I didn't know a whole lot about anarchy. I knew the word *anarkismi* in Icelandic, but not really what it meant. The Antichrist was the Devil. I knew the UK was Britain but didn't fully understand why. But the song was good. Johnny Rotten screams in it, and laughs too. That felt good. The only big difference between me and Johnny Rotten was that I wore glasses. That wasn't cool. Only nerds wore glasses. Punks don't usually wear glasses. I didn't even get to choose the frames for my glasses. I'd seen a picture of Johnny Rotten with tiny sunglasses. Sunglasses were cool. I wanted round glasses, but the eye doctor said my myopia was too severe for small glasses and I had to have big, square glasses. That was fucking lame. But Mom liked them, so she bought them. I'd rather have large, round frames like John Lennon. Though I didn't think John Lennon was all that. He was kind of a hippie.

But he had better-looking glasses than me. Sometimes when I went into town and was trying to be tough, I took off my glasses and put them in my pocket. But I couldn't see properly and ended up waving about in a foggy world. But at least I didn't look silly.

One time I went over to Óli the Stud's, he wanted me to listen to a song through the headphones. When the song started, it was like it had always been somewhere inside me; my spirit felt a distinct harmony with it. I felt like this was somehow my song. Like it was written both for me and about me. Restive feelings shifted within me. I wanted to scream and cry as I listened. But I didn't. I just lay there, fascinated, with closed eyes, listening to the song again and again. I lay on the floor in his room for hours and listened to the same song over and over again. Óli the Stud came and went and left me quite alone. We didn't talk at all. Finally he nudged me and said my mom had called and I had to go home for dinner.

The band was called The Clash. The song was called "Bankrobber." After it, there was no turning back. Punk had infected me. I wouldn't listen to anything else. I wanted more.

"Did you get your grades?" asked Mom at the dinner table.

"No," I lied.

"Why not?" she asked, suspicious.

I'd prepared an answer.

"They weren't ready. I think they're sending them to us at home."

She looked at me searchingly. I looked questioningly back at her, trying to look as innocent as I could.

"Look at me!"

"What?"

"Are you lying to me?"

I looked down at the plate.

"I'm not lying about anything."

"What did you do with your report card?"

"Nothing."

"I'll talk to your teacher."

"Sure," I replied, as if nothing was out of the ordinary, as if I was a man with nothing to hide. I didn't feel like discussing it. I just wanted to be left alone. I didn't want to talk about school. I wanted to talk punk. I wanted to ask Mom what anarchism and Antichrists and antipasti really were. But I knew she didn't know anything about that. I didn't feel like being nagged over something that didn't matter.

"Why are you conducting yourself so badly?"

"I don't know."

"What is your ambition, your goal in life?"

"I don't know."

"What do you know?"

"I don't know. Nothing?"

"Stop being lazy, Jón! You're absolutely able to make something of yourself if you try. What do you actually plan on being?"

"Nothing in particular."

"Do you think you'll get into college at this rate?"

"I'm not going to college."

"What are you going to do, then? You can't just stay at home all day."

"No, of course not. I'll work or something."

Mom sighed.

"I don't know what to do with you."

She gave up a long time ago. She's grown tired; I've exhausted her near to death. She's about to turn sixty. My dad is sixty-three. An old man. They don't know what's cool and what's lame. They don't know what punk is. They have no idea what's going on. I can't talk to them about anything. I've stopped talking to my dad altogether. I try to avoid him if I can. When he tries to talk to me, I pretend I don't hear him, and I go to my room. It's awkward, and it troubles me. I stopped asking him for money. I can't bear to see the expression on his face, the allegation in his eyes, or listen to the whining tone of his voice.

"Money? Didn't I give you money last week?"

I want to scream at him to keep his dumb mouth shut. I want to tell him that I find him awkward and annoying. But before I ever could, he'd slay me with a look. I'm always hurting him. He often makes me promise things I can't achieve. Sometimes he makes me promise things I don't even understand. Like promising to always be diligent or to keep an eye on the garage. What does he mean, "keep an eye on the garage"? Keep an eye that the kids in the street don't kick a ball at the garage door? He made me promise to talk to the kids and ask them kindly not to kick the ball against the door. I couldn't say no or tell him it would be stupid because that would hurt him. So I agreed to do it. But who does he really think I am? Some idiot who walks over to some kids and asks them to please not kick the ball against his father's garage door because he finds it a pain seeing the marks of their ball on the door? Dumbass! He doesn't own me. I'm not afraid of him or his weird promises.

I just don't bother talking to him. I steal money from his wallet when he isn't looking. I go through the pockets of his clothes and steal leftover singles. He'll never figure it out. By contrast, Mom would know instantly if I stole money from her. Sometimes Mom doesn't have any money and needs to ask Dad for some to buy food, clothes, that sort of thing. Each time, Dad treats her just like when I ask him for money.

"Potatoes? Didn't we buy potatoes only last week?"

Mom always gets annoyed when she has to ask Dad for money.

"We're out of potatoes."

"Out? Who finished the potatoes?"

"Ah, Kristinn, I can't be bothered with all this nagging."

Then Dad sighs, reaches into his wallet, pulls out some money, and gives it to her with puppy eyes. He's getting irritated with Mom.

I buy candy and soccer picture cards with his money. If I have enough, I go to the movies. I take the bus downtown. If Mom asks where I'm going, I say out to the soccer pitch or to see some school friends. If I told her I was going to the movies, she'd ask where I got the money. She's stopped being able to work out when I'm lying. I'm getting very good at it. Though maybe she's just stopped bothering to get involved.

Little by little, I stopped buying soccer cards. I didn't like soccer. I started buying punk pictures instead. I didn't know half the people in the pictures compared to the soccer cards. But it was still a step up. I was determined to find out everything you could find out about punk. Some of the characters in the pictures didn't seem like they were particularly punk. For example, I got lots of copies of the card with Dr. Feelgood on it. "Feel good" means being content.

That's not punk. Punk means feeling bad and angry, not putting up with any assholes. Punks don't believe in the future. For them, there's no future, only an endless decline. There's no point trying because everything's all going to hell. Nuclear war could break out at any moment. Anyone not wearing torn clothes isn't really punk, was my opinion. It wasn't enough to simply play at a loud volume to be punk. What's more, punks typically didn't wear ties. The Brits didn't even have collars on their shirts – they tore them off. David Bowie wasn't punk, nor Madness, nor Ian Dury. Yet there were pictures of them on the punk cards. It was like the makers of punk cards weren't quite clear about what punk was. I threw those pictures away immediately. Tenpole Tudor and Adam Ant went the same way. They weren't punk, though many people seemed to believe they were. I couldn't believe Johnny Rotten would be friends with Adam Ant. Adam Ant dressed in some stupid costumes. Some bands were still a gray area. I didn't know if they were punk. There were bands like The Jam, The Police, and Blondie. I kept their pictures until I knew for sure.

The first few days of summer vacation were spent mostly hanging about. I stayed inside my room, reading and listening to records. I read the lyrics of the songs with an English-Icelandic dictionary at hand, looking up and underlining words I didn't know. I got a picture of Johnny Rotten from my punk cards and put it on the wall. I turned around the award I got for Best Performance in Sports at a competition at the National Scout Convention and scrawled on the back of it with a big, black marker. The award was made of leather. I wrote JOHNNY POTTEN in large letters then put a big A inside a circle. I was done with Scouts. I'd been in the Venture Scouts. I was only there a year. The group dissolved. We'd started by learning knots and reading Baden Powell and memorizing various rules. I never completely got knots. I didn't know how to tie a single one. I cheated on the knot test by having a pre-made Bottle Sling in my pocket. The only knot I knew how to do properly was the hanging knot. Then our troop leader took up smoking and we started messing about with that, too. Scout meetings began to change, little by little. Our interest in Baden Powell declined steadily until it fell off completely, and instead of reading *The Boy Scout's Handbook,* we started looking at porno mags the older boys were resourceful enough to bring along. The area leader became some sort of big-shot winemaker and bootlegger. Finally, the bottom fell out of the Scouts. Meetings were mostly hanging out, smoking, looking at dirty magazines, and talking about sex. I felt okay talking and smoking, especially when I could grub a cigarette and a swig from the older boys. Of course, I was also interested in the pages of the dirty magazines. But masturbation didn't sit well with me, and when people started to get out their dicks, then I made myself scarce. There's something especially embarrassing about talking to people who are masturbating at the time, especially when they're wearing scout uniforms.

I left the Scouts. Baden Powell was standing with crossed arms in the hallway and looking at me, a strict expression on his face.

"What's wrong with you, boy? Aren't you a man?!"

Some days, I went over to Fat Dóri's and hung out at his house or went over to Óli the Stud's to listen to records. Sometimes Kristján

Þór came over and we played Risk. Kristján Þór was part of a past I was trying to get rid of. He had no idea about or interest in punk but was trying to be like me. He tried to keep our friendship going while I neglected it. I felt lame around him. He was a dork, and I was trying to be tough. I avoided him and made endless excuses for not being able to play, or pretended to be tired or on the way to something he couldn't go to. I also enjoyed being on my own; when no one was around to see, I fetched my Action Man, which was hidden under a pile of clothes in my closet, and played with him. I often went to the library and hung out there. I'd already read all the books in the children's and teenage section—including the girls' books, Alistair MacLean, Desmond Bagley, Sven Hassel, and all the adult books I thought were interesting. I greedily paged through *Melody Maker* and drank in everything I could about punk. I researched the bands I'd gotten on the punk cards and was persuaded were actual punks. The staff, most of whom knew me well after years of frequent visits, even let me cut out articles and pictures from old magazines. But I needed more information about anarchism. I read a biography of Peter Kropotkin. I found it abstruse and frustrating. The book described various parts of Kropotkin's life but shed little light on anarchism itself. The only other books on the subject were weighty scholarly tomes in English whose titles I could not even pronounce. I borrowed *Anarchism: From Theory to Practice* and pored over it at home. My study of English until now had not offered me more than tiny insights into song lyrics, newspaper articles, and interviews. Faced with a textbook, I was baffled. I'd never read a book in English, let alone such a complex one. And although I understood some of the phrases, I couldn't get the gist. I paged through it, looking for familiar slogans like "Fuck the system," but didn't find anything. For chapter after chapter, it was all about some workers in Spain hundreds of years ago and some wars. I threw the book across the room, disappointed. What a buzzkill. This couldn't be what Johnny Rotten was interested in.

I always slept badly—I'd lie awake late into the night. I read or played Risk on my own until morning. Only then could I sleep. But I didn't sleep long. There was so much I had to do, to try and find out about. During the day, I was tired. As soon as I lay in bed at night, I started to think. It was like my brain couldn't see any purpose in sleep. Thoughts came in waves, and I couldn't deal with them. My brain was continually producing new thoughts, ideas, and questions; I had no control over them. I felt like an observer standing at a busy intersection watching cars he couldn't affect. It didn't matter how I tossed and turned and tried to get rid of the thoughts and empty my mind. None of it worked. My brain totally overwhelmed me; I was merely its feeble accessory. I tried to think of one particular thing, like when I was little. I'd built an imaginary city in my mind, planned out the network of streets, furnished an entire house. That was how I fooled my brain so that it wasn't out of control in every direction. When I had trouble falling asleep, I imagined I was in this city. It hid all kinds of dangers: wild animals, robots, automatic guns with motion sensors that fired when approached. If I was able to lose myself here, my brain's other thoughts weren't able to reach me any longer, and I'd manage to fall asleep. But it had stopped working. The brain had contrived to take total control; it had overcome me.

By evening, just as things were quieting down, my imagination burst into a fireworks display and a circus where everything got mixed together. Endless questions and no answers. What is anarchism? What will happen in the future? Is there life on other planets? Is there a God? Some thoughts went in unceasing circles, turning around one another and giving rise to new thoughts and questions. Some exploded with loud bangs the way rockets do, then disappeared. Others came like cars or planes, loud and quick to disappear but returning just as swiftly. It was like an entire carnival was being held in my head every single night. Dadadararadadara. Sometimes, I had a realization; the answer to a question I had been wondering about a long time ago would suddenly appear. I scrabbled to write it down so I wouldn't forget. But when I woke up, I couldn't work out what I'd written; I'd never know why or in connection with what I'd been writing. This caused me anxiety and despair. What can you do in such a situation? My mind was like a busy airport where aircraft took off and landed, vanishing over the horizon as new planes came in to land, employees dashing about on this or that task, and everything flowing continuously on and on. Never at rest. Everyone always had to be somewhere. No quiet moments when everything would fall silent. The airport in my head was never shut. Are people good or bad? How do you say *hallærislegt* in English? Will I ever get a girlfriend? Am I crazy? Will I get put in a loony bin like Cousin Kiddi? He was awake day after day, got up to all kinds of nonsense, and was subsequently sent to the loony bin when he could no longer help himself. One day he'd had enough; he snuck out in the middle of the night, went swimming in the sea, drowned, and was dead.

The future lay open in front of me like a black cave, full of uncertainty and risk. I feared it, without knowing quite what I was so afraid about. I feared the unknown. I feared that this world wasn't made for me. I feared loneliness, being always alone and left out, feared that no one would understand me or love me. Would I always be odd? Would I always be like an alien from another planet? My brain sent me sentences, parts of books, or even things someone else had said. There was a constant weight over my chest; I couldn't fill my lungs with air. It was like a death-sized fist was inside me, squeezing and pinching—like someone was trying to crush my heart. When thoughts struck me, the weight on my chest increased, and I had to gasp for breath. Mom was always wanting to take me to have my lungs scanned, but I took no notice. I feared I might have a horrible disease that couldn't be detected. Uncle Gulli died of lung cancer. Maybe I had some new type of lung cancer? It didn't matter how tired I was when I lay down on the pillow. Thoughts roused me. Numbness and fatigue turned to perceptiveness and activity. I dreaded going to bed because I knew I couldn't sleep.

Sometimes I would sneak out at night and walk around outside to calm myself down. Anything was better than lying awake indefinitely. It felt good to be out when no one was up and about. It was so bright that it was like it was day, except there were no cars and no people around. I wandered the streets aimlessly. I often went down to Fossvogs School and wandered around the school grounds. If someone came, I hid and spied on them, lying in the grass and holding my breath. Usually it was newspaper delivery guys, but sometimes older teenagers or adults who were walking home.

Night after night, I went down to the school grounds. I'd been there so many times, but it was strange to be there like this—weird but somehow immediately comfortable. Some nights, I hung out for hours. I often climbed on the roof, lying there looking up into the sky. One night, I went over to an open skylight and climbed through. It was a strange feeling, being alone in the school in utter silence. I prowled about and rummaged through things; I went to my old homeroom and examined the pictures hanging on the walls. I stared at the class picture, scrutinizing the other kids and myself. I grubbed through everything I could find but didn't damage anything.

The staff room was locked. I walked past it and went into the gym. The empty auditorium echoed uncomfortably. I went into the dressing rooms and the shower. The shower brought up bad memories. I'd so often been made fun of there; nowhere were you so vulnerable. The fat kids were always targeted, for example, and laughed at. I hit puberty pretty early, which was also an end-less source of teasing in the shower. Worse, my hair sprouted red, continually my curse, offering the mean jerks teasing me infinite opportunities for torment. I hated the showers. They were a place of torture. I went into the girls' dressing room. A forbidden place, one you were prohibited from entering. I sat on the bench for a good while. The girls' dressing room smelled different.

I snuck out the same way I came in. I liked being back home before Mom and Dad woke up. I opened the door super care-fully, snuck into my room, closed the door gently behind me, and crawled into bed. When they got up, I fell asleep.

One night when I was strolling through the streets of town,

I decided to break into my old pre-school. I took a screwdriver, forced a window, and crawled inside. There was little that reminded me of anything, only a familiar smell, the sides of the building, and the primary colors on the walls. I walked around and looked about, picked some things up, contemplated them, sniffed at them—especially the clay stuff. On one table there was a hamster in a cage. I picked him up and petted him. He was soft and sweet. So I stuck him in my pocket and took him home with me.

I hid the hamster inside my wardrobe, in an old fish tank covered with clothes. It was incredibly exciting. Not only had I stolen the hamster, but I was also hiding him from Mom. The hamster was like Anne Frank. My mom was like the Nazis, and I was one of the people who tried to help Anne Frank. Soon, though, my thoughts wandered to all the little kids in kindergarten who were undoubtedly sad that someone had taken their little hamster; guilt became the dominant emotion. I saw before me a group of small, innocent, sad children weeping beside an empty hamster cage. Maybe they thought he was dead.

A few nights later, I broke back into the pre-school and returned the hamster to its cage. On my way through the pre-school, I spotted a Smurf village that had been set up on a table. I was fascinated by all the Smurfs and their Smurf houses, by Gargamel the Wizard and his cat. It was absolutely wonderful. I found a plastic bag and swept all the Smurf stuff into my bag and took it with me. It was only fair that I got something for my pains since I had been so kind as to return the hamster. I hid the Smurfs inside my wardrobe. I felt like a true hero. I had safely returned a hamster to its home. In a way, you could say I'd saved him. I could see the expressions of the little kids before me: a look of surprise and delight over their little faces when they came to school and saw that their hamster had returned. Their faces shone wonderfully with joy. I smiled to myself at the thought. I'd done something truly good. A good deed.

A few days later there was an article in the newspaper *The Face*: "Burglary Epidemic in Fossvogur!" All kinds of burglaries were named, in places I'd not gone, but it also mentioned the hamster and said that the thief had apparently felt guilty and returned it. They were talking about me! The story focused on me! My hands trembled as I read the piece. I felt like Robin Hood. It was a bit like there were two Jóns. One was evil and broke into places and stole things. The other was good and returned the things evil Jón had taken. But to be good Jón, I first had to be evil Jón. Still, I hadn't hurt anyone, and I hadn't damaged anything, either. Good Jón made sure of that.

The following night, I broke back into the pre-school; I'd decided to return the Smurfs. I snuck out again, as so often before, but with the Smurfs in a bag. I forced the same window as before, clambered in with the bag, then took out all the Smurfs and arranged them on the table, although differently than before. I had the Smurfs talking to Gargamel the Wizard. Gargamel's cat was with Papa Smurf, and I put Grouchy Smurf inside a house looking out the window. How astonished the kids would be, and so happy, to see the Smurfs had come back! I was looking forward to reading all about it in *The Face*: "Robin Hood Travels Through Fossvogur!" Maybe everyone would think I was someone who stole from thieves. That I was some invisible hero who loved to steal from evil thieves and return things to their homes. Kind of like Batman. Punkman? I was deeply immersed in these thoughts as I left the pre-school. I opened the door cautiously and was confronted by a terrible sight. Two policemen. One of them slammed the door and rammed his shoulder into me.

"What the hell are you doing, fucking vandal!"

I was speechless with terror and stared at him like a deer in the headlights.

I tried to lie about it to my parents and say I'd found the Smurf stuff somewhere and decided to return it.

"I found it in a garden and decided to return it so the kids wouldn't be upset."

Mom was mad and yelled at me.

"Stop lying, Jón!"

"I'm not lying."

But I soon saw it was hopeless; I knew from experience how difficult it was to lie to my mother. Mom couldn't see the good in what I'd done and gave me no credit because I'd broken in to deliver toys. No, she only saw the negative. I had, for example, nothing to gain by returning the toys. Dad was more concerned about his reputation than the fact that I'd now become a criminal and a known Smurf thief.

"Why do you do this to me?" he asked tearfully.

"I don't know," I muttered, like so often before.

"Exactly right! You never know anything!"

The next day a detective came and searched my room. He opened all the drawers and peeked into all the cupboards. He took my Action Man stuff and looked accusingly at me.

"That's mine," I muttered.

Then I had to go with him to the Department of Criminal Investigation. My fingerprints were taken. They suspected me of having broken into several other places and believed, among other things, I'd broken into some work shed and trashed it. I was supposed to have broken everything and destroyed things and sprayed a fire extinguisher. I'd never do that. I wasn't evil. I wasn't a criminal. I was just a curious kid who liked to see, touch, and smell things. The officer didn't believe me until I broke down and burst into tears. He stood up, talked to the cops, and I heard him tell them I wasn't the person they were looking for. I wiped away the tears and snorted through my nose. The officer drove me home. Along the way, he informed me that he had never in all his investigations had to deal with such an idiotic case.

"What exactly were you up to, kid? Who breaks in and steals things just to be able to return them?!"

"I don't know."

He asked, with a pitiful tone of voice, as though I was a bit special:

"Is something wrong with you? Breaking and entering to steal from small children. Is this something you plan to continue doing?"

"No."

"Why did you do it?"

"I don't know."

"No. Exactly right."

UNBEHAGEN

Oh we're so pretty
Oh so pretty we're vacant
Oh we're so pretty, oh so pretty we're vacant
Ah but now and we don't care
—seX pIstOlS, "pretty vaCanT"

They were going abroad. I saw the travel brochure on the table, so I asked:

"Who's going abroad?"

"We are," Mom replied, like she didn't mean me.

"Where?"

"Bulgaria."

Bulgaria? I'd never heard of the place until now. I didn't know where it was. I didn't even know if it was a country or city.

"When?"

"In July."

I'd not totally managed to learn the months. I couldn't remember what they were called or the order they came in. July was summer, so it had to be happening soon. Maybe it was next month.

"Where am I going to be?"

I knew I wouldn't get to stay home.

"You're going to the country."

I thought with horror of my last time in the country. I wouldn't go back there. I got tears in my eyes at the thought.

"I won't go back to that hellhole!"

"No," said Mom, sadly.

I was relieved.

"Can I stay with Runa?"

"No, you can't stay with Runa."

I didn't feel like going to some crappy rural dump and hanging out there. I wanted to go stay with my sister up in Kjalarnes.

"Why can't I stay with Runa?"

"Because you can't."

"Why not?"

"It's too close to town. And I'm not going to be worrying about you on my holiday."

"But I won't do anything."

Mom looked at me with a resolute expression.

"You're not going to Runa's. End of debate. You're going to the country."

"Where?"

"You're going to Þrastarhóli with your aunt Bondi."

"Where's that?"

"Up north."

"North? Whereabouts?"

Mom sighed.

"It's in Eyjafjörður."

I wasn't any better informed about the north of Iceland than about Bulgaria. I had no idea where it was. It was as far off as Farawayistan in *Duck Tales*. Geography was a closed book to me. I doubted whether I could even point to Iceland on a map. I had a very faint picture of the world in my mind, and I didn't know directions. I didn't know, for example, where the sun came up and set. I knew that it was either in the east or the west, but I never remembered which. What little I knew of the Icelandic map was Reykjavík, Vatnajökull, and the Vestfirðir. Out west was, inexplicably, up. The Vestfirðir were fists that grew out of the land. Paradísarhellir, the cave where Hjalti had written his book about Anna from Stóruborg, was out in the east—so too was Suðursveit, though given the name it should have been in the south; that's where Þórbergur Þórðarson was born and brought up. I was still unclear, though, exactly where "east" was. As for "north," I hadn't a clue.

I had driven the ring road with Mom and Dad and Aunt Gunna many years back. Dad was in a hurry, as usual, and drove like crazy. Mom and Gunna chain-smoked, listened to the big car stereo, and sang along excitedly to "The Song of Nína and Geira." I read *Donald Duck*. I had no interest in seeing anything or paying particular attention to the environment. I was cold the whole time. It was really cold everywhere. I thought Iceland was ugly and boring. The mountains weren't like mountains, but more like a pile of rocks. It felt like Mount Esja was everywhere. Sometimes we stopped because they wanted to look at a mountain, or some lake, and take photos. I stayed inside the car. Dad would hurry everyone along. The weather was miserable the whole time, typically rainy and windy. At night, we slept in a tent. Dad pitched camp while we sat inside the car. The cold didn't seem to have any effect on him. He was out in the cold in just a T-shirt. I lay awake between them and listened to them snore. In the morning, we woke up cold and wet and had asparagus soup and bread for breakfast. Dad heated the soup on a Primus stove while we dried our butts inside the car. We drank the soup out of tins and then continued along gravel roads. Iceland rushed by, blurred and faintly gray through dusty car windows. Everywhere was windy. We stopped to see some waterfalls. They went out to see the falls but instantly came running back to the car, drenched from the water, which had blown directly onto them. When it finally let up and the wind calmed, we hit thick fog. One morning when I crawled cold and wet out of the tent, it was starting to snow.

"Where is Eyjafjörður?" I asked Aunt Gunna.

"In Akureyri. You've been there, haven't you?"

"No."

"You know where Akureyri is?"

I kept quiet. I had no idea where Akureyri was. It couldn't be a very interesting place given that I'd supposedly been there and didn't remember it. I didn't ask anything else. I was outside time, bewildered, captive in time's vacuum. It didn't matter anyway. Mom had made up her mind. The trip was over. We were done driving around Iceland. Nothing about the trip stayed with me, except perhaps conversations between Mom and Aunt Gunna. Gunna would sometimes tell Dad to shut up when he was nagging on and on. That was funny. Dad hung the tent to dry in the garden, and the mattresses and sleeping bags went back up into the attic.

One night, as we were eating dinner, Mom announced that I was going to the country the next day. She packed my clothes into a bag. Very early the next morning, some guy appeared, a guy I didn't recognize but who was going to drive me.

The journey seemed endless. We drove all day. It was bright, sunny weather. Iceland was just as ugly as the first trip: gray and monotonous. Piles of stone and withered grass, fences and ditches.

The farms struck me as ugly. I thought them all alike, unassuming stone houses with corrugated iron roofs. They were silly colors, yellows and blues. Some were even orange. Around them were piles of all kinds of machines for harvesting hay, some tractors, gutted cars. And then pens for cows. I hated farms. I knew the smell of them, the smell of dogs, of sweaty feet, of old potatoes and sweet soup. A cloying, mildewed odor. I tried to imagine the surroundings of the town I was headed to. It'd be like any other rural Icelandic town. I could just imagine the people who lived there. The father was definitely a hick, always unshaven, with gray stubble. He'd be dressed in baggy terylene pants that were way too big on him and were tucked into his boots. He'd be wearing a sweater with holes in it and a blue jacket over the top. He'd definitely own a Land Rover. When he spoke, he'd talk loudly and curse a lot. His wife would be wearing stockings, woolen socks, and a mustard yellow skirt; she'd always be pissed. When she went out, she'd wear the ugliest coat she could find. The farmer's wife would have the ugliest coat in town. Her windbreaker would be torn here and there so you could see through the lining. Their kids would also be dressed stupidly. The boys would be wearing oversize jeans and rubber boots; the girls, too. They'd strap their pant legs into wool socks and wear work shirts fastened all the way to the neck.

Rural people have no sense of fashion. They're not hippies, though. They just all wear men's clothes, even the kids and the women. It'd be like me wearing Mom and Dad's clothes, cut down for me. I was always embarrassed by my parents, especially my dad. I couldn't imagine how I'd feel if we lived in the country.

I suspected I'd be ready to kill myself. I certainly wouldn't know anything about punk. There aren't any libraries in rural areas. Then again, I probably wouldn't learn anything about sheep and that crap if I lived out there, either.

The old man driving didn't say a word to me. We were silent the whole way. In the evening, we reached a town. I had no idea where we were. The old man opened the trunk and handed me my bag.

"Well," he said, and we went inside.

Everything looked the way I'd imagined. The farmer was in oversized terylene pants and woolen socks. There was a hole in his sweater, and he had stubble. His hands were covered in cuts. The woman was also in pants, though not oversized, but narrow. There was an old guy there, also in terylene pants. There wasn't anyone else in the household. They welcomed me with open arms and asked for good news about the family. I assured them that all was well, though in fact I didn't know what the question meant. Isn't everything always good news unless someone is dying? Obviously it's never all good; you can always find something, like for example someone is sick. But no one talks about that. People aren't interested. They just want to hear that everything is okay. In every way. Everywhere.

The next few days were spent getting to know the people and seeing the place. It wasn't your typical farm. They didn't have any sheep and only a few cows. The farmer was sick in some way and couldn't work. The farmer's wife had a job in Akureyri. I didn't need to do anything: didn't have to shear or drive cows or shovel shit. It was a quiet life. I liked being in the country. I could hang about somewhere all day and read and didn't have to do anything

I didn't want. No one woke me in the morning; I had my own room. The food was plain, and people ate like in Reyjavík—they even had spaghetti. I'd been worried about that. I had so often been sent out to the country, where I was forced to eat all kinds of food that I thought nasty—like lumpfish, colostrum pudding, pickled meats, porridge pancakes, hræring (a mix of porridge and skyr), even udders. In rural areas, people eat all kinds of disgusting stuff Reykjavíkers wouldn't even think you could eat. But not in this part of the country. I could eat what I wanted, and if I wasn't hungry then I didn't have to eat anything. It was almost possible to think country life was wonderful.

I discovered that the old guy was my mother's brother, and I suspected that the farmer's wife was his daughter. I knew very few of my extended family members. I didn't really know who was who and didn't quite know why. Periodically, I met people on the street who said hello and asked how my parents were doing. I always told them the same thing—everything was good.

"Good afternoon, Jón."

"Hi," I'd say, pretending like I knew the person.

"How's your Dad doing?"

"All well and good."

"Please give him my very best regards."

"Yes, of course," I'd say, convincingly.

I never knew who these people were, but they often turned out to be Mom or Dad's siblings. I've always had great difficulty telling people apart and find it very difficult to recognize faces. My brother Óskar once came to visit; he'd recently shaved off his beard. I said hello to him and introduced myself.

Everyone started to laugh.

"Don't you know your own brother?" Mom asked, teasingly. But I saw these people so infrequently. Mom and Dad rarely took me with them on visits. You couldn't take me anywhere because I was such a prankster. During the summer, I was usually in the country. At family reunions, I was usually absent. As far as I was concerned, my parents' siblings were strange and distant, and so were my own siblings. It was like everyone else was from a different generation than me.

Sometimes we drove into Akureyri. It was almost like going into town back home. There were shops and even some teenagers hanging outside the convenience store. I went to the bookstore and bought a copy of *Bravo*. The next day, I hunkered down with the magazine. It was in German, so I didn't understand any of the writing, but I examined the pictures carefully. I carefully discerned who were punks and who weren't. That's how I discovered Nina Hagen. It was love at first sight. I was absolutely fascinated. She was without doubt the most beautiful woman in the world. There was a folded poster in the magazine that I hung up as soon as I got home. She was definitely punk. I sat and stared at her. I was in love. I loved this woman. I knew nothing about her, but she was definitely awesome and definitely knew all about anarchism.

The only newspaper they got on the farm was *The Times*. The back issues were stacked in a pile inside the kitchen. I scrutinized each and every edition, cutting out anything that had to do with punk. I put the clippings up in my room, all around Nina Hagen. *The Times* called punks tramp rockers:

"We play tramp rock because we're bored!" said the Danish queen of tramp rock, Camilla Cool. Tramp rock came to Copenhagen about a year and a half ago; it came, of course, from the Sex Pistols in London. Those few who took up tramp rock in Copenhagen were treated badly and most people wanted their bands to go away and die. But their members didn't slink off because it's part of the *fílósófía* of tramp rockers to shock others and turn the public against themselves. Tramp rockers color their hair purple or green and wear clothes so torn to pieces that the hippies of the past decade would be ashamed of their outfits. What's more, they often stick safety-pins through their ears or cheeks.

I cut out the picture of Camilla Cool and hung it on the wall. I read the story again and again and again. What was *fílósófía*? I had no idea, but I knew how fun it was to shock people and turn them against you. For example, it's okay to make fun of hippies. They're lame.

Shortly after I got to the countryside, The Clash toured Iceland and played gigs at Laugardalshöll. There was a lot written about them in *The Times,* which published pictures of them taken at the airport. "London Calling" was played on the radio. "Bank-robber" would definitely have been played at the gig. I longed with all my heart to go but couldn't because I was so far away. I was gutted about this; I cried. That was my song! The most magnificent event of my life was taking place, and I wasn't there.

Nina Hagen looked reassuringly at me. Camilla Cool, too.

Punk was shaping my life. I scrutinized punks and tried to imitate them in the way I dressed. I found safety pins that I pinned to my T-shirt, and then I scrawled the Anarchy sign on it with a ballpoint pen. I scrubbed the knees on my jeans with an emery board until they were ripped and destroyed. Then I knotted a hangman's noose from soft rope like I'd learned in the Scouts and put it round my neck. Finally, I cut off the torso below my ribs and also the sleeves. People on the farm watched, fascinated by the transformation, by the birth of punk amid the rural calm. They were particularly pleased with the hangman's noose. The farmer was pretty cool, even lent me his marker so that it was easier to see what I'd written on the T-shirt, and the farmer's wife got me some bigger safety pins, like I wanted.

Mom's brother smoked Camel cigarettes. Inside the panty was a cardboard box full of cigarette packs. I snuck into it and stole a single pack. I hid the pack out in the barn and slunk out occasionally to smoke. I trained myself to smoke like a real tough guy, to let the cigarette hang carelessly down from my mouth, to blow smoke rings. I practiced flicking flaming butts with my finger. (I made sure I didn't flick them into the hay.)

Since I couldn't go see The Clash, as compensation, I went to a youth concert in Akureyri. I was extremely excited that I was going to Akureyri alone. I got myself ready, put on lots of pins, and wrote Nina Hagen's name on my canvas shoes with the farmer's marker. Although it was raining, I refused to wear an overcoat. I would rather freeze to death from the cold and rain than be seen in some ridiculous windbreaker. I was just in my school shirt with the rope hanging around my neck. The farmer took me to Akureyri, dropped me off, and said that he'd come get me after the concert. Once he was gone, I took a big safety pin I'd kept in my pocket. The next step I had prepared and planned very carefully. I undid the pin, pinched my right ear lobe, stuck it through, and fastened it. I was ready. I went to the venue. I immediately attracted considerable attention. I was both an out-of-towner and, moreover, they thought I was a bit odd-looking. Some openly gaped in astonishment. I pretended I was accustomed to drawing attention and didn't let it affect me but walked around in front of the stage and looked out for other punks. I got out the Camel pack and carelessly lit myself a cigarette.

It wasn't a punk concert. The bands were dressed normally. Some played heavy metal, and others didn't even have a singer, just solo guitar. The lyrics were usually about girls or the weather. Shitty music. Few of the songs were original; most were rock versions of old Icelandic melodies. In addition, some tried taking popular foreign songs and adding Icelandic lyrics. What a disappointment! No songs about anarchism or how unbearable it was to live in the shadow of the atomic bomb. No "fuck the system." Most of the musicians wasted more time adjusting their instruments than playing them.

The rain pounded on me, and I was freezing cold and wet through by the time the last band came onstage. The headliners are always last; the other bands are just warm-ups. The band ending the concert was called Just Party. They were a bit older than those who'd played before. The singer sang original compositions in English. I thought that was pretty cool. Finally, a little recompense for missing out on The Clash. I was filled with joy, nodding in rhythm to the music and clapping between the tunes. Maybe Just Party were punks?

"Nice!" said a thin, gangly guy next to me.

"Yes," I said.

"Are you from Reykjavík?"

"Yes!" I replied proudly.

After the concert, I walked to a convenience store. I was starting to shiver from the cold and the weather. I positioned myself at the window and kept a lookout for the farmer. Several kids who were inside the convenience store were paying me close attention. They were clearly talking about me and whispering and laughing; they were a few years older than I was.

"Are you a punk?" one of them asked.

"Yes."

"Can I spit on you, then?"

"No," I replied, indignant.

The others laughed.

I'd experienced similar situations a few times before.

"If you're a punk, I can spit on you!"

I was silent. Was that really true? Can you really spit on punks? When did that happen? I refused to believe it. People would hardly go and spit on Nina Hagen when she went to the convenience store.

The kid walked right up to me.

"What's that around your neck?"

"A hangman's noose. It's the same knot you use to hang people."

He gripped the end of the rope and pulled. The kids laughed.

"Stop it!" I said.

"What, aren't you a punk?" asked another kid.

"Leave me alone," I muttered.

I was a little scared. I kept looking desperately for the farmer.

"Leave him alone," said the girl in the store.

"Can't I talk to him?" asked the boy.

I wanted to tear myself free and run behind the counter.

"You have to leave if you're going to act like that," she continued.

The boy let me go and went to his friends. The kids laughed and looked at me. I smiled, grateful to the girl who'd saved me, and moved closer to her.

"Are you from Reykjavík?" she asked.

"Yes, I'm staying in the country, nearby."

"You listen to punk?"

"Yes!"

The question was pleasantly surprising. She knew about punk?

"You're into Nina Hagen?"

I could scarcely believe my ears. Nina Hagen! This girl really knew who she was? Perhaps she even knew Nina?

"Yes," I replied cheerfully, pointing at my shoes as proof.

We both looked down at my shoes and then she looked questioningly at me. The ink had run in the rain and become a faint, black blob.

"I wrote Nina Hagen on my shoes with a marker," I said, to make it clear.

"Oh, okay."

"Nina Hagen's my favorite singer," I said boastfully. "I've got a poster of her at home."

The truth, though, was that I'd never heard a song by Nina Hagen. I'd just seen some pictures of her. I thought she was so beautiful and cool.

"I've got one of her albums," the girl said. "*Unbehagen.*"

I nodded like I knew exactly what she was talking about. In fact, I had no idea. *Unbehagen?* What did that mean?

"My favorite band is The Clash," I said, to say something.

"Did you go to the gig?"

"No, I didn't."

"They were awesome," the girl said.

"Did you go?"

"Yes," she said, as if nothing could be more natural.

I looked at her curiously. She didn't seem to be a punk. Her jeans weren't ripped, and she was just in a long-sleeved T-shirt. Her hair was normal and in a ponytail. She didn't look punk, but she listened to punk. Then again, Óli wasn't a punk, but he still had more punk albums than I did. I didn't have any. I was filled with awe at being confronted with someone who had gone to see The Clash live.

"I have their album, too," she added. "What albums do you own?"

I couldn't admit to this wonderful person, who was not only a guardian angel to the persecuted but also a passionate punk, that I didn't own a single album.

"I don't have any albums with me. There's no record player where I am in the country."

"Bummer! I couldn't stay anywhere there wasn't a record player."

"Yes, but at least 'London Calling' was on the radio the other day."

"Is there a cassette player out at yours?" she asked.

There was in fact a combined cassette player and radio in the living room—kind of like the one Mom had.

"Well, but I don't have any tapes," I added, as an excuse.

"Bummer!" she said again.

"Yes," I mumbled awkwardly.

"I can record it for you!"

"Really?"

Three days later, the farmer drove me back to Akureyri. I went back to the store and got a cassette. It was in a box. On the outside she'd written in blue ink: NINA HAGEN. UNBEHAGEN. What a beautiful thing! We drove back home, and I borrowed the cassette player and took it into my room. With quivering hands I opened the capsule and pulled out the jewel that stored the mysterious songs of the most beautiful girl in the world. UNBEHAGEN. On a black TDK cassette, high position type 2. Sixty minutes of wonderful punk. I opened the cassette player, put the tape in, shut it, took a deep breath, and pressed play. "African Reggae" filled the room. I was hypnotized by love. I had never heard anyone sing like that. My sweetheart variously muttered in a deep voice or shrieked like an old woman, then suddenly broke into being an opera singer. She was wonderful in every way. The only problem was that she sang in German. All I could understand about the song was that she wanted to go to Africa.

I listened to the whole album. Over and over again. The tunes ran together, one long and incessant sequence of screechings and deep-voiced falsettos. She spoke rapidly and in a torrent. I couldn't even distinguish words. I tried to listen specifically for whether she ever said "anarchy," but I never heard it. The musical instruments sounded great, too. The men in her band were great musicians but didn't look like they were punks. They were just dressed normally, based on the pictures I'd seen in *Bravo*. It was like Nina Hagen was the only punk in the band. In most of the songs, there was a guitar solo. I had not heard many punk songs, but somehow I still knew that there's a rule against guitar solos in punk. My disappointment was huge. I found it very sad. This wasn't really punk, but something else. Why was she always changing her voice? Nina Hagen appeared to have no interest in anarchism or in overthrowing the system. She just wanted to go to Africa. I could hardly see the punk in that. Was there something punk about Africa? Were there punks in Africa? Why didn't she go to London instead? I just didn't get it. The music got on my nerves. I found it boring, and I didn't understand the lyrics. I turned off the music, took the cassette out, and put it back in its case. What a disappointment. Nina had failed me. But love is blind. I looked at the poster, ashamed. She was beautiful and she was tough, real cool. I decided to forgive her for her bad music. No one is perfect. I couldn't stop loving her even if she was really boring. I decided to hold out hope. Maybe she would release another album that would be better and that would be called Anarchyhagen—and be in English. Maybe she just needed a new band. Maybe someone needed to point out to her that the guys in the band with her were lame and needed replacing. Maybe she could sing with the Sex Pistols. Her look would fit in. I definitely wouldn't be ashamed if she were my girlfriend.

I would happily go around town with her. But my first love was superficial. I loved Nina Hagen just for her appearance.

VALLEY LIFE

I'm just a victim of your wildest lies
Send in my photo with another name
I'm society's victim
Nobody has to get you to buy it now
That's your concern and I don't vote
I'm society's victim
I'm just the subject of discussion now
The one no one admires
I'm society's victim
I'm not just sufferin' from paranoia
It's invented by you and them
I'm society's victim
—DISCHARGE

I came back home from out in the country the same day Vigdis
Finnbogadóttir became President of Iceland. It was also the same
day that Italian terrorists blew up railway stations in Bologna,
killing 85 people, reducing the earth's population to four billion,
four hundred and thirty-four million, six hundred and eighty-two
thousand. Icelanders numbered two hundred and twenty-nine
thousand, one hundred and eighty-seven of that. Jimmy Carter
was president of the United States but was about lose to Ron-
ald Reagan in the presidential election. The Soviets had invaded
Afghanistan. The US supported and trained the terrorists who
fought against the Soviets. The terrorists would later evolve into
the Taliban and seize power in Afghanistan. War would break out

between Iran and Iraq. The United States would support Iraq and give them food, money, and weapons. With their support, Saddam Hussein would invade Iran.

Icelanders were just beginning to use credit cards and would go on to take the lead in their use around the world. The Social Democratic Party, which later turned into the Alliance, was in power. The prime minister was called Benedict Gröndal. Inflation in Iceland was at one hundred percent and showed no signs it would stop rising.

None of these issues mattered to me. For me, the world was going to hell no matter what. I had no future. I was unsuccessful. I didn't fear the future; I just didn't care about it. I avoided thinking about it. I was killing time. The atomic bomb was waiting to be used and could explode at any moment. It was just a matter of time before the end of the world. Americans had thrown atomic bombs down on Hiroshima and Nagasaki. It could happen again. People talked about it. The US military base in Keflavík put us at risk. If there were a war between the US and Russia, the Russians would shoot a nuke at Keflavík Airport. The whole of Reykjanes would burn up. Everyone would die. A shock wave would hit Reykjavík and the houses would collapse. Then the radioactivity would kill those of us who hadn't died in the explosion.

By now, I'd become a complete punk. One of my first tasks as such had been to go to the pet shop on Grensásvegur and buy a dog collar with spikes—I put it on my neck instead of a hanging rope. Since I had always hated my hair color, I wanted to dye my hair green. Mom forbade that. But because I had repeatedly stuck safety pins through my earlobes and kept getting infections as a result, she agreed I could get a piercing on the condition that I go to a professional in a beauty salon. That was my next task. With a stomachache of anxiety, I sat in a chair in a salon. The beautician first cooled my earlobe with ice. Then she pinched a "gun" on my lobe.

"Are you ready?" she asked.

I held my breath, closed my eyes, and clenched every muscle in my body. I nodded my head.

Much to my surprise, it didn't hurt at all. I had a real earring! I felt my character grow by half. When I walked out, I felt everyone staring at my ear. Everyone I met stared at my ear. The bus driver stared. I thought I felt the gaze of everyone on the bus directed at my ear. It was amazing! I went through my room and took hold of everything that was childish or not punk. Some of it I threw away; the rest I put in a closet. I hung up the poster of Nina Hagen and the newspaper clippings I'd collected.

Next, I went carefully through my clothes, picking and cutting. I junked most of them. I held onto some jeans, T-shirts, and long-sleeve shirts. I got the jeans and rubbed at the knees with coarse sandpaper until the material gave out and I had ripped knees. I cut the cuffs off the long-sleeved shirts. Then I went over everything with black markers and drew an A in a circle here and there and wrote "Anarchy" and band names I felt were right.

But I needed a decent coat. Punks didn't usually wear windbreakers. They had leather jackets. Problem was, I didn't own one. I called Óli for information on where I could get a leather jacket cheap. Óli said I could have his brother Friðjón's old leather jacket.

I ran over to his house in my newly-cut T-shirt and got my jacket. It wasn't a real leather jacket; it was made of artificial leather. And it wasn't black, but brown, with cuffs. It wasn't the right style, but beggars obviously can't be choosers. I cut the cuffs off it and tore off the toggle that adjusted the fit.

I put on my gear and went to where Mom sat playing solitaire.

"Good God! What have you done now, child?"

"This is punk," I said resolutely.

Mom sighed deeply and shook her head.

"Can I have some money?"

She went back to solitaire and said, downcast as usual:

"Ask your Dad."

That was something I wanted to avoid at all costs.

"I can't be bothered to talk to him. Can't you let me have some money?"

"Why do you need money?"

She didn't look up from her game.

"I want to buy patches and an album."

"What will it cost?"

I mentioned the amount. Mom thought for a while, then heaved a sigh and got to her feet. She took out her wallet and handed me the money.

"Here you go."

"Thank you."

I was grateful not to have to talk to Dad and ask him for money. He would never let me have money to buy patches or albums. I had to lie to him that I was going to the movies, then stretch out my hand towards him and let him hold me there in his firm grip, stroking my cheek as he whispered and muttered something I couldn't hear although I nodded my head anyway and smiled in a friendly way like I was a really good kid. He'd even started talking about the break-in and how inconvenient it was for him, and I had to promise not to do it again. And I promised beautifully, not because I meant it, but because I was suffocating and wanted to get away from him as quickly as I could.

I took the bus down to Hlemmur and went to the only store on Laugavegur that sold tags. It was a variety store, specializing in products for kids and teenagers. An old Arab ran the shop. It stocked everything between heaven and earth, all kinds of fashion clothes, posters, spiked belts, patches, logos, and incense—but also stink bombs and practical jokes. I'd often been to this store, usually just to look around and fantasize. Sometimes I bought things. Once I bought a fake turd. That was a source of endless pleasure until it was confiscated by teachers at school. I'd also often bought stink bombs, which I then threw through windows or put through the mail slots of people who had annoyed me.

The store had wised up to this new era and had become a true punk heaven. It had everything a punk could have dreamed of: pants that had been torn apart and put back together with safety pins and real leather jackets with thick, red linings. And patches. On one side were cloth patches you sewed onto your clothes and on the other breastpins or brooches you pinned to yourself.

I looked at everything carefully and asked the prices. The Arab responded in his exotic accent with a wise, patient demeanor.

After much speculation, I bought a Crass patch with the anarchy sign to sew on my clothes and three small buttons: one that said

SEX PISTOLS, one that said FUCK THE SYSTEM, and one with a picture of The Clash. Then I bought several iron spikes to attach to my clothes. I couldn't afford any more since I also had to buy an album. I fastened the iron spikes to my leather jacket, put on my buttons, and sauntered out to the record shop.

I could afford just one album. I looked through all the punk albums in the shop carefully and listened to them. I took care not to buy an album I could borrow from Óli. Also, most of the records only had one good song on them. I listened to Sham 69. They were fairly popular. I wasn't a big fan. The Dead Kennedys had a few good songs like "California Über Alles" and "Too Drunk to Fuck," but I still didn't think it was worth buying the whole album.

After careful consideration, I decided to buy *Inflammable Material* by Stiff Little Fingers. I'd seen a program about them on TV. They were from Northern Ireland and seemed to have fairly strong opinions on life and existence. That carried a lot of weight— plus the lyrics came with the album. But what determined that I bought this album rather than another one was that the lead singer was wearing glasses. He had square steel-frame glasses like I did, and I immediately felt a connection with him.

There weren't many punks in Fossvogur. There were many who liked the music yet who weren't willing to go all the way, like the girl in the convenience store in Akureyri. They wore normal clothes but owned albums by punk bands. Then there were the fake punks. They thought they could be punks by listening to the music, but they lacked the core mentality, i.e., they'd neither given up on the future, nor were they furious at the system. For these people, punk was just a superficial, entertaining fashion. They even listened to Adam Ant and considered him a punk. They usually had no interest in anarchism, and I didn't want anything to do with them. You had to be careful of fake punks. For me, punk wasn't a fad but a lifestyle. The clothes were a surefire way to be part of a definite group and to make it possible for other punks to recognize me. They were also a firm statement and expression of one's state of mind and ideology. What mattered to me most was the deep meaning of what it was to be a punk. That meant being an outsider, incompatible with the masses, dreaming that one day I would be dead in peace, no longer needing to take part in any fucking shit. Anarchism was a strong part of it. To the normal world, I was a dangerous freak—ugly, stupid, silly. But in the world of punk rock, I was an equal—attractive, intelligent, exciting. Punk gave my life purpose. The rules no longer defined me. According to punk rock's terms, I could do what I wanted. I could write without someone making fun of it when I wrote badly. It was punk to write badly. I could play the guitar without having learned it. I could say and do things the system rejected because punk rejected the system. Punk rebelled against the system and against systematic thought. The system I knew best was the school system. I hated it, and I feared all systems that might be trying to force me into a future. I hated everyone who lived by the rules. I hated the values that deemed desirable that which I didn't know and held all my qualities worthless. The system wanted to peg me as an abnormal deviation. I didn't belong in the school system. But I didn't belong with the dunces, either. The system thought I was stupid, but I wasn't. Perhaps I was simply too smart for the system. The Punk overcomes the system: I realized I didn't have to learn all their damn rules. I didn't believe half the crap. I saw no point in learning math or Danish. I didn't care about other people's opinions of me. I refused to keep letting others define me. Punk delivered me from all the invisible demands on which school, Mom, and Dad insisted. I wanted to express myself, talk and even scream. I wanted to tear myself free. I wanted peace. Punk was a ship setting off from a boring shore, and I jumped on board toward a new adventure.

I started going to the youth center at Bústaðir to try to find other punks. I ran into Alli there. He lived one street over. His father was a teacher at Austurbæjar School, and Alli went to school there, so we didn't really see each other except during the summer. Alli had become a punk. He was wearing an old suit jacket with patches on it. I checked them carefully. They were all punk except one: The Police. The Police weren't a punk band, but New Wave. Their lyrics were asinine and not about anything important. One song was called "Walking on the Moon" and was about some idiotic people who were walking about on the moon. There were endless songs about girls like Roxanne. Real punks didn't whine about girls. Still, Alli was enough of a punk to kick around with.

Most kids at Bústaðir were either disco freaks or normals. Most were fine and left me alone. But there was a certain group of boys I called the Morons. The Morons were boys who thought they were really funny and witty and were always playing pranks and fronting around each other. But they were annoying, hanging out in groups and talking loudly. The Morons were always cheerful but also really annoying. In winter they would wrestle in the snow and try to cram snow inside each other's mouths and stuff. Their favorite music was comedy ska, like Madness and Bad Manners. They went to films like *H.O.T.S.* about cheerleaders in high school and thought they were brilliant. They didn't have girlfriends; they just hung around with each other. Their lives seemed to pass in scuffles, screeches, and bad jokes.

When the Morons were preparing a prank, their behavior changed. They'd start whispering and giggling and tense up with the exertion of stifling their laughter. Their pranks always ended up being somehow related to girls. Sometimes they played with a tampon or pad, dipping it in ketchup and throwing it at each other and screaming with hilarity. Condoms, however, were a total fascination to them. Sometimes they showed up with a condom they had spat in and threw it amongst themselves, or pretended to discover it on each other. When they were done throwing it around themselves, they threw it at me. The Morons had a particular interest in me.

Every single night, the Morons taunted me. They jeered at me, pushed me, and tried to trip me when they ran into me. I asked them to leave me alone but that just got them more keyed up, so I learned to keep quiet until they were done. Usually, some girl came to my rescue, or an employee. I endured it without ever complaining to the staff. I knew that if I did, I would simply get beaten up later. Before I left, I made sure that they weren't outside. Inside, I tried to sit where employees could see me, and I never went to the bathroom alone. When I needed to go, I seized my chance as soon as some employee did, or snuck away when my enemies weren't around or weren't looking.

I was never invited to join in with any of the stuff that was going on. I didn't want to, either; I simply wasn't interested. Generally, I thought teenagers were boring and stupid. Most of them were caught up in pointless and superficial stuff. The girls seemed most concerned about their looks. The boys thought about nothing but the girls. If they had hobbies, it was sports. I despised sports.

I hung out in the corner, watching and waiting for a punk to walk in the door. The one I most hoped to meet was Siggi the Punk. He was the most famous punk in Reykjavík. He was in the band Masturbation and was from the neighborhood. He was a real punk, with earrings and a leather jacket and marked-up jeans. I'd never met him. I'd only seen pictures of him in the papers. I'd heard stories about him and seen graffiti by him on bus stops. He drew anarchist signs in black ink and wrote short slogans like "Fuck The System" and "Down with the police!" I really wanted to meet Siggi the Punk, get information and advice from him, and even become his friend. But he was a few years older than me, so it was pretty unlikely that he had any interest in befriending me.

I wanted to meet someone with whom I could talk, someone who understood me. Someone in the same boat. I wanted to talk about the system and how it was trying to kill my spirit. I wanted to meet someone with an understanding of anarchy who could tell me more about that phenomenon. I wanted to explore the mysteries of life. I wouldn't be at ease until I could get some answers. Maybe there was some anarchist country somewhere where people could go and be left alone. I craved knowledge the way a thirsty man longs for water. But not those pointless facts taught in school. I had no interest in them. I wanted my knowledge.

There were no answers in the newspapers, either. They all seemed busy with anything but what mattered. I wanted to find books that might possibly contain some answers for me. But what books were there? There weren't any in the library. They were old and outdated, dry and boring. Þórbergur Þórðarson was dead. If he'd been alive, I would have tracked him down. I'd read most of his books. I felt in harmony with him. He had understood me and guided me. Why was I always so nervous, anxious, and uneasy in my soul while everyone else seemed relaxed and worry-free? Was I abnormal? Was I insane? Or was it perhaps that they were abnormal?

So I sat there evening after evening and put myself through endless suffering in order to find answers to the mystery of life. My anarchist tags and buttons became the source of endless comments.

"Are you an anarchist?"

"Yes."

"You don't know what anarchism is!"

"Sure."

"What is it?"

"It means being left alone and doing what you want without the police or the authorities messing with you. It's about being against all the rules."

"Against all the rules? Are you against traffic regulations, too?"

"Errr, yes."

"So, can someone in a car just drive into you if you're on the sidewalk?"

"Errr, no…"

"You don't know what anarchism is at all."

"Yes, it's being left alone by idiots like you."

I usually ended up helpless. My basic knowledge of anarchism didn't allow for debate. I went back to the library and pored over the books on anarchism. I stored the key names and theories in my memory and decided that I probably wasn't a Bakuninist but rather a Proudhonist. Next time I was asked if I was an anarchist, I was on top of things:

"Yes, I'm a Proudhonist."

This was a completely new tactic.

"What's that?"

"It's a theory within anarchism that's named after Pierre Joseph Proudhon."

Proudhon got me neatly out of any discussion of anarchy. People got the impression that I'd done my homework. If that failed, then I dropped in Bakunin's name, referring to the conflict between their theories. After that, they stopped looking at me like some kind of half-wit, and more as a mentally disturbed genius. But although that tactic stopped debate, it didn't stop the Morons. They didn't care how much I knew about Proudhon or Bakunin or anarchism. They just thought it was fun to pick on me.

I tried to avoid Alli if I could. If we were both together, the tormenting was so much worse. We were on sale, two for one, ripe to be bullied. It didn't improve things that I was the son of a cop and Alli was a teacher's son. The Morons for some reason found it more fun tormenting Alli than me. Sometimes they got at him and left me more or less in peace. He also took the teasing more personally than I did and got angry. That was, of course, grist to the Morons' mill, and they got all the more provoked and excited. I didn't get stirred up. I didn't care, even when Coke was poured over me and used chewing gum thrown at me. I had a goal. I was on a secret spy mission. My assignment was to gather data about punk. And if this was part of my martyrdom, so be it. When I'd got to know more punks, we'd get together a big clique, and no one would dare do anything to us. One day, punks would control everything.

The only person I spoke to was Eiki the Druggie. He was a disabled kid who was three years older than me. He was called Eiki the Druggie because he was always so stupid that it was like he was always on drugs. I liked Eiki. We had often played together when we were small and knew each other well. I had more in common with him than most others. There was some mysterious force connecting us. We were both outsiders. Deviations from the norm. The genius and the imbecile.

Finally, the evening came when the year-long toil yielded the desired result. Siggi the Punk came into Bústaðir. He was even more magnificent than I'd imagined. He was really thin and withered and a whole head shorter than me. His dark hair was cropped and patchy. He'd evidently cut it himself. It was obvious that everyone had a lot of respect for him. Even the worst of the Morons went and talked to him and asked him for news. He was tactful and reserved, speaking low, answering questions, and sucking in through his nose. Then he came and sat on the couch. I stared at him. This was the first real punk I'd met and the first person I'd found who was more punk than me. He had a dog collar around his neck, and his leather jacket was the coolest thing I'd ever seen. It was black and sewn together from a number of smaller leather pieces. A leather jacket like that was a real possession. His jeans were torn into pieces from the knees up to mid-thigh and scrawled all over with black marker. On his feet he wore tattered army boots. He must have been sixteen or seventeen years old. His eyes were dull and dreaming. He smelled of strong patchouli perfume. That was something I'd have to get hold of for myself. He looked at me. I was totally paralyzed by fear and didn't dare speak to him.

"Hey," he said.

My heart surged. He'd said hello to me!

"Hey," I said, absolutely rigid with admiration.

We fell silent.

"Siggi, isn't it?" I asked.

"Yes," he said, and hocked.

I couldn't think of anything else to say. What kind of idiot was I? What could I say, really?! Mostly, it was absolutely invaluable for me just to get to watch him and to observe. One of the employees came over and said hello to him. He was very respectful. He was apparently well liked by everyone. I noticed that he had a speech impediment and struggled to say *gl-* or *cl-*; he said *tlothes* instead of clothes and *dlasses* instead of glasses. I was determined to practice so I could speak the same way. When the employee went he turned to me:

"Got a cigarette?"

"Yes," I said and picked up the crumpled pack of Winstons I'd stolen from my mother. I smoked at most one or two cigarettes a day, so a pack was enough to last me a month. I smoked more to be tough than out of any need.

We went outside and smoked. I read all the writing on his pants and checked out the patches on the jacket. He just had two patches: Anarchism and Crass. He showed little interest in me but just stared right ahead, empty and indifferent.

"I bought a Stiff Little Fingers album the other day," I said, to say something.

"Yeah," he said, indifferent.

There was no curiosity in his voice. It was like I'd reported something that was common knowledge, that didn't matter. How could it be unimportant to have bought the Stiff Little Fingers album?

"They're very good," I added.

He was silent and just smoked. Now and then he sucked through his nose and spat. He didn't seem to have a cold. It was more like a tic.

"What music do you listen to?" I asked, curiously.

He didn't answer immediately.

"I don't listen to bubblegum," he declared in a low voice.

Bubblegum? I'd no idea what that meant. Bubblegum? Were they some band I'd never heard of? I desperately wanted to ask but didn't dare expose my ignorance. So I nodded like I completely understood. Maybe this was a New Wave group? Definitely.

"I don't listen to New Wave," I said, just to be sure.

He said nothing, just sucked in through his nose.

"Some punks listen to Adam Ant and The Police," I added, to make sure he didn't think I did that sort of thing.

"That's not punk," he muttered.

"No," I echoed.

He was the first person I'd met who shared this understanding with me. Something wonderful was happening. We finished smoking and stubbed out the ends.

"Shall we go back inside?" I asked.

"No, I just came in to get a cigarette."

"Okay…"

"I'm heading home. Want to come?"

I hardly believed my ears. Siggi the Punk was inviting me to his house? Were we becoming friends? He was accepting me?

"Yes, yes," I said, trying not to sound too eager.

Siggi lived in a terraced house in Smáíbúðahverfinu. His mother, a short and fat old woman, greeted us as we entered.

"You're home, Sigurður?"

Siggi slammed the front door with all his might.

"Shut the fuck up, hag!"

I reacted more than his mother. She seemed used to him speaking to her that way. That was something I had so often longed to tell my dad but never dared. And I had never dared say anything remotely similar to my mother. Mom never lectured me about anything. What little she said was usually spot-on. I followed Siggi into his room. I said hi to his mother on the way. She didn't answer me, just looked at me angrily. He closed the door and locked it with a key.

"Gnarled old crone," he muttered.

His room was a little cubbyhole with a single bed. The walls were scrawled over with anarchist symbols and all kinds of slogans. Above the bed hung an upside-down cross; under it had been written in black ink "JESUS DIED FOR HIS OWN SINS, NOT MINE."

Over the tiny window hung a dirty sheet. The room was dark and dirty and covered with rubbish, newspapers, comic books, and empty cigarette packets. On the bed was a giant ashtray packed with cigarette butts. The patchouli smell was overwhelming and hung in the air like a thick cloud. Siggi sucked in through his nose and spat on the floor. Spat on the floor in his own room! I made a mental note of that. This I was going to try! Then he went over to the record player and put an album on the turntable. A piercing guitar-screech and fast drum rhythms resounded from the single small speaker. The singer screamed so fast that you couldn't work out any of the words except an occasional "fuck," "system," and "death." I liked it a lot.

"Which band is this?" I asked, full of expectation.

"Discharge," he replied without looking at me.

I nodded like I knew absolutely who that was and tried to store the name in my memory. Siggi took a pipe out of his ashtray and began to scrape the ash from inside with a pocketknife made from the aluminum foil out of a cigarette packet.

"Want a pipe?"

"What is it?" I asked.

"Scratch."

"Is it hash?" I asked, surprised.

I had never seen hash before, let alone smoked it.

"Scratch," he said again.

Here I had to admit my ignorance.

"What's that?"

"It's hash that has already been smoked."

Huh? Hash that has been smoked but that you can somehow

smoke again. Ash from previously smoked hash. I was happy to try it. I was willing to try anything. My life up to this point had been pointless.

"Do you have a cigarette?"

I handed him a cigarette. He tore it into pieces, crumbled the tobacco into the aluminium foil, and mixed it with the ash. He held the foil in the air and heated it over a lighter flame. Then he tipped everything into the pipe and lit it. He took a big hit. He held the smoke inside and handed me the pipe. The bitter smoke burned my throat, and I was coughing. Siggi blew out and took the pipe.

"You've got to keep it in if you're going to get high."

He took another hit of the pipe and handed it back. I took a small drag and held it down inside. We took turns smoking until there was nothing left but ashes. Siggi threw himself on his bed and put his hand over his eyes. I sat on the end of the bed and waited for something to happen, for euphoria to pour over me. Nothing. Discharge just kept screaming from the player.

"They're good," I said.

He did not answer.

"Siggi?"

"Huh?" he murmured.

He seemed to be asleep. I sat on the bed, embarrassed, waiting for something to happen, until I realized that nothing was in the cards.

"I'm thinking about just going home."

"Yes," he said.

He obviously had no intention of getting up and following me out, so I just went.

"Bye," I said before I closed the door.

He didn't answer and was apparently asleep. I said goodbye to his mother on the way out. She didn't answer me, but instead looked at me with contempt in her eyes. It was midnight but still bright and warm. I walked home, where my mother greeted me with hands on hips.

"Why are you home so late?"

"Uhh, I just am."

"Where have you been?"

"Bústaðir."

"Why were they open so late?"

"A table tennis competition," I said and took off my shoes.

She was skeptical but didn't say anything. I'd become very good at lying.

I said good night and went into my room. I put the Stiff Little Fingers album on the record player and turned the volume to the lowest setting. I lay in my bed. A turning point had occurred in my life. I'd become a real punk.

And so began my relationship with Siggi. He was older than me and clearly not all there. I talked to him every chance I got. I'd ask him things about punk or anarchism or how you should draw logos with markers, for example, what the different types of anarchist logos were. He always treated me really well. He wasn't ever patronizing or anything like that and seemed to look at me as an equal. I thought he was great, and we got to hang out more and more together—just shooting the breeze. It gave me a bit of protection, since Siggi enjoyed a certain respect that I didn't. I was left alone when I was with Siggi. We hung out, a little pair outside

Bústaðir, smoking and talking about punk. I asked, he answered, teaching me the various facts of punk rock, helping me find out what was punk and what was not. We wandered around a lot, went down to the bus station at Hlemmur, hung around downtown.

Sometimes when Siggi and I were wandering about, we broke into unlocked vehicles. We were looking for coins and cigarettes and stuff, even sometimes grabbing cigarettes directly from ashtrays. Those days, all cars were unlocked and almost invariably contained cigarettes. It was the norm. Everyone smoked and cigarettes were everywhere, so it wasn't like we were surprised when we found them. We weren't vandalizing anything, just taking the smallest items, bits and bobs, coins and cigarettes.

Several times, the police stopped us. One night, when we were on a journey through Bústaðahverfið, messing about in cars and things like that, someone called the cops. We were at a place somewhere near Réttarholtsvegur and were scrawling the anarchy sign on the walls. Suddenly the police turned up in the form of a Black Maria that braked hard: out jumped several cops. We sprinted off, cops on our heels. I was scared but also tremendously excited; I felt like I was someone important. I was on the run from the police with Siggi the Punk! We ran into the forest behind Bústaðir Church, which everyone calls the Big Wood. Siggi ran in one direction and I in another. The place where I ran out of the woods there was a garden. It was summer, around midnight. In the middle of the garden was a house and, behind it, two trashcans. Without thinking about it, I clambered into one of the trashcans and pulled the lid down over me. I was awfully breathless, sure the whole neighborhood must be able to hear both my breathing and my heartbeat as I hunched down in the trashcan. The can was empty, but the smell was disgusting. I put myself through it, however, in the name of freedom, so that I wouldn't be captured by the police. I was certain that at any moment the cover of the can would be yanked off and the fists of the police would appear and pull me up—but nothing happened. I squatted there and tried to listen for any sounds. To hear cops running about, talking or something. But there was absolute silence. After a long wait, I decided to lift the lid slightly and check around. I raised the lid super carefully and looked about. There was nothing, absolute silence. I went back down into the can. The police had indeed run past without knowing I was there. So I stood up in the can.

"So, are you done being in the trashcan, pal, or do you want to stay there a bit longer?"

I turned around. Behind me were three cops who had been standing there the whole time. The cops had had a good view of the whole thing and were standing grinning at me. They had seen me clambering down into the trashcan and had waited for me to come out again. I, of course, was looking right at them and all three knew perfectly well that I had no chance of escape.

"Uhh, no, no..." I answered and clambered out of the barrel. I was led to a police car where the cops accused me of breaking into cars and graffitiing walls. I flat out denied it.

"I'd never do such a thing! Neither break into cars nor steal anything! I'm not a thief!"

"So you weren't writing on the walls?"

"No! I would never!"

"And you don't have markers on you, or anything like that?"

"I do have some markers but I don't use them for writing on things. I don't write on houses, I just write on paper."

Then they had me empty my pockets. I had a pocket full of cigarettes from six different packets. It was clear that I wasn't innocent of stealing from cars. I had a bunch of singles and two markers. Guilty. No way to wiggle out of it. The cops took me down to the police station, and I was made to sit in the corridor. They knew, too, whose son I was. Dad came to pick me up.

"Well."

I got up and walked to the car with him. My father was silent. Mom was waiting for us at home. She sat me at the kitchen table and began the interrogation. I was asked what on earth I'd really been doing. Had I really been breaking into cars and stealing cigarettes? I tried naturally to dispute it and gave the impression that the police were exaggerating, that I wasn't up to much and the police had confused me with some other boys. I blamed the graffiti on Siggi and told them I would never do such a thing. Then I tried my utmost to convince them that the only thing I'd been guilty of was being in the wrong crowd, and that I'd avoid those kinds of people in future. After I'd uttered this lie, my mother became even angrier.

"Do you know how embarrassing this is for your father?"

"Yes."

"And do you think that's okay?"

"No, I'm absolutely never ever going to do this again."

Mom sighed.

"Go to your room and stay there."

One time I got involved in something with Siggi that even I thought a big deal, but fortunately it never came to light. My dad was a really good marksman, and, like many police officers at the time, he was trained to use a rifle, too. He competed in rifle contests and won lots of awards. He even made the news once for something that happened when he was driving his police car. Back then, sheep rifles were the norm on police cars and were used to take down dogs and cats. Dad saw a mink, took a single shot with the sheep gun, nailed the shot, and killed the mink from a long way away. It was quite an accomplishment and was on the cover of *The Face*. They printed a picture of Dad with the sheep rifle.

Dad also had a pistol he kept at home. It was a Sportsman, not dissimilar to the guns cowboys used. I had often taken it out and looked at it when home alone. It was kept in a locked cabinet, but I knew where the key was. There were also lots of bullets. I sometimes played with a blank; it was really fun to pull the trigger and shoot the blank from the gun. Once when Mom and Dad were out and I knew they would be gone late into the night, Siggi and I were hanging out at my house. We were putting carpet glue on a rag and breathing it in. The euphoria caused us to swim about—we were half-passed out, giggling and stuff like that, but that state always ended rather quickly. We'd been huffing up in the attic and were on our way back down to my room when I saw an opportunity to impress Siggi and said to him:

"Want to see something? A real gun!"

Siggi was more than willing, so we went downstairs and I opened the cupboard and pulled out the gun. Siggi had never seen a real gun before, and we were playing around with it without any bullets inside until Siggi asked:

"Why don't we get some bullets and go outside?"

I didn't think it was a good idea, but I couldn't say no.

"Sure," I replied, as if it was no problem.

We took the gun, loaded some bullets, and headed out. Siggi kept hold of it, and we went up to Ósland. I was really nervous. This wasn't a good idea. I was still a bit heady from huffing and wanted it to stop it altogether.

"Why don't we just go back and return the gun?"

"No, we have to fire it!" said Siggi, excited.

"Nuh-huh," I replied.

Without discussing it any further, Siggi lifted the gun and fired at a lamppost. There was an appalling crash. My heart skipped a beat. I'd never seen a gun fired, and I'd never imagined how violent the crack was. Our ears were ringing, and we ran straight back home like frightened rabbits. I took the gun off him immediately, emptied the round, put the gun back into its bag, and put everything into the closet. I expected to hear the wailing police sirens at any moment. My hands trembled. Siggi didn't care. It was like he thought it was just fun and no big deal.

"Well, I'm heading home."

"Yeah, okay, bye," I said in a trembling voice.

I stayed in my room and peeked out the window every other minute to see if the police were coming or if something was going to happen. But nothing did. There was no one. But after that, I stopped hanging out with Siggi. I didn't think he was all there. I'd also learned enough from him.

PERMANENT MARKER

Police man in the street
arresting those he meets
why he does I can't see
but I can be care if he doesn't take me
—NEFRENNSLI, "Policeman"

I wanted to learn to play an instrument and become a member of a punk band. Most people wanted to sing, like Johnny Rotten or the singer of Stiff Little Fingers. But I was too shy and withdrawn. I'd never dare sing in front of people. They'd simply laugh at me. I thought I'd probably be a good guitarist. A punk guitarist doesn't need to know much, just some cross grips, to be able to play punk. The guitarist in Crass, for example, places his fingers across the top of the guitar neck, and not below the way a good guitarist does. A punk guitarist doesn't know how to tune his guitar. The less he knows, the better. As punks become better musicians, they become worse punks, and before they know it, they're no longer a punk band but a New Wave band, having forgotten their purpose and ideals. Their music is no longer raw but polished and stuffed with sweethearts. The lyrics are no longer about the injustice of the system and anarchism—instead, they are increasingly sentimental and philosophical reflections on life. The first sign that a punk band is changing is often when the band adds a keyboard player. You can't do punk with keyboards. That's why I never was into The Stranglers. I felt they weren't punk. Although their bassist was quite punk, they had a keyboard player. In the end, they betrayed their true colors by turning not only into a New Wave band but even an all-out dance band. I despise everyone who betrays punk. Sellouts! Any band that added a keyboard player or was in some way questionable was immediately taken out of the sacrament. Either people were punk or they weren't. And as musicians went ahead and developed their music, more bands got tossed out from my record collection. Bubbi Morthens was the first to get tossed. I decided to give away all of his albums. The Clash betrayed me when they released *Sandinista!* And the Sex Pistols were over. Crass even said that punk was dead, that its fashion had become a commercial product, that the bands were more interested in making money than changing society. Gradually, I stopped listening to anything but Crass. I hadn't bought a lot of albums to date. I just borrowed them and copied them onto cassettes. The advantage the cassette player had over the record player was that you could take it everywhere, into the bathroom and even out to the yard or garage. That is, you could put batteries in it!

I met up with Alli, and we talked about the need to establish a properly Icelandic punk band. We were sorely lacking in that area. There were just three punk bands in the country, The Spunks, Disappointment, and Masturbation. I found them all annoying and felt they lacked the essential emphases. It was like The Spunks didn't really take punk seriously. They didn't even dress like punks. I'd gone to one of their concerts and hadn't enjoyed it a bit. Disappointment barely functioned and hardly ever gigged. They also lacked any identity and basically only had one good song, "Reykjavík O Reykjavík." Masturbation had both the looks and the songs to back it up. The whole band had shredded jeans and leather jackets and Bjarni the Mohawk even had, as you might expect, a mohawk. But they didn't seem to take themselves seriously, and even started to fool around in the middle of songs. Siggi the Punk was in Masturbation.

Alli could play the guitar and even had an electric guitar his brother had given him. He'd also learned the violin for several years, so the guitar wasn't that exotic as far as he was concerned. I didn't know any musical instruments. I tried to write songs. It wasn't easy. I didn't really know how I was meant to word things when there wasn't a tune. But the publicity materials were a cinch for me: anarchism, the school system, police, the peace struggle, and punk.

I tried becoming a drummer. We put together a drum kit in my room out of sweet tins, cans, pots, and pot lids. Alli played guitar, and I drummed with homemade wooden drumsticks. It went badly. I seemed to be completely devoid of any rhythm. Alli tried to explain the structure of music to me and how the drums were meant to supply the foundation for the rhythm but I didn't know what he meant. He made me listen to all kinds of songs where I had to listen for a drum beat. I never heard any beat, just a series of noises. The sounds that came out of my kit were nothing like the sounds from a real drum kit.

"We're missing a bass player, of course," said Alli.

I realized that it was a little harder to play punk than I had thought. Alli suggested that I play bass since it was the easiest instrument to play. I liked the idea. Sid Vicious was the bassist. He knew nothing about his instrument when he started playing for the Sex Pistols. He was just hired because of his appearance, and so he was allowed to play the bass. Even so, he was the main man in the band, after Johnny Rotten. He was so much cooler and tougher than the guitarist. The bass is a simple instrument, much simpler than the guitar, just four strings and no frets. I went to see my friend Óli the Stud, who had just bought an expensive bass and had started playing in a dance band.

"Would you teach me to play bass?" I asked.

He was up for it, so we sat down and he showed me his bass, a handsome black Fender. He showed me how I should hold it and how to pluck the strings. Everything went great, and I quickly realized that the sound of the bass changed depending on where on the neck you pressed the strings. I was a natural and would definitely be playing like a chief in no time. Then Óli put a record on the turntable and told me to listen to the bass on the song and play along. I tried to listen but couldn't hear anything no matter what I focused on. Óli tried to help me out with gestures and facial expressions. No luck. I just heard a jingling, like someone was shaking an iron tin full of screws. At first, Óli thought I was pulling his leg, but when he realized that I was serious, he said that I had to go to study music.

"You need to learn the basics of music."

I was up for that. But what did it mean?

"Can I learn the bass?"

"No, I don't think they teach bass anywhere."

"But I just want to learn the bass."

Óli stressed that I needed to learn the fundamentals of music and added that I should go to Óli Gaukur's Guitar School. There, I'd get training in the basics and learn the guitar, and as soon as I'd mastered the basics of guitar I'd automatically be able to play bass.

This sounded like a rather tortuous path, but since Óli said that it was the way, it probably was. I quite liked the idea and went straight home to my mother with my message.

"Can I go to Óli Gaukur's Guitar School?"

"Why?"

"To learn the bass."

Mom reacted pretty well to the idea and found it constructive that I wanted to learn something. So I got permission to enroll in a six-week course. My father took me to Rín, the musical instrument shop, to buy the cheapest acoustic guitar they had. I thought it was an ugly, stupid, hippie guitar. I had never seen a punk with an acoustic guitar. I was, however, willing to use it in private to practice and sat up all night inside my room and strummed on the guitar. I had no nails, so instead I used one of those plastic things they put round the necks of bread bags. I put my index finger flat across the strings, the way the guitarist in Crass did, and moved it up and down the neck while I struck the strings relentlessly with the plastic neck-tie. Perhaps this was the beginning of a phenomenal music career. Maybe I was about to become a world-famous punk guitarist.

I went to guitar school for the first time the next day. The students sat in a booth with headphones on their heads and electric guitars in their laps. Óli Gaukur walked among us, giving instruction. We all had to do the same song. He taught us a specific chord and made us practice it again and again until we knew it. Then he taught us another chord. I confused the chords with one another and found it extremely difficult to find the right place for my fingers. At the end of the session, he had us playing "Old Noah."

We didn't use our nails, but we had to use our index fingers to strum the strings. I found it dead boring. I both found the chords difficult and the song pointless and annoying. Even worse, however, was that I hurt my fingers. I got a cramp in my hand from holding the neck tight and had sore fingertips from strumming the strings. I'd rather learn cross grip since that was more what punks used, and I asked Óli about cross grip. He said he didn't teach any such thing and we would not need it if we learned real chords.

The second time was even more of a test than the first. Óli assumed everyone could do what we'd learned the first time around and had been diligently practicing at home. Most of the others clearly had practiced. However, I had no interest in this and had forgotten the chords. Óli tried to go over them with me while I informed him about the pointlessness of any kind of stupid chord when you just wanted to play in a punk band.

"To be able to play in a band, you have to know the instrument."

I told him the importance of a person not knowing too much, and that a good guitarist could easily ruin a proper punk band and subsequently turn it into a New Wave band. Óli Gaukur had no interest in or sense of punk but nodded patiently, then tried to focus my attention back on the chords.

The third time, we were once again playing "Old Noah." Each in their own booth. I didn't. I nodded my head while he gave us instructions, but as soon as he turned away, I took the plastic piece and strummed the guitar. The sound that came through the headset was great. I closed my eyes and enjoyed strumming the strings. I strummed so hard that I snapped a string. Óli came over with a disappointed expression and took my headphones and guitar from me.

When the session ended, he asked me to stay behind.

"Why are you here, Jón?" he asked, with a friendly tone.

"To learn to play the guitar."

"Then why don't you do the things I teach you?"

It was a good question. I, of course, hadn't come to learn the guitar, but to learn the fundamentals of music and how I should play bass.

"I want to learn to play punk."

"I don't teach punk, Jón."

That was incomprehensible to me.

"Why not?"

"I teach people to play traditional guitar, the important chords, so they can play popular songs."

That was something I had no interest in. I was clearly in the wrong place. Chords and songs sounded about as exciting to me as long division and Danish. I was definitely not going to sit around a campfire with an acoustic guitar like an idiot, singing "My sweetheart, come to me." I wasn't going to sit in the kitchen and play "Old Noah" for Mom and Dad like some moron. I wasn't a dork.

Óli suggested that I quit guitar school and even offered to repay me. We were both extremely happy with the outcome. My dad had already paid up front, so I could even pocket the cash. I told Mom and Dad, on the other hand, that everything was going extremely well in guitar school and that I'd become really good at guitar. Neither of them had any interest in it, and I knew they would never come and ask me to play for them.

I gave up on trying to play an instrument. If I was going to be in a band, I'd just have to be the singer. It was my only hope, since

I was devoid of any musical talent. Alli was a guitarist, so now we were only missing a drummer, a bassist, and some rehearsal space. We were aware of one guy who knew the bass. He was called Maggi. We didn't really know him well, but nevertheless we went to his house and rang the bell. His mother came to the door.

"Is Maggi home?"

After a little while, Maggi came to the door, a bit unsure.

"Want to be a bass player in a band?" we asked.

"What sort of band?" Maggi asked.

I was quite certain about the fact that it was a punk band we were forming. This wasn't a comedy ska or New Wave outfit. This was not, importantly, any old rock band. This wasn't only going to be a punk band, it was supposed to be the best punk band in all of Iceland. Alli, however, was less certain. He listened to punk and dressed like a punk, but he was still not particularly interested in the philosophy of anarchism or punk rock. He was more in it for the music and the look. I knew for a fact he listened to New Wave: to Gang of Four and the B-52s.

"A punk band!" I announced resolutely so that there would be no confusion.

Maggi wasn't a punk. He was quite far from being a punk. He had little interest in music and didn't know the difference between Duran Duran and the Sex Pistols. He was mainly interested in motorcycles and spent all his spare time building motor scooters in his garage at home. He was allergic to something that meant his nose was running nonstop, and he was constantly sniffing and blowing his nose. But he'd learned bass from his older brother and was willing to join us.

Now we just needed a drummer. We'd gotten our bass player. The drummer fell into our hands as if by a miracle. One day when we were hanging out by the garages in Alli's street smoking, we heard the beat of drums carrying from within one of the garages. Someone was clearly practicing drums. The same rhythm sounded repeatedly at short intervals. Dunk dunk dunk dunk klassh. Dunk dunk dunk dunk klassh.

"Who's that?" I asked.

"I don't know," said Alli.

We weren't bold enough to knock on the garage door but waited and waited around for the drummer to show himself. After some waiting, the garage door opened and a boy, a little older than us, came out. To my great disappointment it wasn't a punk, just some regular kid.

"Who's that?" I asked again.

"Some kid who just moved into our street."

He looked at us out of the corner of his eye and went straight into his house.

The next day we went and knocked for him. An older woman came to the door, and we asked for him.

"We're looking for the boy who lives here," I said.

"Hannes!" shouted the woman.

After a while, Hannes came down with a curious expression, though he obviously remembered us from the day before.

"Hey," he said.

"Aren't you a drummer?"

"Huh? Yes, sort of..."

"We heard you playing in the garage."

He smiled, ill at ease. I got straight to the point.

"Want to join the band?"

"What band?"

"A band we're forming."

"What's its name?"

We hadn't come up with a name yet. We'd been thinking about it a lot but weren't going to decide anything until the band was fully formed. I thought Anti-Police was a striking name, but Alli wanted something Icelandic like Brjálæðingarnir (The Madmen) or Kleppararnir (The Lunatics). His mom worked at the nuthouse, but my dad was a cop.

"We're not ready to christen it just yet," explained Alli.

"Is it a punk band?" Hannes asked, after looking at us.

"Yes," I replied immediately and with some determination. I wondered whether it was possible to transform Hannes into a punk. Maybe you could trick him into getting an unusual haircut then stuff him in some torn jeans.

Hannes shrugged his shoulders and seemed pleased.

"Okay," he said.

The band was formed. Hannes invited us in and we went into his room, which was covered in albums. I'd never in my life seen so many albums, not even in the record store Karnabær. He had hundreds of albums, and his room was like a record library: all the cabinets and shelves were full of records. On the wall hung a poster of Joan Jett and the Blackhearts. I had never heard of them before and had no idea who they were, but judging by the picture, they didn't look like punks.

"What sort of music do you listen to?" Alli asked.

Hannes smiled, uncomfortable. He was a quiet, placid, composed kid.

"I just listen to all kinds of music," he said.

"Punk?" I asked, with excitement in my voice.

"Yes, yes, I listen to a lot of punk."

I was relieved. That was good news. It turned out that Hannes knew all the bands in the world and even knew the names of the members. He was a music freak, and his only hobby was listening to music and collecting records. He had just moved to Fossvogur from Vogunum. His father had recently died, so he lived alone with his mother.

"Do you have somewhere to rehearse?" he asked.

We didn't have anywhere and were on the lookout for a garage. We couldn't rehearse in Alli's garage because his brother had been in a band, and his parents didn't want any more bands in their garage. We also couldn't use my garage because it was full of crap. Dad had recently received, free, more than a ton of old issues of the *National Will* that were being thrown away. Twenty years of antique *National Will*s now filled the garage. No one understood why he had salvaged them. Mom was both shocked and pissed.

"What the hell are you doing with this crap?!"

"It's valuable," Dad insisted.

"It's crap!" Mom shouted.

Then Dad shook his head like Mom wasn't making any sense, like she had no understanding of complex political issues. Like she came from a long line of conservatives and didn't understand the multifaceted value of old copies of *National Will*. My dad got it. In the first place, the newspapers had sentimental value for him because there were articles about the political struggles of people on the left and the ideals in which he had participated. What's more, the papers were interesting sources. In the great nothingness of his retirement, Dad planned to sit down there in the garage and go over the papers, cutting out interesting articles and pasting them into a scrapbook. Third, he thought it a crying shame to throw such a remarkable paper as the *National Will* out on the trash heap. Moreover, he feared that if the papers were thrown away, someone might possibly forever lose some article. But it was not only the ideals that attracted him; he also saw a financial benefit. If he kept them long enough, the papers' rarity would potentially mean they could be sold for good money later. For him, these were valuable. But ultimately Mom would insist they move out of the garage. So Dad, all by himself, took all the papers up to the attic where they lay for years, until the two of them moved from Fossvogur into service apartments for the elderly. Dad hadn't yet taken the time to go through the piles with scissors and a glue-stick, and Mom didn't want to fill their little service apartment with old *National Wills*. Dad then spent a few evenings ringing round all the conceivable inheritors for the piles of newspapers. It was a vain effort: my father couldn't find anyone who cared about a whole ton of old *National Wills*.

"Who do you think would want this crap?!" Mom shouted as he searched for phone numbers to call.

After numerous unsuccessful calls he gave up on it and gave up, finally, on the dream. Several energetic delivery van drivers came a few days later and carried the treasures away in their cars and drove them to the dump. Dad watched and sighed sadly.

"So, they're getting chucked away after all."

"And it could have been far earlier!" Mom shouted.

Dad stood by powerless, unable to avert this great cultural misfortune.

All this took place, however, long after the days of Nefrennsli.

"We can rehearse in our garage, for sure," said Hannes.

We couldn't believe our own ears. Garages that are open to musical types don't grow on trees. Most garage owners have enough in their garages already. People keep camping equipment and forgotten stuff. Bands cause disturbances and noise and bother beloved neighbors—especially at night. They draw smoking and spitting crowds of teens no one wants to see near their property and valuables.

"We don't have a car and don't use the garage for anything," he added. "Mom definitely won't care."

A rehearsal space needs sound-proofing. The main things people use are old carpets, egg boxes, and foam mattresses. I remembered a leftover foam mattress Dad had gotten for free from some place many years before and that remained rolled up in a storage closet. It was something various people at various times had wanted to throw out, but as usual Dad was confident he'd eventually find a use for it. He even tried to sell my Mom on the idea that they could use this remnant as a tent mattress for camping, but she wouldn't hear of it: it was exceptionally ugly foam, melted around the edges and with bubbles and holes. I knew that there was little point asking my dad about the mattress, so I followed my own advice and asked Mom if I could take the foam.

"Yes, please do!" she said, very relieved to get rid of it. "It's just some junk your dad picked up. I don't understand why he's always collecting such rubbish. Just don't let him see you taking it."

I snuck the foam over to Hannes's garage, and we put it on the door and under the amplifiers and drum kit. Dad never missed it. Alli and Maggi fixed us up with carpets. They managed to get hold of a very thick floral rug from the recreation room on Suðurlandsbraut and bring it over on the bus, to the annoyance of the other passengers since the carpet smelled of old urine and vomit. It went down on the floor. Alli gathered egg cartons and hung them right on the walls along with pieces of foam and foul-smelling leftover bits of the rug. It was all very punk, and finally the rehearsal space was ready. We were drenched with sweat but satisfied with our successful efforts. Now there was nothing left to do but to get started.

There were no windows or ventilation in the garage. We had covered the door with foam, so it very quickly became stuffy and hot inside the punk womb. The sweat poured off us and when it warmed up, it stank with terrible emissions of vomit, urine, and sweat. Alli was particularly easily nauseated and had to run out from time to time to retch. But little by little we got accustomed to the smells and eventually stopped noticing it. We smoked and burned incense and also hung up some posters to make it homey.

We held our first formal band meeting. The first item on the agenda: Name. We needed a name for the band, and it had to be punk. Anti-Police was eliminated with three votes to one. Maggi was keen on a short name like Farting or Ass. I thought that was naïve and too much like a joke. This was not supposed to be a prank band. Hannes was the one of us who had the greatest experience with bands, and he'd even read books about bands.

Despite the fact that his favorite band name was Bay City Rollers, he still had greater insight into music and punk rock than the rest of us put together. Hannes suggested that we call the band Punk Icelandic Land, abbreviated PIL. That way we wouldn't have to come up with a logo and could instead use the logo of the British band Public Image Ltd., which Johnny Rotten founded after the Sex Pistols split. Hannes also pointed out that it was in the spirit of punk to repurpose, and why not repurpose a name? I thought that it was in many ways a fascinating idea but noted that this was dangerously close to another band called Danceband Reykjavík and Environs, abbreviated as DRAE, which was in homage to The Co-operative for Reykjavik and Environs, or KRAE. I didn't want to be like them in any way. I wouldn't want anyone to think we were in some way influenced by DRAE. Many good bands never get past the initial stage in which the members agree on a name. It's crucial that the name is good. Finally the meeting dissolved into an argument between Alli and Maggi, who continually suggested names like The Runs, Pussy, and even Cunt. We were clearly on the wrong track with Maggi, who didn't fit into the group and was immediately fired from the band after he declared he'd only joined the band to impress girls. With that statement, he was completely lost to me. It was more than we could tolerate—and then Maggi gibed that there was little chance this band would attract girls anyway.

"Why on earth does he think he could get a girl when he's always sniffing and his nose runs constantly?" Alli asked in amazement after Maggi had slammed the foam-lined garage door behind him.

"You know, his nickname's Snotty, because his nose is always running," I said.

Hannes, who had not been very engaged in the conversation about a name, mainly sitting silent and pensive at the drum kit, suddenly asked:

"What about Nefrennsli?"

"What?"

"Why not call the band Nefrennsli? It's cool."

Nefrennsli? The name sounded very good. If we got popular abroad, you could easily translate it; we'd become Runny Nose. I rolled the name about. "Jón—or Johnny—the lead singer of Runny Nose" sounded just fine. Alli nodded. It was the name of the band. We were Nefrennsli. The hottest punk band in Iceland had formally begun work. Nefrennsli.

The next days and weeks were spent rehearsing. We practiced from morning to night. We started out playing songs by other bands, "Public Image" by PIL, "Do They Owe Us a Living" by Crass, and other easy songs. Again and again I couldn't keep time. I was terrible at knowing when I should come into a song and where. The boys nodded encouraging heads in my direction, but I got confused over the ongoing beat and came in either a beat too early or too late. I was like a blind man in a maze. If I managed to get into the song by sheer chance, sooner or later I lost the beat unless the song was both easy and slow. So what happened was that Alli and Hannes played all the songs extremely slowly. Whenever I was meant to start singing, Alli nodded his head to me really obviously and counted me in silently as I read his lips, or else he sang the opening line of the song with me. In this way, I sometimes got to hang on through the song. But this would never work onstage, where you need to be jumping and dancing around with your eyes on the crowd, not standing like a stone staring at Alli all the time.

This peculiar inability to keep the beat was paralyzing and exacerbated by my timidity, reserve, and stage fright. I felt extremely uncomfortable standing up while I sang; I'd rather sit in the corner and look down at the song lyrics and watch for instructions from Alli. Worldwide fame, which had seemed so close, was now rapidly disappearing. How would I be able to show up at a gig? I could hardly sit in a chair and mutter something in the corner. Maybe it was just a matter of practice? Maybe I could learn the songs? If we practiced enough, maybe it would all suddenly click.

Soon our first original song was born. Alli started out with a simple, rhythmic melodic line and even wrote some lyrics which he called "Onetime Hippie." The song was about a stupid hippie who went about in a floral dress and didn't realize that hippies were dead. The song was almost as simple as a child's language, and I even got to sing with some passion and without having to stare at Alli. Amazingly, I got up from my chair and screamed at the end of the song, in the direction of the sponge on the garage door:

"Onetime hippie, always a fucking hippie!"

Hannes also had an idea for a song. He hummed the melody for Alli, who tapped it out on guitar and added to it. They played the song and I recorded it on tape. I was given the task of composing lyrics. That night, I sat down with a notepad and pen and listened to the song over and over again while I wrote the words:

Anarchy and Freedom

Anarchy and freedom is what I want
Fuck the government!
You can't say I can't do what I want
Fuck you fascist pig!

Everybody thinks they know
What is right and what is wrong
But they don't know shit
And that's why I'm singing this song

Fuck the police and fuck the schools
They are just a bunch of fools
Fuck the armies and the church
Anarchy and freedom rules!

I could scarcely believe my own eyes. I'd written my first lyrics. They weren't even that bad. This was an authentic punk song. I played the song and crooned the text. I was no longer just a spectator but a participant. I was so excited that I didn't sleep until dawn.

And so songs were made one after the other. Alli and Hannes wrote melodies, and lyrics came from here and there. One, for example, we borrowed from the poet Stein Steinarr. I wrote a few, and Alli's dad wrote one. It was called "Battle in Beirut." The song was slow and gloomy, and although I had no idea where Beirut was on the map, I sang mournfully and gravely:

Battle in Beirut
bombs hover
houses collapse as carrion-fire tears
people fleeing rockets firing
in crazy fear
lies a crazy world

After a few weeks and incessant practice we'd gotten a few songs. We'd become a real band. Alli and Hannes were excited to go play somewhere, but I was hesitant and rejected the idea. Although I wanted to stand onstage and scream, like a rock star, "In crazy fear lies a crazy world," I also had no enthusiasm for doing it. I felt stupid and ugly. My glasses were silly, and I couldn't take them off because then I couldn't see anything. What's more, I had these weak, dull, pale eyes. And then there was that damn lack of timing. I knew that it would only get considerably worse when I was nervous. I would drop out in the middle of a song and totally spoil it or embarrass myself. I was even nervous if some friend of ours was in the garage. I found it awkward, and I began to get distracted even more than usual during songs, forgetting lyrics and garbling. But I couldn't admit it to anyone. I couldn't tell Hannes and Alli that all their relentless practice would be for nothing because the singer was shy and would probably never sing onstage. I made up countless excuses, claiming to have a headache or coming up with something I said was bothering me, either about the lyrics or the tune. There was always something to fix before we could play in public. I went round in countless circles in my head, thinking about anything that wasn't quite right, and

JÓN GNARR

the more I thought, the more I became unqualified to change it. The boys showed an incredible understanding, waiting patiently for me to be ready to step onstage. As a compensation, we celebrated with a concert in the garage and recorded it on tape. Then we sat in a room and listened, fascinated, to the best punk band in the world, which had never played in public because the chief instigator was too shy.

Since we couldn't launch the band with a gig, we launched it another way. We all bought thick markers and wrote NEFRENNSLI wherever we could; on bus shelters, shop walls, road signs, and any place that had already been defaced. The band's logo was N with a ring around it and an arrow out; little by little the band became famous even though no one had heard of it. I was even widely known as "the singer of Nefrennsli." I was a recognized singer in a punk band that had never held a concert. As the band's reputation and mine grew, I became more of a wallflower, grew ever more anxious about launching. Wasn't it just fine this way? Couldn't we just hold a concert for ourselves in the garage? Did we need some launch somewhere hanging over our heads? It was better that people thought I was going to be great than if they saw that I was lousy. But more and more people asked about the band, and we got requests and invitations to play at gigs. Alli and Hannes were excited, but I always found some excuse.

"We can't play this weekend: I'm definitely getting a sore throat."

We decided to send a tape recording of our music to a radio station. We sent them the song "Bad World," which we thought was our best song so far. We thought this song would be a hit, not only in Iceland but also overseas, since it was in English. A few days later, a manager from the radio program rang Hannes. He said he'd listened to the song and wanted to interview the band. Full of awe and with thundering heartbeats we walked into the radio station on Skúlagata. We were ushered into the studio; the host welcomed us and offered us seats. I felt like I was standing on the precipice of world fame. I was doing an interview on national radio. Every Icelander would hear us interviewed and listen to our song. We'd become famous. When the interview began, I was seized with a choking tension. My mouth dried up and my palms sweated. My heart was pounding in my ears. The presenter introduced the band for the listeners and said something about a growth in Icelandic garages. Then he turned to us and asked us to introduce ourselves and say what we played. All the descriptions and cool phrases we'd planned to use were forgotten; shyness took over. We stammered and mumbled over one another. The presenter tried to start with something light and asked us about the name of the band and whether we always had colds. We didn't really understand his point. Alli said yes and I said no. I was so nervous and agitated my ears felt stopped up. He told the audience that he had listened to our demo, and I tried to get a sense of what he felt about it, but there was no way to tell.

"You know something about playing instruments, boys?"

"No," we muttered unanimously. "Nothing at all."

"Nothing at all?"

"I just know how to play guitar," said Alli softly.

"We just do what we can," I muttered.

"Don't you need to know how to in order to play?"

We flat out disagreed that it was necessary.

"Don't you need a lot of money for musical instruments?"

I went bright red. What he was really talking about? Why was he asking us about this? Where exactly was he going with this? Why didn't he ask us about the lyrics?

"You can just borrow instruments," said Alli, loudly.

The old man looked at us playfully.

"Can you all simply become musicians without knowing a blessed thing about instruments?"

"Yes," I said.

"No," Alli stated.

I looked accusingly at Alli.

"You might have to know a little tiny bit," he added.

"Maybe some chords," I said cockily, by way of explanation.

"And a drum line," Hannes shot in.

"That's enough," I said.

The presenter looked searchingly at us for a while. We were silent. Outside, the Icelandic nation was sitting, breath held, listening. I struggled to find something interesting to say, to bring up some cool slogan or something like that, but the stress weighed too heavily on me. I could barely get my breath, and the familiar feeling of suffocation poured over me. My hands shook, and I was afraid that listeners could hear my heartbeat booming in their radios.

"How do you compose the lyrics?"

"He writes them," Alli said, pointing at me.

"I write them," I said.

Alli and Hannes nodded their heads in agreement. I felt that the lyrics affected everything and considered them more important than the music. To my mind, the music was just a framework for the words.

"You write in English or Icelandic?"

I'd never considered this a particularly special thing for me and didn't know how to answer.

"Just depends," I said.

"You like singing in English?"

"It's much better than singing in Icelandic."

"Why?" he asked, curious.

"It always sounds so ridiculous."

In my mind's eye I saw all those ridiculous lyrics I'd tried to compose in Icelandic and the struggles I'd had getting translated lyrics to fit their tunes. The sentences were always too long or too short. I burst out laughing at the thought. I didn't want to laugh but I couldn't help it. The excitement and feeling of neurosis were too strong for me.

The program host smiled like he was trying to figure out what was so funny.

"Why ridiculous?"

"It makes you seem like an imbecile," I said by way of explanation and giggled.

Now he started to laugh. I got the strong impression he wasn't laughing with me but at me, like it was me who was being ridiculous, and I stopped laughing in an instant.

"It's not possible to find the proper words…it just ends up in some kind of confusion," I stammered, beginning to feel significantly ill.

"But is it a source of pleasure for you, messing around with language so that no one understands it?" he asked.

What did he mean now? What kind of question was that? Why didn't he ask anything about punk or anarchism? What exactly was the man talking about? Didn't he know how to interview? I looked awkwardly at the boys to see if they had an answer to this question. They clearly didn't and were looking questioningly at me. I felt like I was going to explode. Was the interview turning into a disaster? Was the nation going to turn off their radios? I waited for my head to explode and my brains to splash across the studio walls.

"Huh?"

He repeated the question.

"Do you enjoy messing around with language so no one understands it? Perhaps you don't understand it yourself, sometimes?"

"Yes and no," I said, just to say something, although I still didn't know what the man was getting at.

There was an awkward silence.

"But is there a meaning to your lyrics?"

Finally a question worth answering! Finally the guy had said something a person could understand.

"Yes, of course," I answered, certainly.

"And who are you most trying to reach? Are you trying to reach out to your peers?"

What the fuck were these questions? What did he mean now? Were we trying to reach out to our peers? How would we reach them? Didn't the man get that we were a punk band? There are no other real punk rock bands in Iceland. We were the first real punk band singing about anarchism. Reach out to our peers?

"The politicians," said Hannes suddenly.

"The politicians?" asked the program host, just as startled as me.

I could not imagine that there were many politicians who'd bother to listen to us. Politicians? How did that pop into Hannes's mind? We were playing for politicians? I seriously doubted it would be possible to find politicians who liked Nefrennsli, and I saw before me the guys my dad watched on TV. They were definitely not men who were into Nefrennsli.

"No, everyone," I said.

"Everyone?"

"Yes."

"Are you trying to influence the older generation at all?"

"We aren't exactly expecting any interest from them," I said.

Alli and Hannes joined in.

"The old crowd is finished," Alli muttered.

"So no point talking about it?"

"No," we responded unanimously.

"But what do your parents think? Do they enjoy this music?"

We all shook our heads. Mom and Dad had never heard of Nefrennsli and would surely not have enjoyed the music. I don't think my mom would even classify this as music, and I doubted that my dad had any inkling in his head that I was in a band.

"Mom doesn't care," said Hannes.

The host soon realized that he wouldn't get any interesting answers to this question, so he changed the subject.

"Do you work?" he asked next.

Do we work? What kind of question is that? Where was this

topic headed? What did it really matter whether we were working or not? It was a totally frigging absurd question! He might as well ask us whether we had any living grandparents.

"We were in the youth employment program," said Alli.

"Well, two of us were," he added, looking at Hannes.

The radio host stared at me. It was clearly time for me to say something in this media interview. The nation sat tensely at their radios and waited.

"I was a carer for my sister," I said.

Then silence. Maybe we were just too tough and cool for this guy. What did the old fellow know about punk? Clearly nothing! Asking about language and work wasn't talking to someone. Why didn't he ask us something about the song? Talk about how cool it was and how it was awesome that there was finally a real punk band in Iceland, a band comparable to the major UK punk bands.

"Well, guys… What can you tell me about this song we're about to play?"

At last! The Icelandic nation would finally hear real Icelandic punk. This unbearable nightmare was finally complete.

"It's called 'Bad World,'" said Hannes.

"He wrote the song," I said, pointing at Alli. "And I wrote the lyrics."

"And do you think the world is evil?"

"Yes," I answered with conviction.

"But surely it must be good when anyone can play without knowing a thing about musical instruments?" said the man, pleased with himself.

Again! Yet another absurd question about something unimportant.

Was he simply asking this to confuse us? Was he intentionally trying to get us off balance by asking us questions we didn't understand?

"Huh?" I said.

"Yes," said Alli, at the same time.

"That's totally good," said Hannes.

We were losing control again. I made a last-ditch to save the interview. It was do or die.

"It's not enough to play. You need someone to listen," I said resolutely.

He turned away from us and poked at some buttons.

"Let's just hope someone is listening. Thank you for coming, boys," the host said finally and turned on the track.

> *Why is the world so bad*
> *Or is it just that I'm so sad*

We floated out of the radio station. We felt like rock stars as we walked around the city center. We all agreed, however, that the interview had not gone well. The old codger was an idiot and had only asked us questions that made no sense. But our song had been played. All the people had listened and heard the song. We all had high hopes that people would mob us in the city square at Lækjartorg and insist on autographs. But it was cold in the capital that evening, and people were apparently too busy hurrying home to the warm to notice the three punk rockers waiting—full of expectation and dressed lightly—for fame. Wearing T-shirts in the frost, hands in pockets and backs to the wall. Like the Sex Pistols with runny noses.

At that time, I tended to wander about a lot, around the city, both day and night, either on foot or by bus. That was how I came across Outreach, a project run by the city of Reykjavík and located on Tryggvagata. Outreach comprised adults who drove around town and looked out for down-on-their-luck teenagers like me. Several times over the years, they'd grabbed me up in their arms, hurried me to the shelter on Tryggvagata, jabbered at me, and even managed to drag me into various activities and resources. They were especially concerned to work out teenagers' interests and would try to find assorted ways to enable kids to enjoy those interests. I had a few good times there. My main hobby was anarchism, so in my case it meant their resources mostly involved chatting with me about things related to anarchism. But they perceived more than I revealed and clearly saw that I was a tortured soul. I had become badly damaged due to all the bullying I'd suffered without being able to process it. I just felt I deserved it and, what's more, it was completely understandable since I was stupid and boring, ugly and ridiculous. I was a ridiculous person, and of course people bully ridiculous people. The folk at Outreach were more interested in discussing that with me, and not anarchy.

"How are you, Jón?"

I didn't know how to answer. I'd never had anyone ask me how I was. I really had no idea how I felt. I was stressed, always stressed. I was anxious, I longed to be anybody but myself. I wished I was calmer and didn't have red hair. The people inside Outreach tried hard to motivate me and did what they could to increase my confidence. They often talked, for example, about the future, but all the talk about the future stressed me out even more.

I would rather not think about the future.

"Can't we just talk about anarchism? Do you know the difference between Proudhonism and Bakuninism?"

They didn't know.

"What do you want to be, Jón?"

An unpleasant, anxiety-inducing topic. What did I want to be? I wanted to have dark hair. I wanted to be calmer. I also wanted to be a singer. But all the same, I knew that what I wanted would probably never come to pass. I was just unfortunate, neurotic, redheaded, and ridiculous. A half-wit in glasses. When I grew up, I'd certainly end up in the loony bin like Cousin Kiddi. Perhaps there are lots of folk like me who come into existence and get born by mistake, the way some things that are manufactured are defective and never work. Useless from the start. All you can do with such things is throw them away. Maybe I was like that, just a copy of a person. I never spoke about this with anyone, not even the people in Outreach. In a certain way, maybe I didn't realize it. I thought it was self-evident, and I was afraid that if I said it out loud, they would agree. The main reason, however, was shame. I felt ashamed. Ashamed to be myself, the way I was, so I didn't talk about it. I really didn't understand why they were so concerned to get involved with me. Sometimes when they sat and chatted with me, I wondered why they were wasting their words on me. Did they feel sorry for me? Yes, they probably felt sorry for me, but it was also their job. One time when we were sitting and having a chat, and I was talking about anarchism and punk while they tried to get me to talk about anything else, the future came up in conversation, as so often before.

"What do you want to be when you're older, Jón?"

That single question awakened feelings of suffocation in me; my chest tightened, and I felt pain in my forehead.

"I don't know, just anything."

"Don't you have a sweetheart, Jón?"

Me? I was the ugliest and most awkward boy in Reyjavík! What girl would want to be my sweetheart?

"Noo-ee, I think the girls are really nothing special," I said, as an explanation.

"How strange that you don't have a girlfriend, such a cute kid like you!"

The words reverberated around my head. A cute kid like me? I looked at the woman questioningly and considered her words. She smiled and seemed to mean it. It looked like she really believed it, and her words weren't just an expression of sympathy. Incredible! She was cool, though she wasn't, of course, punk—but she wasn't a hippie, either, more like plain, sweet, and she had a boyfriend. She was just some twenty-odd-year-old chick, everything figured out, and she found me cute! "Such a cute kid like you, Jón." That a person like her could say something like that about me was frankly unbelievable and caused a revolution in my wretched soul. I found her much more interesting than the people who had so often in the past told me I was stupid and ugly. Her words far outweighed theirs. I had never reckoned on anyone ever saying I was cute. I was filled with unprecedented confidence. The staff at Outreach, had caught wind of the fact that I was in a band. Sometimes concerts were held in the courtyard outside Outreach and they would from time to time ask me if Nefrennsli didn't want to play.

I deftly handled their questions and made endless excuses. Sometimes we weren't well enough prepared, or else I had a cold or the flu and couldn't sing, and then I argued that there weren't enough punks to play in Outreach's yard, and it wasn't right for a punk band like Nefrennsli.

"See, we're the real thing, a true punk band."

I definitely wasn't going to play a concert with a bunch of ridiculous bands. Then Outreach decided to hold a real punk festival. By this time, all my excuses were exhausted. There was going to be a punk festival, and Nefrennsli simply had to go onstage. The concert would be for punks only. There weren't going to be any idiots who would laugh at me and mock me. Alli and Hannes jumped high for joy when I told them what was in the cards. The concert was organized, and the names of the bands that were playing were written on signs that were hung on the lampposts outside Outreach and nearby. REYKJAVÍK'S BEST PUNK BANDS. PUNK FESTIVAL IN OUTREACH COURTYARD ON TRYGGVAGATA, 1–4PM NEXT SUNDAY! Among the band names was Nefrennsli. The big moment was coming. The anticipation and excitement carried me away. I was going to take the step I'd always wanted to but never dared.

When the day of the festival arrived, I'd not slept a wink for two days. I wanted to cancel. Should I pretend to be sick? No, I couldn't do it, it was arranged, and there was nothing for it now but to bite the bullet and jump off the cliff. I put on my finest punk clothes, which consisted of the most torn jeans I had and a Sid Vicious shirt, and put safety pins through my ear. There was no way I was going to wear my glasses; I decided to sing without them.

That meant, however, that I wouldn't be able to see Alli, so I would have to rely on myself totally for the songs. I was very myopic: minus six in one eye and minus seven in the other. And I didn't only have severe myopia, but also a significant astigmatism. Glasses-less, I could see about one meter in front of me; everything else was a haze. Maybe it would be better this way, since I wouldn't be able to see the audience and therefore wouldn't get nervous if there were some kids who were hiding there, looking at me funny, or who weren't really into Nefrennsli. Before entering the courtyard, I took off my glasses and hid them behind a trash can and then went into the haze. Alli and Hannes were extremely cheerful and full of expectation and almost jumping out of their skins because they wanted to get onstage. I, however, was absolutely paralyzed with fear and didn't speak a word to anyone. I just followed them at a distance, hoping I would not end up a lone wanderer, lost and wild, completely dry in the mouth and absolutely confused. The bands got onstage one after another and played their songs. Between the bands, an announcer came up onstage to introduce the band that was next up and present them to the audience. Before I knew it, we were up.

"Next onstage are three young boys from Fossvogur who call themselves Nefrennsli."

Clap. Clap. I succeeded in clambering up onstage with the boys, bone-dry in the mouth and with a thundering heartbeat. My hands shook from the stress. I could barely make anything out.

"Okay?" I heard Alli ask from somewhere in the haze.

"Umhmmm," I muttered.

I wanted to die, to disappear into the stage or somehow jet

up into the air. Without warning, Hannes struck his drumsticks together and launched into the first song. Someone had handed me a microphone and I held it firmly, both my hands clamped fast to its sides. I was paralyzed. The song kept going, but I stood rigid like a wooden figurine, wearing an expression that suggested I'd just forgotten something. I had no idea when to come into the song. Alli moved closer to me and shouted:

"Why don't you have your glasses?"

"I forgot them," I called back.

They continued to play. Alli moved right up next to me, energized but with a questioning expression, and gave me a signal to start singing. I brought the microphone up to my lips and put my other hand in my pocket. As soon as I started singing, it dawned on me that I'd started singing the wrong part of the song. I was so shocked to hear my own voice on the speaker that I immediately fell silent again, turned around and gaped somewhere into the emptiness, acting like I was worried about some technical issues. The song carried on and I mumbled incoherently, half a sentence here and another bit there, unable to remember the lyrics and sure my face was blushing beetroot. With about this much success, we scraped through two songs; the boys played on, inspired, and I walked awkwardly back and forth, muttering things in odd places into the microphone. Between words, I looked confusedly out into blue yonder. I tried to pretend I was a bit distracted due to some technical problems, but it was clear nothing was wrong. I just couldn't deal. It was a complete flop. Then it was time for our third and final song, "Bad World," which was also our best-known song, the one that had the greatest chance of becoming popular.

I knew I was both physically and mentally unable to perform the song. I just wanted it to end. How the hell was I going to get myself out of this dilemma?

"Isn't that enough?" I muttered toward Alli.

Wasn't it blindingly obvious that I was about to have a heart attack?

"No!" said Alli, determined.

"'Bad World,' man!" said Hannes, encouraging.

I wandered up and down the stage, which was more or less made out of pallets. Hannes launched into the song, beat together the drumsticks, shouted one, two, three, four! I had these thundering headaches that got worse with every second; added to this were the convulsions of nervousness. I rambled about without any purpose and stubbed my toes on something. That was the solution! I took a snap decision and decided to fall. It didn't matter if I just fell or severely injured myself. Anything was better than this hell. When the idea popped up in my mind, I was filled with joy. It was all finally going to end. I tripped forward and collapsed with a ton of noise right off the stage, landing on some bits of wood then rolling from them down onto the pavement.

"Jesus Christ!" shouted someone.

"Are you all right?"

I had fortunately not hurt myself at all, but I played it up in dramatic style. The staff of Outreach helped me up, and I appeared totally maimed.

"I just crashed into…"

"Do you think you're hurt?"

"Yes, I'm sure I've hurt something," I replied and acted like my ankles and hands were painful, sighing and weeping from the sham pain. They helped me to my feet and led me inside. I was off the hook, lawfully so. The boys in the band didn't let their heads drop and performed the song without lyrics. With the help of the staff, I was comfortably positioned on the couch inside. A heavy weight had been lifted from me. I decided to bring Nefrennsli to an end because I no longer wanted to be a singer in a band. It was clear that I had no future in music. Music was definitely not for me, and from now on, I would try not to listen to it or play it. But despite the fact that I was finished with the band, it continued to exist thanks to the felt-tip pens. Since only a small audience was at the concert, there weren't many stories about my performance. The little article about the concert that appeared in the paper didn't give the impression that Nefrennsli had performed their music any differently than the rest of the bands.

A long time later, people still thought Nefrennsli had been a rather powerful band. The felt-tip pens sketched the road to fame and fortune. All the bus shelters in the city were graffitied, NEFRENNSLI, NEFRENNSLI WAS HERE, NEFRENNSLI RULES, NEFRENNSLI next to anarchist signs. People continued to think that the group must have been a real band to be splashed all around town. Alli and Hannes kept practicing in the garage, but I'd lost all ambition and interest. In the days after, I went thoroughly through the music in my life and decided to only listen to Crass. According to my understanding of what a punk band was, they were the only thing I could accept as genuine punk, so I kept their records but either gave away or threw out all the other albums I had. The Clash, the Sex Pistols, and all those bands that

I'd previously esteemed so highly were now nothing but traitors in my mind, sellouts who had betrayed their ideals. Crass were the true punks. From that moment, I also made a distinction between myself and other punks by defining myself as a Crass-punk. If I was asked if I was a punk, I'd affirm that I was, but add by way of further explanation that I was a Crass-punk or even an anarcho-punk, a punk who focuses primarily on anarchism, an evolved version of a punk. I didn't feel like listening to any more bands that performed songs about some kids who messed about in town and acted like fools or about girls or about things overseas that don't matter. And I didn't feel like listening to songs that dealt with something that was happening in the US, such as who was going to be governor of California—that wasn't really important to me. Anarchism was an integral part of punk rock. That was what punk had to stand on. Punk was supposed to be a tool for the spreading of anarchism, and the punks who didn't circulate anarchist ideology were therefore not punks, were in reality working against punk. Punk was a way to draw young people to think about anarchism and its importance. My idea of anarchism was something to the effect that I could do what I wanted as long as I did not hurt others and that others could do whatever they wanted so long as they didn't hurt me. These were the messages that punk bands had a duty to spread through their music.

PUNK

At school there was a little boy
The teachers thought him slow
He slunk along the walls
Even the walls bullied him
—UTANGARÐSMENN, "Thor"

At this point, it would be appropriate to write something about fall. I could describe in long words the way the light changed, the days shortened, and the nights extended. I could describe the leaves collecting in piles. I could describe the silence in the morning when it gets so cold that birds stop singing. I could describe, too, the rain. But I'm not going to. I don't look forward to fall.

In the fall, I started a new school for the first time. Réttarholt School had tracking. I was in D-Class. Still, that wasn't the dunce class. That was the F-Class. A and B were the hotshots. I was pleased to end up in D. Those who ended up in F-Class had no chance and were labeled idiots. The school system gave up on them and mainly tried to keep them away from other students. I don't know why I didn't get put in F. My scores weren't exactly impressive. Maybe it was just difficult to analyze them using the system Réttarholt School relied on. Fossvogs School didn't give ratings but instead gave reviews. Perhaps I got points for attendance since I'd always been there at Fossvogs School. I just never learned anything.

Rétto had a bad rap. Most people I knew were nervous about starting there. It was a rough school. There were many stories of teachers who seemed bad tempered, and there were several older students who were famously violent. In my class were some kids who had been with me at Fossvogs. The rest I didn't know. Rétto was a kind of gathering school where the kids from both Fossvogs and Breiðagerði School and several other middle schools ended up. Everyone had changed and grown considerably during the summer. I'd not paid much attention before. The girls had changed the most, and all of a sudden they looked a number of years older than the boys. They were also beginning to wear makeup, which they'd left alone until now. I felt like I'd aged ten years in a single summer, so much had happened. I'd often heard kids talk about Rétto as being for "big kids." Now I was one of them. I wasn't a child anymore. I was growing up. I had become what I'd feared and despised most: a teenager. I'd become one of them. I was even starting to get acne. I was fourteen. I was turning into an adult. I'd started smoking and drinking and had gone on my first bender.

I was the only punk at Rétto. Most kids were just ordinary, and some were pranksters. They gawked at me. Some were even afraid of me. I was immediately picked on by some of the older kids, who stopped me in the corridor and made fun of me and asked if they could spit on me and why I was the way I was. I tried to answer them as clearly as I could and conduct myself well. But they weren't looking for debate or an explanation any more than on previous occasions. They simply didn't like me and saw to it that the little interest I had in attending school was wiped out. Most of these boys were the same ones I'd had trouble with at Bústaðir, but a few new ones had joined the group.

"Why are you so ugly?"

"I don't know."

"Are you a retard?"

"No."

"Okay if I spit on you?"

"No."

I don't know why they didn't leave me alone. I'd never done anything to them. I meant nothing to them and never picked a fight. They simply didn't like the way I was and went out of their way to make that clear. The random attacks I'd experienced in Bústaðir became daily events at school. All day long I'd keep running into these gangling youths in all sorts of places around the grounds. I tried to hide myself away, but then they sought me out, usually two or three together. I was always on my own. Sometimes they were waiting for me at the front door when school was over. Sometimes they even waited outside the school grounds in places they knew I would go. When they stepped forward, I just stopped. There was nothing else I could do. Fleeing just increased the humiliation. I was powerless to do anything against them. They'd waited the whole time for a chance to beat me up. So I just stood there silently and waited until they were done, had gotten their kicks, and took off. The ritual always began with verbal insults:

"Hey, carrot top, what you doing?"

"Nothing."

"Why are you so dumb?"

"I don't know."

Then the practical part of the bullying would start. Either they'd shove me or grab hold of me, laughing and amusing themselves. When they couldn't think of any more brilliant insults to say, they'd push me around between themselves and try to knock me to the ground. Their favorite method was when one held me and turned me around in circles while the others stood around and tried to trip me as I was flung in an orbit. When they let me go, the one holding me grasped me in such a way that I rolled down the street. I never said anything and actively tried to show no emotion. Begging for mercy was in vain. Usually they didn't stop until someone came and asked them to stop or some adult saw them. But often no one came. So it didn't end until they got tired and walked away laughing.

I started to hate them. I didn't know why they put so much store in hurting someone they knew nothing about. I couldn't understand why they despised someone who hadn't done anything except choose to live his life a certain way. Why couldn't I be the way I was? I wasn't bothering them. Were they afraid of me? What were they afraid of? Did I threaten their existence in some way? Did the independence of my peculiarities somehow challenge them? Perhaps my character was too complex for them? Standing face-to-face with violence in this way, day after day, deepened my understanding of it. Perhaps the violence in the world all stems from the same root but takes on different complexions depending upon the nature and circumstances. It begins as a thought and a glimmer in the eyes that becomes words, and then words become acts. Talking smack about someone or humiliating him with words is just the same as violence and physical abuse. It can hurt the same, because the same thinking lies behind it. Violence is all the same even though it takes a variety of forms—it hurts just as much in Reykjavík as in Paris.

As much as I hated these guys, I was absolutely unable to be mean to them. I dreamed about punching them and beating them to pieces, but I couldn't do it because I was afraid of injuring them. I was afraid that if I punched someone in the face, I would break his teeth. I feared, too, that if I hurt them, they would respond by hurting me more. And where would I punch them? I couldn't even think about punching someone in the face. Punching them anywhere else seemed pointless. The only thing I really considered was kicking them up the ass. But it wouldn't have achieved anything. They kicked my ass, and if I did it to them, I'd become like them. I decided that the best thing I could do would be to continue the way I was and not change myself a bit but instead to fortify myself, to become more myself, to never give up and so overcome them eventually.

I tried to arrange my journeys so that I ran into my tormenters as little as possible. After school, I went out the back door and snuck home in a roundabout way. In the morning, I waited outside school and didn't go in until the school bell had rung and I was confident that everyone had gone into class. Outside of school, I avoided all shops and other places where I knew my tormenters often passed their time. I didn't talk to anyone about all this. I didn't want to. I didn't complain. I also feared that if I tattled it would just get worse. Then they would just have more reason to beat me up, and I feared that what they wanted most of all was to beat the shit out of me.

If I resented Fossvogs School, I hated Rétto. I got a knot in my stomach just seeing the building. I was only ever safe in lessons; I dreaded recess. I made a few acquaintances in class and tried to hang around with them as much as possible and make sure I was never alone. But though I attended class, I learned the littlest amount possible and usually didn't even have books with me. I didn't want to learn. I didn't want to be there. School wasn't for me. I made a silent agreement with the teachers: you leave me alone, and I'll let you off the hook. They were mostly satisfied with that; they were burned-out and weary. They all went by nicknames. Pills taught Icelandic. He was a fat, middle-aged man who behaved very strangely. Pills got his nickname because he walked around with a medicine box and sometimes took pills in the middle of class. The story went that he'd once gotten a shock in the middle of a lesson, dropped to the floor, and been taken away in an ambulance. But Pills was a humorist. He thought I was a funny guy and often smiled at my word-twisting and my retorts. He got that I didn't want to study, and he didn't try to force any lessons down my throat. In his class, I could come and go freely. If I wanted to go out and smoke, I just stood up and said I was off.

"Okeydokey," muttered Pills.

He was continually out of breath, and when he spoke he puffed out his words in his exhalations. He expended no unnecessary energy forming sentences, and he spoke quietly. When he talked, he had a strange mannerism of cleaning his teeth with a house key or a pen. This meant that most of what he said was pretty incomprehensible, running together like some porridge of loud respiration, smacks, quieter mumbling, and teeth-scraping. If any other student tried to play the same game as I did, standing up as if to leave, Pills was quick to make the person sit down again. Once a student asked how it was that I could always go when

I wanted to, but no one else. Pills answered without looking up:

"It's because it doesn't matter whether Jón is here or not, he never learns anything."

Pills also had a quick temper if he didn't like something, and he even hit students. Once there was a boy in the class who was trying to throw a glove at another boy but accidentally threw it at Pills. He blushed deeply, grabbed the glove, slapped the boy's face with it, and yelled at him:

"You are an idiot!"

Although Pills was strange, I liked him a lot. In his own way, he was a punk. He respected my opinions and even admired the way I fought hard against getting an education. Maybe he had, after decades of experience in the school system, come to the same conclusion as me, finding it both inhumane and depressing. Maybe his role as an emissary of the system had destroyed his happiness and his will and made him so depressed that he couldn't get through the day without drugs.

Most teachers were pretty indifferent and physically exhausted. Some had a reputation for drunkenness and had even been seen hammered somewhere. You could often smell the booze. This was usually very exciting. The Danish teacher was called Bacon. He was as fat as Pills; unlike Pills, he didn't pop drugs, but he drank wine. Bacon was always drunk in class—a really strong smell of alcohol emanated from him. He kept a hip flask in his jacket pocket. When he took a sip, he turned his butt to the class and pretended to be trying to remember some word or other; he had his sip, turned back, and pretended to remember the word. Usually he only got tipsy, but from time to time he drank a little more than he intended and spoke incomprehensibly, unsteady on his feet and clearly inebriated. We sat right there, watching, thrilled, and tried to keep from laughing. Once he drank so much that he nodded off at his table. He muttered something unintelligible while his head slid down onto the desk. When his forehead touched the table, he paused. We looked curiously at each other, and no one said a word. After a brief silence, he started snoring deeply. Then we all left the room.

The English teacher was called Sprint because he walked fast. He was a neat and decent man and a good teacher. Sprint put himself about, was enthusiastic and patient, and showed us respect. He was gay, something that was a great embarrassment at the time. Everyone knew, but it was still a secret. If his sexuality had been official, he would certainly have been fired. Sprint proved to be a true supporter of mine. There was finally a person in my life who understood English. I asked his opinion about books and phrases, and he taught me about British culture. He had even lived in London and was able to explain the class system and the structure of British society. There was so much that was sung about in punk songs that I didn't understand; he taught me, among other things, that Brixton is a neighborhood in London, Cockney is a dialect, and Ulster is a county in Ireland. These words came up often in punk songs. Patient and gentle, this fastidious, middle-aged homosexual sat reading with me lyrics by Stiff Little Fingers and Crass. English classes were no problem. I saw a real purpose in learning English because it was the key to the solution. By knowing it, I could understand lyrics and read books in English and even one day move to England. I got ten on all my exams in English and was far ahead of my classmates. Books that were meant to take three months to read, I finished in a few days.

Besides English, there was only one other subject in which I applied myself. That was Christian Studies. I'd totally lost all faith in any God, and as a devout anarcho-punk, I was opposed to religion. I found all those holy stories revolting. Anarchism was against religion and so were punks. Religion was just another system that had to be overcome. And though I didn't believe in Jesus and thought this all extremely childish and lame, I colored in pictures of him and studied at home and was well-behaved in class. The reason was simply that the teacher was such a kind and wonderful man that I couldn't bring myself to disrupt him. He showed me consideration and respected my atheism as an opinion. He was totally free from sentimentality and pretentiousness and was simply down-to-earth. He was the only teacher without a nickname; he was just called Ingólfur. What's more, Ingólfur Jónsson from Prestbakka was famous because he'd written the poem "Bright Over Bethlehem." So I colored and I read everything I had to read and I never got up and went out. I never aired my ideas about divinity with Ingólf and never ever asked him whether God could create a rock so big that he needed to get me to help him lift it, which was a favorite question I always asked of believers.

But in the middle of winter, Ingólfur fell ill and stopped teaching, and a new teacher replaced him. I thought he was an arrogant and annoying dude in every way. On top of everything else, he was a priest. He talked down to the kids and was clearly unable to stand me from day one. I stopped coloring at once and didn't study at home. There were only two people in my life that had gotten me to see something good and positive about faith. They were Grandma and Ingólf Jónsson from Prestbakka. Everyone else seemed to be an idiot who preached Christianity but was unable to live that way themselves. What I had heard and read about Jesus seemed in glaring opposition to all that was done in his name. I found people who seemed totally infatuated by him were almost always snobbish and pretentious and, most of all, boring. Christian Studies changed absolutely. The priest kicked me out of class on the smallest provocation, and I asked fiendish questions. The question of God and the stone came up time and again without answer. I didn't stop, and when I asked if Hitler had believed in Jesus, I was sent to the principal.

The principal had a nickname like most other school staff. He was called Baglet, and I was a regular visitor to his office. Baglet was an elderly guy, bald, with particularly prominent, large ears and eyes that were on stems like they were about to pop out of his head. He didn't ask me anything, but in a screeching voice announced that I was rude and a dunce, untidy to boot, and it was only a matter of time before I would be expelled from school for my attendance. Then I was allowed to go. I never said a word; I sat quietly while he recited over me, then stood up and went. But one day I got expelled from Christian Studies forever. It was a class about the creation of the earth according to the teachings of the Bible and how God created humans and the animals. I thought it was absolute nonsense. Someone asked who had created God. The teacher wriggled skillfully out of it by saying that God was eternal and had always been there. I couldn't resist.

"That's not we learned in biology from Gandý."

"And what did you learn there?" he asked, patronizingly.

"We learned we were descended from monkeys."

He grinned sarcastically.

"And who created the monkey?" he asked.

"They simply evolved from animals."

"Well, yes, and who created the animals?"

"They evolved from more primitive animals, according to Darwin's Theory of Evolution."

The Christian Studies teacher clearly did not care about Darwin.

"And who created these primitive animals?"

I thought and remembered.

"They evolved from fish."

"And who created the fish?" he asked.

"They evolved from lizards."

"Who created these lizards?"

I recalled a clear image of Darwin's system that hung inside the biology room.

"They came into being from insects, which came into being from organic matter."

"And who created this organic matter?"

We locked eyes. He grinned and waited for a response. He clearly had played this game before, and I saw where it was headed.

"I don't know," I replied after some deliberation. "Maybe it's simply eternal."

Someone giggled. It was like I had hit him with a wet rag in the face. His face distorted with anger; he steamed over to me, and I thought he was going to beat me. I froze with fear.

"You're repugnant, boy!" he yelled.

He pulled me to my feet and threw me out of the classroom with so much force that I struck the wall opposite the door.

"Never let me see you in here again!"

Then he slammed the door behind him. So concluded my formal studies in Christianity.

One noteworthy teacher at Rétto was the biology teacher, probably the most memorable teacher I've ever met. Gandý was an odd bird through and through; there were no drugs or alcohol or fundamentalism involved. He was middle-aged, rather thin and short, but highly educated. His eyes were slightly slanting, and he had a small mouth and large teeth, misaligned and protruding. He was bald but combed his hair over his bald crown and gathered it at the sides. When he got a bit overheated, his hair got all rumpled and stood on end. In our first class he distributed the textbook. It was a light yellow book with the inscription BIOLOGY on the front.

"Do you know what book this is?" he asked with a sarcastic expression.

"Biology," someone said.

Then he grinned and shook his head. There was no other way to guess, so we just fell silent and waited for him to tell us the name.

"The sequel to *Little Yellow Chicken*!" he cried and beamed.

The teachers' pets who knew their lessons smiled as though they understood the joke, but most of us just stared at one another. Then he rolled out a full-size skeleton of a man standing on a wooden podium. Someone had written Gandý on the skeleton's forehead in black marker, and it hadn't been possible to clean it off properly, so the outline of the letters was clearly visible.

"And do you know what this fellow is called?" he asked, and grinned again, full of expectation.

One girl immediately raised her hand.

"Gandý?" she asked cheerfully, like someone who knows she's ready with the absolutely correct answer.

It was like she had splashed a piss-pot over him. He stopped smiling and jumped one step away from her. We all understood that something had happened, but we didn't know what. He stared angrily at her, his eyes shooting sparks. Then he suddenly pointed at the door with his index finger and said loudly:

"Be gone!"

The girl jumped to her feet, looked uncertainly around, and went. When she was gone, Gandý gathered himself and went back to smiling.

"Well, let's try again. What do you think his name is?"

No one dared to say a word for fear of saying something wrong. Some shook their heads. When Gandý found the excitement enough he cried out:

"Straightie!" He couldn't keep from laughing, so much that his large teeth shone.

Lessons with Gandý were a veritable circus. At the beginning of the class, he stood by the door to the room and waited. As soon as the school bell fell silent, he closed the door and locked the room. Those not present couldn't enter. He didn't even wait for anyone hanging up their coats outside, he just closed the door on their noses and gave them no chance. Anyone not already inside the classroom when the bell fell silent couldn't get in. It was that simple. He rarely opened it for those who knocked except just to tell them to go to the principal. Sometimes only half the class was in the lesson while the other half waited outside the locked door. And the most striking thing about this was that Gandý wasn't angry; on the contrary. It was like he thought it was fun, beaming with joy and anticipation and with a mischievous expression over his face. When he quarrelled with students, he enjoyed himself so much that he grinned.

Gandý was an enigma. The story went that he was a professor and even had multiple degrees, but he'd read so much he'd gone mad. He had that kind of look. He resembled a lunatic scientist out of science fiction. No one knew where the nickname Gandý came from. And no one dared ask him about it. Doing so got you chucked out for sure. He answered any question about his identity with a series of fabrications. He said he was an inventor who had a laboratory up on Vatnajokul where he grew square tomatoes. And then he said that he had invented a new plant.

"What plant do you think it is?" he asked, full of anticipation.

When no answer came, he answered himself:

"Seven-Up trees!" And how he laughed.

He embellished his story, saying that it was a tree that he grew somewhere on Vatnajokul. The tree bore fruit once a month, when Seven-Up bottles grew on the branches. One time he even brought to class a mysterious hexagonal apple he showed us, saying that it came from his laboratory on the glacier. I occasionally enjoyed being in class with Gandý. He mostly left me alone. I sat by the window and sometimes smoked out of it behind the curtains, but he didn't protest and pretended not to notice anything. The lessons went on and I only understood bits and pieces, both because of my lack of interest and because of Gandý's eccentricity. He did admittedly explain Darwin's Theory of Evolution clearly, but mostly he focused on making us learn the Latin name for "buttercup" by heart—we wasted countless lessons on that. It was like this was some kind of obsession with him, and he wrote it on the blackboard and made us recite it over and over again out loud: *Ranunculus acris*. He even wrote a few words on the board to help us remember: ran, uncle, less. His method achieved its intended goal. It was probably the only thing I learned in his class. I have waited for a moment in my life where I could show off this evidence, but the opportunity has never arrived. One day when we got to class, several of the upper class students had taken Gandý and hung him on a hook by his belt. There he dangled, unable to touch his toes to the floor. I decided to make myself scarce, disappeared, and went out to smoke. I heard later that the ones who helped him down had been sent to the headmaster.

Arni Njalsson taught sports. He was known either by the nickname Arni Nails or simply just Nails. I could not even think of going into the showers after sports because of what took place there. Fighting and torture were found more there than anywhere, so I made sure never to show up with my gym clothes, and had to sit on the floor while others worked out like mad. Arni never called me anything but Punky. He had no real expectation that I would bring my gym stuff. Since I was of course unable to do anything during these times, I got given the task of taking his daughter down Bústaðarvegur to Fossvogs School.

"Punky?"

"Yes?"

"Got your gym kit?"

"No."

"Take the girl to school."

So I walked to his house, got the girl, walked her down Bústaðarvegur, and accompanied her over the pedestrian crossing. After that, I had free time.

To become more punk and to gain respect and peace from those persecuting me, I started trying to become more disgusting. I had a unique talent that I had often whipped out many times over the years: I could vomit when I wanted. I found out when I was trying to talk while belching that I could also vomit. The difficulty of it depended on what I'd eaten. Coarse food like potatoes, meat, and apples were difficult to puke. But soup and beef and the like are easy to bring up. The best thing to throw up is ice cream. When someone was annoying me, I vomited up food and spat it in their direction. This came in handy. Most thought it was so unpleasant they avoided me. I also would spit on a windowpane and lick up the sputum and swallow it while everyone watching got nauseous. I used the same defensive strategy as skunks and fulmars do. This often brought me peace. I even became quite famous for it and was known as the disgusting punk who vomited on people if they messed with him—Jónsi Punk.

Everything that happened at school decreased my interest in studying. I was far behind in the curriculum, and instead of revealing my inabilities, I covered them with misrepresentations, jokes, and indifference. In English, I was actually far ahead of others in the curriculum. I found that punk taught me more and was more useful to me than the English at school. I didn't bother to read what I was assigned. Icelandic was annoying. The course was dead dull and was centered mainly on spelling and spelling conventions and endless rules. The words and phrases were just silly, like "Ingunn disgraced herself when the farmers in eastern Skaftafellssysla went to Þingvellir." Damn, this Ingunn is so clearly very boring. What did she do to shock the farmers in eastern Skaftafellssysla? Danish and math I refused to study at all. I took an unofficial free period during those classes. Physics and chemistry I found similarly pointless. I stopped bringing my schoolbag and schoolbooks entirely; at best, I had a pencil with me. At times I hung forward on the table, scrawled something in a notebook, or tried to launch discussions with the aim of getting myself thrown out of class. Some days I didn't show up or went home immediately after the first class. I distanced myself from the school, and my peers grew more and more alien to me. I went up to the city library, hung out there, and read *Melody Maker*. Then when the time for school was over, I went home and it seemed like I was coming home from school. I felt like an extraterrestrial on an alien planet. Everyone but me seemed to enjoy it okay. I didn't understand why I was different from everyone else. It was like I had no connection with others and was sentenced to hang about alone in a world that seemed based on principles that I either didn't get or found to be incorrect and unfair. Then my mom got a call from the school. Baglet the principal called her and expressed concern about me and my attendance and behavior. Mom sat down with me and demanded a response. But I had nothing to say. There was nothing I could say to her. She didn't understand me. She would not understand my side. She was on Baglet's team and not mine.

JÓN GNARR

She wanted me to do what Baglet wanted me to do. What right did this disgusting loser have to call her and say they were worried about me? I despised him. He didn't give a shit about me. Why didn't he say to her what he always told me, that I was a disgusting slob and rude? Why couldn't I just quit this damn school and stay home? What was so stupid about wanting to be like Johnny Rotten when I grew up? Johnny Rotten was famous. It was better than being like Pills or the Christian Studies teacher.

The system wants every single person to be like all the others and only do what it wants them to do. One should always be evil and annoying. One may eat pills as much as one wants, and one never need smile or say anything fun to anyone but just listen and be where one is meant to be and go to bed on time and be awake and arrive at work when the system starts up. It doesn't matter how you feel. Reykjavík is a ghost town. It's inhabited by ghosts and robots.

No one is really in favor of this. But that's just fine because the system does not want people to be human. That's awkward for the system. It wants ghosts, living dead people who are like suitcases on a conveyor belt just waiting to be sent somewhere. If someone does something different than the others, the system turns against him, at first softly, with advice, and then with increasing hardness. At first, with corrections, and then with threats, and finally punishment. If you dare to be different, you get taken out. Get in line, dress like this, not strangely, don't say this and don't say that and preferably shut up. And above all: learn these damn rules inside out! If you learn them, things won't go badly. Or else you'll never get a job unless it's something depressing. You've no chance.

We'll close all the doors on your nose. Nobody will want to be your friend, and the only people who will want to marry you are ugly, stupid people like yourself. If you try any funny business, we'll send you to jail. And you'll never escape from there because we don't want you back. We'll stigmatize you, and you'll never see kindness or joy in our eyes but only hardness and suspicion. The system is simply one, one totality. All deviations are faults. If something doesn't match, it's discarded. All deviation damages the regulatory system and confuses the organization. The system organizes all the disorder and deviations. The system is what everyone expects, and everything must be straightforward. We don't want any variety. We don't want change. All houses should be identical. All people should look alike. We don't want punk. We want the Savanna Trio. Regular, calm music. We want to sleep. We want to watch stories on RÚV television about how it's nice to live out in the country. Wouldn't it be simply marvelous if Reykjavík didn't exist and we all lived out in the country? Your existence is like a barking dog in our dream. Do what we tell you or you'll be the worse for it. Sit! Stand! Shut up! Kumbayah! This is what's fun. This is what's right. Eurovision. "Little boxes on the riverbank, little boxes of dingalingading, all made from dingaling, and they're all made just the same." And we all want the same. The system is God. Those who worship God are acceptable to him and go to heaven, but those who deny him or don't trust him go to hell. And hell is the darkness that surrounds you when we close our eyes to you.

I couldn't say anything. Mom shook her head in submission and sighed.

"Phsh, I don't know what the devil to do with you, then."

A tone of defeat in her voice. Mom was a representative of the system, and this was a way to make me feel guilty. The system uses my parents to get the system's large fists inside me and grab me by the guts and squeeze as needed. It puts slabs on my chest until I'm suffocating—but they're clean and tidy slabs. The system knows that it can control people through their nervous systems. Pangs of conscience break you down from within. The system's toxic warfare. Invisible, intangible, ubiquitous. Doesn't leave fingerprints. Just a look. A tone of voice. A word. Ambiguous words. Sharp words. Judging words.

There was a kid with me at Rétto who was gay. At that time, the system did not accept gays. Disgusting gay devil! The system tried to crush out his homosexuality with all kinds of advice and action. Bullying, looks, contempt. There's no place for you here! School, family, peers, and neighbors joined forces. Conscience pangs, mocking, contempt, violence, fear, intimidation, shame, and, finally, exclusion in hell. Rumor was that he hanged himself in the garage at home. The system breathed relief. Deviation deleted. He was faulty from the beginning. The parents had acquired a defective child who died in infancy. Yet in reality, he was drowned. No one did it. It just happened. The system saw to that. Robots and ghosts were able to continue their journey along the colorful conveyor belt. They didn't have to worry about anything. They never needed to, since the system was pleased with them. They never lost any sleep. Relaxed, half-sleeping their way to heaven.

I was not on the way to heaven; that much I knew. Hell was my destination, calling on the Department of Psychiatry, unskilled labor, drugs, and Litla-Hraun, the prison. I had long been ready to take my first steps on the criminal path. That was the way to judgment. Everyone knew nothing would come out of me. I was a defective copy. My crime was to be different and to behave differently than required. Still, I wasn't doing anything to anyone. I didn't harm anyone, but I was still a threat. I was the punk song on the radio station that otherwise played elevator music for department stores. When people spoke, it was like they didn't hear the words being said, but instead they went on like a pleasantly babbling stream. Was my curse to hear every word? From the outside, from the other point of view, I was like a zombie, but inside I felt like the carnival in Rio de Janeiro was taking place. My brain was like a nuclear power plant producing endless ideas and words. The words were three-dimensional, and under each word were sentences, new meanings, possibilities. The words swapped, merged, formed new sentences. The words played on the emotions like a harp. Each word had its own sentiment. Nothing was immutable, everything renewed and transformed continuously. But others didn't see me with my eyes. They couldn't. They just saw me with their eyes. They lived in prison, but I was outside. I was free, but they were closed off. It was impossible for me to step into prison and leave myself locked inside. And they could not understand that I didn't want to step into prison because they saw the prison not as a prison but as a home. They were blind because they did not see.

I was sent to the school psychologist, who came to the school once a week to talk to students who were in trouble. I had never been before but had heard stories about him. Those who'd gone to him said he was insane, or at least close to it. The psychologist was a little guy with an enormously long beard. Friendly enough, he told me to sit.

"Well, how are you doing, Jón?" he asked, kindly.

I noticed that he had to look at a piece of paper to know what I was called.

"Fine," I answered and wondered if I would now be sent back to the doctors at Dalbraut or whether I had grown too old to go there? Perhaps he would put me in ECT? Would I maybe be sent to the nuthouse, Klepp? I wonder whether you have to be a certain age to be accepted at Klepp?

"Fine, yes," he said thoughtfully. "Do you feel you're getting on well in school?"

I thought about it. I felt things were going rather well. The only problem I could see was the taunts I got from the kids. Most of the teachers left me alone. I was just waiting for the school system to give up on me so I could go and do what I wanted.

"It's working out quite well," I said.

I could have told him about the kids and how maddening it was that they messed about with me and that the teachers were crazy. But I simply had no confidence that it would change anything. Bacon would not be fired if I said something. Bacon was not considered a problem. The system was fond of Bacon and pleased with him. The psychologist did not come to help me but to check on me. He was an emissary of the system and vigorously sucked at its teats.

"How's the situation at home?"

I didn't know what he meant, and he rephrased the question.

"What are conditions like in your home?"

How was I meant to answer that? Did I have to tell him about my dad? That it was crazy when he held fast to my hand and stroked me on the cheek as he whispered to me that I should promise him this and that? Would that change anything? Would Dad then get called to a school psychologist? Mom was fine, except perhaps when she was mad about something I had done. Other than that, she never got up to any nonsense. The doctors at Dalbraut had, for example, wanted to put me on some medication. Mom had forbidden it and said she would rather have me as I was than doped up on some drugs.

"I don't know," I said.

The psychologist thought about it and stroked his beard and read what was on the piece of paper. What was the piece of paper? Who had let him have it? I didn't believe any teacher would write something about me. Maybe this was simply a blacklist of everything I had done. Was it perhaps the report the detectives took from me?

"How do you get along with your parents?"

What could I say? We were like three strangers living together in one room and speaking three different languages. Mom and Dad didn't understand one another. Mom understood me a bit, but I didn't understand them at all. We were each from a different planet.

"All right," I muttered, to say something.

The psychologist looked at me and stroked his beard, nodded and muttered, distracted, like he'd accept anything I said. But I remained silent.

He stood up and walked over to the sink that was in the room.

He told me to come over. He put the stopper in the sink, turned it on, and filled it up with water. We were both silent as the water flowed and I watched, curious.

"What's this?" I asked when he turned off the tap.

He handed me a glass and a spoon and pushed the trash can toward me with his leg.

"So, Jón. How would you go about emptying the sink?" he asked, looking at me questioningly.

That was amusing. What did he want me to do? What was he really interested in? It would undeniably be funny to scoop water into the glass with the spoon and pour the glass into the trashcan, or scoop water with a spoon into the glass, then drink it and throw it up into the trashcan. It would also be funny to simply drink the water straight from the sink. I understood what was going on. He was testing to see if I was stupid. Okay, this was what you call an intelligence test. I was seized by a pressing need to do something weird and I really, really wanted to give him something he wasn't expecting. What if I sucked up the water in my mouth, spit it into the glass, and poured it from the glass via the spoon into the trash can? And then drank it? But the therapist was so serious that I dared not clown about.

"Can't I just take the stopper out?" I asked, carefully.

He looked searchingly at me and lifted his eyebrows like he was asking me whether I thought I was right. I was silent and looked down. He emptied the sink, sat back at his desk, and wrote something on a piece of paper. I stayed put and waited. If I could go now, I'd be able to go out and smoke before the main recess started and all the idiots came out of class. During the main recess

I tended to sneak out the back door, go over into the garden opposite, and smoke there in order to get some peace. But it was fun to smoke with someone rather than alone. The only one who smoked outside the back door with me was Fat Dóri. He never got any respite from the bullying. And there were often some amusing kids outside smoking during classes. They were boys who were cutting or had been thrown out of class—like me.

The psychologist looked at me.

"Jón, where do elephants live?"

The question caught me by surprise. I had instead been expecting a question about what hobbies I had. I was entirely prepared to tell him all about anarchism. It had also occurred to me when I first saw him that he reminded me considerably of Peter Kropotkin. Perhaps they were related? Or perhaps he knew who Kropotkin was and was trying to imitate his appearance? I would also have been very happy to tell him about Crass and the difference between Crass and the Sex Pistols. In addition, I really wanted to tell him about all the Crass slogans, like "Jesus died for his own sins not mine," and "Fight war not wars." I was quite willing to discuss what they meant with him. Didn't that mean you ought to fight against war but not in it? Or did it mean that one should fight in a particular war, not in all wars in general? I had not met anyone that I could talk to about this. But he didn't want to talk about anarchism; he wanted to talk about elephants. I knew a lot about elephants. I had both watched a documentary about them and read about them in animal books. I thought elephants were charming animals. I owned a big book about animals published by Fjölva and there was a chapter about elephants I had often read.

The Icelandic translation of elephant was *úlfaldi* because the word had been matched to the picture of a camel back in the old days. Someone had confused camel and elephant—the name camel had been put on the wrong animal. But I knew that it was "elephant" in English. There are two species of elephants, African and Asian. The African elephant is bigger than the Asian. I doubted, however, that the psychologist wanted such detailed explanations. He was just checking whether I was an idiot. It was asinine.

"Africa."

I was hoping that would suffice. I couldn't be bothered with this. I hoped that he wouldn't ask anything else. He nodded his head like I'd guessed the correct answer in some quiz. But it wasn't completely right because I had omitted the Asian elephant.

"But where do whales live?" he asked next.

I also knew a lot about whales. In the Fjölva big book of animals, there was a picture of orcas that had killed a blue whale that leapt out of the sea.

"The sea."

He nodded and wrote something. Then he looked up and told me I could go.

"Thank you," he said and hunkered down into his papers.

I was relieved. Fat Dóri was outside, standing in a corner and smoking. We had stopped meeting outside school. I bummed a cigarette and told him about the psychologist.

"He made you do the test with the sink?" Dóri asked.

"Yes?"

"Me too."

I giggled. Dóri took a big drag from the cigarette then shot the stub into the air with a flick, down into a puddle.

"Fucking idiot!"

Mom was sitting in the kitchen when I got home. She looked at me strangely—something was up. There was something wrong. And when something was wrong, then it was always connected with me in some way. Usually it was something that I had done. On such occasions, Mom was sat at the kitchen table when I got home; she called to me and asked me to come and sit with her—or, rather, ordered me to.

"Would you come and sit here with me, Jón!"

Two crumpled cigarettes lay on the table. I knew immediately that they were my cigarettes. I'd been smoking since going to the country. I hid cigarette packages that I bought outside in the garden, but it still sometimes happened that I left them in my pocket. I tried to have a surprised expression like I didn't understand what was going on and knew nothing about these cigarettes.

"Are these your cigarettes, Jón?"

I put on a shocked face and opened my eyes wide like I was totally astonished that she could think I had any cigarettes.

"No," I said, indignant.

"So, what were they doing in your trouser pocket?"

These were stubs I'd found and salvaged. I acted like suddenly I'd remembered something I'd forgotten.

"Wellll, I was keeping them for my friend."

Mom heaved a sad sigh.

"Stop lying to me!"

"I'm not lying at all," I muttered like someone who knows he is lying and everyone else knows it too.

I looked directly at her.

"Have you started smoking?"

"No," I said.

I was trying to be as resolute and honest as I could, though I had started smoking. I was no longer just testing it out. I'd begun to think about cigarettes in the morning and to smoke before I went to school. Sometimes I wanted a cigarette so badly in the evening that I smoked out the window. And why couldn't I? She herself smoked. When I was little, I tried to get her to quit smoking. It was after I found out how dangerous it was. I didn't want my mom to get lung cancer like Gulli, her brother, so I threw her cigarettes in the trash. She didn't give up smoking. Once I took a cigarette from her pack, stuffed firecrackers in it, and put it back in the packet. I did it to show her how dangerous smoking was. Then I hid myself and watched her smoke. She sat at the kitchen table drinking coffee. Then she drew a cigarette from the pack and lit it. The explosion was so intense that the cigarette ripped apart and soot and tobacco were spread everywhere. Mom was so startled that she screamed and struck the cup of coffee off the table so that it crashed to the floor and shattered. She screamed and then burst into tears. That startled me so much that I was paralyzed. I had not expected that there would be such a big explosion. Mom yelled at me:

"What's wrong with you, child! Are you trying to kill me?"

I then explained to her why I had done it, that it was because it was dangerous to smoke and I didn't want her to die. Then suddenly she stopped crying and started laughing. Then she stopped laughing and began to cry again, and so it went on like that. I stood like I was frozen in front of her. Was she having a nervous breakdown? Had I finally managed to over-exert my mother, and would this cause her to lose her wits? Would she be sent to Klepp and would I be blamed for everything? Would I be left all alone with Dad?

"Tell me the truth, Jón. Have you started smoking?"

My sister Runa smoked. All my friends were smokers. Smoking was cool. All actors smoked. Everyone who was in a band smoked. All punks were smokers. It was just jerks who didn't. I decided to lay my cards on the table.

"Yes," I muttered.

Mom nodded her head, and I felt relieved.

"I knew you'd started smoking. I've started to notice you smelling of smoke."

I was silent. Did she perhaps feel that it was okay?

"I hate when you lie to me."

"I know."

She wasn't angry because I was smoking, but angry that I was going behind her back and lying.

"How do you pay for it?" she asked.

I had no great difficulty getting cigarettes. I borrowed cigarettes from other kids and stole money from Dad's wallet to buy packs myself.

"I just borrow," I muttered.

She was no longer angry. She thought it was okay. She had only been angry because I was lying to her.

"What do you think your Dad would say?"

I could only imagine. He was against smoking and would definitely seize on this to the fullest. He would pretend he was hurt, that this was a great shock to him, that I had somehow hurt him personally by smoking. He would be totally astonished, he would hold my hand and stare ahead, appalled. Then would he tear up, look at me, and ask:

"Why do you do this to me?"

And I would answer as always:

"I don't know."

What can you say in response to that? How does one answer such bullcrap? But that was something I would have to go through now that this had become public. Dad grabbed every chance he got to nag. Nagging seemed to be what he most enjoyed. If someone said or did something that displeased him, he appeared to take it personally, like it was done deliberately to shock him. He nagged me, Runa, and Mom. He even tried nagging Mom's sisters, but they didn't listen. He nagged them constantly about smoking and, like that wasn't enough, he also nagged them if he saw them with a drink in hand. Those times, he would get all amazed and put on his wounded look.

"What, are you drinking alcohol?" he said, and always looked at the clock.

They answered him, ever defiant:

"Oh, for God's sake, shut up, Kristinn!"

Dad could do all his annoying with just expressions and word choice. Wine became liquor and dope became narcotics in Dad's vocabulary. Once he tore into Aunt Salla and said there was no difference between smoking and narcotics; he was basically saying that Aunt Salla was a drug addict. He preferred it that Runa never smoked in front of him, even though she was an adult. He never let Runa alone. He used the same techniques on her as on me, being friendly and annoying at the same time. Runa had smoked for many years, but he was always astonished to see her light a cigarette.

"What are you doing?"

She pretended not to know what he meant, although she knew full well. She always tried to turn the other cheek.

"What do you mean?" she asked, cheerfully.

"Are you smoking?" he said, with great uncertainty in his voice, like he refused to believe his own eyes.

"Yes, Dad, dear, I smoke."

Then he was silent, and looked tenderly and oddly at her and said:

"But you promised me that you'd stop."

Runa never remembered these promises, but she had indeed often promised this so that she didn't have to listen to him nag any longer. Dad could always get you to promise something. Everyone except him forgot these promises straightaway. Although he forgot everything else, he didn't forget those annoying promises. He put people in a position where they couldn't help but agree with whatever he wanted them to. Sometimes he simply held you fast and didn't let go until you were ready to promise anything. In most cases, you didn't even know yourself why you were making the promise. A promise to be diligent, a promise to be good, a promise to be fun, a promise to tidy yourself up. A promise, a promise, a promise. The things people said and did hurt him so very much.

Runa was letting him down by smoking. Once she stopped smoking for a while and told Dad about it to please him. Then she started smoking again a few months later. Dad was of the opinion that he had been personally betrayed. Runa never understood how he reached that conclusion.

"You're making a liar out of me!" he yelped.

"How so?" she asked, surprised.

He was indignant.

"I told all my coworkers that you've stopped smoking, but you have not stopped. I was so proud of you. Now no one will believe a word I say. My colleagues will think of me as a liar."

I saw my father before me as he told all the cops the great news that his daughter had stopped smoking. And how all the cops were really joyful on his behalf, how they all shone with happiness and excitement over this marvelous news. I saw my father knock on the chief of police's door and tell him the good tidings. Then I imagined the chief of police springing to his feet and exclaiming:

"This truly is good news!"

That was asinine and weird, like most of what Dad said. I didn't believe that my dad was such an idiot that he told everyone his daughter had stopped smoking. Nobody would care at all. But he took advantage of it just to try to make her feel bad. I'd at long last realized it. He lived entirely for nagging us, giving us bullcrap. Those were the only ways of interacting he knew, and he never acted any differently than the way he was when using us as the audience to retell something that had been in the news.

One time, Runa's little boy was playing with an empty ashtray in the living room. Runa sat right by him reading the paper.

Suddenly Dad shouted out and pointed to the boy:

"Take that away from him!"

Runa sprang to her feet.

"What?"

"He's got an ashtray!" Dad shouted like some emergency was in progress.

Runa breathed a sigh and looked sadly at him.

"Can't he play with it if he's happy?"

Dad got all offended and acted thunderstruck. Then he looked at Runa like she was an imbecile who didn't understand anything at all.

"He might chop off his hands!"

"Oh, for God's sake, Dad. It isn't dangerous. Stop behaving like this."

Dad sighed, leaned back in his chair, and wore an annoyed expression.

"It's not that the ashtray is worth anything," he said, apologetically. "It's just that it has sentimental value for your mother."

The message to Runa was that she was at once hurting his feelings and slighting Mom. Then Mom called from within the kitchen:

"It's got zero sentimental value for anyone. It's a piece of junk I bought at Hagkaup for my fiftieth birthday."

Then Dad got embarrassed, stopped being pissed, and began thinking about something else.

Sometimes Dad behaved like a small child who could never let others be. He was always interfering, jumping into conversations he'd not otherwise been following, and asking about things he didn't get or in which he wasn't interested. If he wasn't involved, he would continually ask Mom about things that weren't important in the moment. It was like he was somehow annoyed if Mom was happy or was telling a story and was always interrupting her in order to ruin the story.

MOM: I'll never forget when my brother—Gulli—came to our home on Skipholt wearing a Santa costume. It was the height of summer...

DAD: Who called you earlier?

MOM: Huh? No one. *(Continuing on with her story).* He tiptoed upstairs...

DAD: So the phone didn't ring?!

MOM: *(Irritated).* It was your sister. Gunna.

Silence.

LISTENER: *(Excited).* And he was wearing a Santa costume?

MOM: *(Smiles again).* Oh yes, with the beard and all. And my mother was sitting in the living room watching *Bonanza*...

DAD: Did she ask for me?

MOM: *(annoyed)* No.

DAD: Am I to call her back?

MOM: Oh, for God's sake, Kristinn, leave me in peace!

Then Dad seemed to get all wounded; he stood up and walked off. Mom was no longer in the mood for telling her story. Everyone had to take care not to offend Dad; it was like being around a child.

If you weren't talking about him or to him, then he interrupted. And there was no point trying to make light of the fact that he was mad.

One time, I went to the basement to paint anarchist logos on a large piece of cardboard I wanted to hang in my room. I was very excited about this project and wanted to paint anarchist signs like those on my Crass albums, where the lines of the A go outside a circle. I found an old brush and used it to paint. Then I hung the cardboard up in my room. A few days later there was a knock on my door. This was unusual. I got up and opened it. Dad stood there with a very grave expression on his face. His features were disfigured by his inner turmoil, his emotional distress. He held up a brush in his hand and extended it towards me. I had forgotten to clean the paint off and now it had hardened.

"Did you use this brush?" he asked, his voice quivering.

He was on the verge of bursting into tears.

"Yes," I said.

"I just found it on the table…useless."

"Yeah," I muttered.

Dad's eyes flooded with tears as he said:

"And now I have to throw it away."

I didn't think it was a big issue. It was an old brush with a plastic handle, and it was small and insignificant. Cheap.

"It's not such a big deal," I said.

He looked at me as if he could not believe his ears. In his eyes I was unethical and impudent, cheeky, shockingly selfish, inconsiderate. I was a person who walked all over other people and left nothing behind except destruction and pain. He stopped being wounded and became angry. He got himself totally worked up over this. His eyes shot sparks. He held on to the paintbrush so hard his knuckles whitened and his hand shook.

"Not a big deal?" he hissed. "What do you know about it?"

I was afraid. Dad was a big guy. His arms were as thick as my thighs. It brought back to mind the times he'd beaten my ass when I was little. I was as lightweight as a bag of wheat in his hands.

"What's that?" I asked, frightened.

"You've ruined my brushes tens of thousands of times!" he yelled at me.

I was startled. It was horrifying and ridiculous at the same time. My father was so emotionally twisted that it verged on insanity. I'd mistreated his paintbrush, and in so doing, I'd mistreated him. The paintbrush was one of those things that had, in his mind, "sentimental value." Countless thoughts zinged through my mind. Was he about to attack me? What did he want me to do? What should I say to him? Should I start bawling, collapse over my mistake, and implore him to forgive me? He would then embrace me and cry, too, squeezing me to him and whispering how he had loved this brush and how the brush had great sentimental value for him. And then we would sit together hand in hand, wiping away our tears, and he would tell me stories about everything he had painted with the brush, and before we knew it we'd both beginning to laugh about how much fun life is. That evening, we'd head outside and bury the paintbrush together in the garden and start crying again. At that moment my thoughts, feelings, and fears got too much, and I burst out laughing. I looked at this strange man standing there with his paintbrush and laughed, screamed with laughter until tears fell down my cheeks. Dad was offended and stormed away without saying a word. He didn't speak to me for days. I didn't care and was just relieved to get rid of him. I didn't care if he was hurt. I refused to participate in this bullshit anymore. This man had been torturing me with crap like that my whole life. Always aggrieved. This wasn't something to get pissed about. It was just a brush, a shitty unremarkable brush. I enjoyed seeing him sulk. He couldn't, at least, nag me in the meantime.

After a few days, Mom came and talked to me.

"Please talk to your father."

"About what?"

"You need to ask his forgiveness."

"Forgiveness? For what? I didn't do anything to him!"

Mom sighed.

"I know. I just can't stand it anymore. Do it for me, ask his forgiveness."

For Mom. I was in it for Mom. She always forgave him in order to keep the peace. Anything for peace. She begged for forgiveness and let him be mean to her. It was her method to survive living with him. An example of this was when she accidently put food coloring instead of chocolate sauce on his ice cream. Dad ate the ice cream with a hearty appetite while he watched the news. When he came into the kitchen with the bowl, Mom noticed that he was all black around the mouth.

"What have you been up to, Kristinn?" she asked, amazed, though she soon realized her mistake and began to laugh. Dad was not amused and said she had done it on purpose. She had hurt him.

"Intentionally? Why would I do something like that on purpose?"

"In order to humiliate me!" Dad said and would not stop until he had got her to promise never to do it again. Mom eventually got fed up and promised him that she would never ever again put food coloring on his ice cream.

"He's not a bad man," she often said. That often happened when she was complaining about Dad to someone. She sounded exhausted but would always end up saying: "He's not a bad man." And it was absolutely true. He was not bad or evil. He was just tremendously weird. I went and asked his forgiveness. I thought it was unfair, but I did it anyway—for Mom. He was sitting in the living room, watching TV, and did not look at me when I showed up. I was embarrassed for a few moments and then muttered:

"I'm sorry."

"Huh?!" he said harshly, like someone who has been deeply wounded and can't imagine any way things will get better.

"I'm sorry I ruined your paintbrush," I said, a bit clearer.

He thought to himself and wondered if he should forgive me, if he could forgive me. I waited. Then he extended me his hand. My breath was labored and my chest heavy. Why was it always like this? Why did my dad have to be this crazy? Why couldn't he just be normal? Why couldn't we just talk like normal people? I couldn't bear this game, this damn script that our relationship was and had always been. Nothing was real. Suddenly I wanted to cry. Not over him or the brush. Not even over our relationship, but over having given up and managed once again to allow him to use me as a plaything in his crazy, sentimental drama. He looked up. His eyes flooded with tears. I barely caught my breath but squeezed out a smile. It was a polite, false smile of encouragement. I smiled like

I was smiling to a bum who I feared was going to hassle me on the street downtown. Then came the embrace. He pressed me to him so that I was standing, half bent, over him.

"You mustn't do this, my dear, dear boy," he whimpered.

"No," I said.

"Will you promise me that?"

"Yes."

Mom didn't tell him I'd started smoking. I didn't tell him either. There was a tacit agreement between us that he didn't need to know. I started smoking in my room. Dad was never in there. I also smoked before he got home. He never noticed anything.

Mom sometimes sent me to the shops for her. I never told her that I got beaten up all the time, and she never asked me anything about it. I went all the same, not least because I got to keep the change. There were several shops in the neighborhood, and I checked whether any annoying kids were around before I went inside. If some dickfaces were in the grocery store, or outside, I slunk off to the next store. One evening, I went the whole way up to Ásgard just to buy three bottles of Coke. The shop was empty, but as I was finishing shopping, two kids who often picked on me suddenly showed up. They were dribbling a basketball between them inside the convenience store. I tried to ignore them, though I could hear them whispering about me. I pretended not to see them and hoped they would leave me alone. When I walked out of the convenience store with the bottles in a bag, they immediately came after me.

"Hey dumbass, where are you going? Why are you so stupid?"

I pretended I didn't hear them and hurried on my way. But they ran after me and blocked my path.

"Were you buying mixers?"

"Yes," I muttered.

It was more cool to say that than to say you were shopping for your mom.

"You owe us booze."

"I do?"

"Yes."

"Why?"

"Are you as stupid as you are ugly?"

I didn't understand the question but answered it in the affirmative to please them.

"You owe us booze as protection. If you don't pay, you get beat up. Understand?"

"Yes, I do."

I tramped past them and walked off. Then one of them took the basketball and threw it so hard at my neck that I fell, dropping the bag; the Coke bottles all broke, and my glasses whipped off. I felt about for the glasses, thankfully located them, put them back on, and ran away. I cried all the way home out of fear and anger. Motherfuckers! What exactly had I done to them? I was nothing to them. Was there something about me that bothered them so much? I told Mom that I'd dropped the bag and broken the stuff. I felt ashamed. Maybe it was simply my own fault that I was always being teased. Maybe I was just calling it on myself. A man doesn't run crying to his mother. What should she do? What could she do? Go and talk to the kids? It would just make matters worse.

BOOZE

From then on, the physical abuse at the hands of kids in my neighborhood got worse. They sometimes stopped me on school grounds, held me down, and demanded:

"Why are you so stupid? Why are you so ugly? Can I spit on you?"

Then they would punch me repeatedly in the stomach. Next they'd kick me. When I got away, they came after me and kicked me up the ass—you could say their shoes imprinted my ass—and then two or three of them together tried to kick my feet away from under me, push me, trip me. Ultimately, they'd succeed and down I'd drop. And still I always owed them booze on my shopping trips. One kid there was really big and strong, and somehow he'd arrived at the conclusion that I owed him some booze; I had no idea what had led him to that conclusion...maybe he just wanted booze. I adopted a strategy of not speaking at all because I soon realized that no matter what I said to them, it always went badly for me. I just remained silent, looked down at the floor and waited for them to do something else. Most of the time, some girl would come up and say:

"Oh, leave him alone. Stop teasing him!"

Usually they stopped as a result. But not once did an adult, a teacher or similar figure, get involved, though presumably they knew what was going on and saw it happening again and again.

Of all the boys who teased me, there was one I particularly feared. He was a brawler who was regularly involved in fights and who beat the shit out of people. He was the sort of kid who didn't think twice about punching you. He was also a real weirdo. He was named Biggi, and people called him Brutal Biggi. And although he was not like the Morons, he was friends with them. The Morons didn't exactly beat you up; they just messed about with you. If, for example, I left my bag lying about somewhere, tthey would take it, dunk it in the toilet, and flush it until it was soaked through. When I was walking home with a drenched bag, they would point at me and laugh. When I was walking home with a drenched bag, they would point at me and laugh.

"Hey ugly, why do you have a dripping wet bag?"

"He had to pee in it."

"Are you so stupid that you piss in your schoolbag?"

The two boys who were on my case the most always hung about together and were called Black and White. They got their nicknames because they listened to ska: Madness and Specials. They were friends with Biggi. One time when they were tormenting me, I tried to push them away from me and shouted out, "Black and White—fuck and fight." That pissed them off, and they told Biggi to punch me. He walked swiftly over to me and punched me straight in the face with a clenched fist. I had never been punched so powerfully; I was terrified, totally paralyzed by fear. A short time later, he beat up Dóri for no reason at all.

Dóri got a black eye and was so frightened that he dared not leave his house for days. Dóri and I discussed it inside and out. It became the only thing we talked about. What were we going to do? Could we do anything to make it stop? Could we somehow speak out? Could we join together, like Black and White, and throw some punches ourselves? Wouldn't they just respond by punching us harder? I was certain, however, that things could not go on this way, with the situation deteriorating, always getting worse. We were shit-scared the whole time and didn't dare do anything, didn't dare go to Bústaðir, didn't dare go to the shops, didn't dare go to school, didn't dare take the bus, even. It hung over our heads at all times. We'd begun to call it hell, hellish hell—everywhere was hell.

I had a knife, a dagger that I had gotten for free when I was in the Scouts. Since I'd gotten so scared, I started carrying the knife with me when I went out of the house because it gave me a little security. I'd managed to borrow Mom's sewing stuff and stitch the sheath of the knife safely into my jacket. I thought to myself that if Biggi ever managed to trap me so I couldn't get away, I could threaten him so that he would run off. My sense of security increased day by day as I wore a knife hidden under my clothing. But I never told anyone about it. The knife was an absolute last resort.

After hanging around one night at Bústaðir with Siggi the Punk, I was returning home. Suddenly Brutal Biggi appeared. When he saw me he sped in my direction. I stopped.

"Where's my booze?"

"What do you mean?" I muttered.

"You owe me booze!"

I stood frozen.

"I don't owe you any booze," I muttered.

He punched me in the shoulder.

"Of course you owe me booze. You owe me liquor!"

He grabbed me and slammed me up against the wall, struck me again and again up against the wall.

"Stop it. Stop it," I implored him, on the verge of tears.

"Get me my booze then. I'll stop when you get me my booze. You owe me liquor, dumbass!"

I was so scared, I started crying. I hoped he would put me down if he saw me cry, but he just got all the more worked up.

"Are you crying, you piece of shit?"

He grabbed me so hard around the neck that I could hardly breathe. I was out of my mind with fear, and without thinking about it, I reached inside my jacket, pulled the knife out, and shoved it menacingly towards Biggi. I fully hoped he would be so scared when he saw the knife that he'd run away. I wanted to say something but couldn't get out a word, just kept shaking the knife in the air in front of him.

"You've got a knife, bonehead?"

He ripped the knife off me in a single motion but was so surprised that he let go of me. I seized the opportunity and ran away as fast as I could. He shouted after me:

"I'm going to beat you to shit, motherfucker!"

Terrified, I ran straight home. I sat totally alone inside my room through the rest of the evening and cried and trembled. My Sid Vicious T-shirt was sodden with tears and snot. This fucking life! Shithead and loser. Why was everything so miserable for me? Why didn't things ever look up? Why couldn't they just leave me alone?

I hate them, hate them, hate them, I murmured to myself. I lay awake all night, trying to come up with a solution.

News immediately got around the whole neighborhood: it was on everyone's lips that I'd had a knife.

"Did you have a knife?"

"What, were you gonna just stab Biggi, or what?"

I didn't know how I should reply. I'd had no idea what I'd planned to do.

"Well no, I just had a knife, see."

I was going to get beaten up. Biggi had already declared that he was going to beat the shit out of me. Everyone was talking about it, and all of my thoughts turned to avoiding Biggi. I'd heard stories about this and that kid he'd beaten up, and the stories had always sparked panic in my mind. Now it was my turn. Brutal Biggi was going to beat me up. I tried to stay at home as much as I possibly could. If I went out, I snuck along walls and darted between houses. I was absolutely terrified. Dóri and I talked yet again about what to do, but we were just as perplexed as before. I spoke to some boys I looked up to and asked them what I could possibly do in this hopeless situation. They said that there was nothing else to do but fight back.

"There's no escape. You just have to face up to it. If you allow a pillock like him to bug you, it won't ever stop."

But how would I be able to beat up Brutal Biggi? I thought of all the possible ways. What could I do? Run up to him and beat him on the head with a lead pipe or something? I decided to talk to a boy who had been with me in the Scouts. He was an impressive fighter; he was known as Gaddi the Fists. He had a reputation for being mental. He was one of those who really threw punches. He was often in fights down at Hlærisplan and didn't hesitate to take on older and stronger boys using his fists and his knees. But he had always been very nice to me, and we had always been on good terms. I told him all the sob stories about the kids who were constantly picking on me and about how Biggi was going to beat me up. Gaddi was no friend to Biggi. He well knew who he was, despised him totally, and said:

"This idiot deserves a good kicking."

So Gaddi was quite willing to help me and not at all fazed. We three should just attack Biggi and beat his ass. We knew that Biggi played table tennis at Fossvogs School two nights a week. Biggi had a precious DBS 10-speed bike he always took when he went to table tennis practice. We knew where he lived and worked out the route he would take to practice. We decided to wait for him in a hidden spot right near the school. I stressed repeatedly that we shouldn't let him know who we were, so we had to wear ski hats and clothes that we rarely wore otherwise. Gaddi was very excited about the whole thing and was looking forward to it. I was apprehensive in the days leading up to it. But it was the only way I felt I could do something to put an end to things. The thought of it made my hands continually shake and made me feel like I was trembling all over inside. My heart beat at double speed. But I couldn't possibly turn down the chance; it was the only way. The plan was to sit on Biggi, attack him, hit him, then set fire to his bike and table tennis stuff. I had emptied containers of washing up liquid, rinsed them, and filled them with gasoline. We'd scare him so much that he'd never dare harm us.

Then came the frightful night. We hid ourselves and waited. I hoped with all my heart that Biggi wouldn't come; I prayed to God. "Good God, please don't let Biggi come," I said over and over in my mind. But God didn't hear me, and shortly after that, Biggi came up on his bicycle. When he was about upon us, we jumped in front of him with ski caps and nylon socks on our heads.

"Death to morons!" yelled Dóri.

As we rushed forward, Biggi lost his balance and fell off the bike. Gaddi threw himself at him and punched him in the face repeatedly while Dóri kicked him as he rolled around on the street. Meanwhile, hands trembling, I sprayed gasoline over Biggi's bike and gym bag and lit it so that it flamed up. Gaddi and Dóri rained down blows on him. I also wanted to kick him, but I didn't dare. Biggi held his arms around his head; his nose was bleeding, and his lip was cracked. I tossed the empty container and ran away. The boys also took to their heels and we dashed off, each in his own direction.

The next few days passed in a nightmare. I didn't know if anyone else knew we had been there. I went to school and saw Biggi with his face all swollen and a black eye. It gave me a feeling of unparalleled satisfaction. He didn't pay me any special attention, but I was sure he suspected me of being one of those who had attacked him. I was filled with confidence. We were the architects of this. We had beaten Biggi's ass, and now he would leave us and everyone else alone. We had taught him a lesson. But then the story started going around that it had been me, Dóri, and Gaddi that attacked him. Gaddi had blabbed. He had enjoyed it and had boasted about it. Kids began to ask, "Did you take part in the attack on Biggi?"

I flatly denied it.

"No! Are you totally insane?!"

I thought that was an entirely believable answer, as there was really nothing that tied us to Gaddi. He was not a punk, not at Rétto, and, most of all, was just not the type of person I was associated with. Gaddi the unpredictable, the dissimulator, the fighter. He was notorious in the neighborhood, and it was even said that he had once beaten his mother when she had criticized him for something or other.

After it became clear that Gaddi had been behind the attack, Biggi challenged him to a fight. It was decided that the combat would take place in the courtyard behind Grímsbæ. Several kids went to watch, but I didn't dare on my life be seen there. It was the biggest fight most had ever witnessed. Gaddi fought bravely, but Biggi had physical advantages over him, and despite the fact that Gaddi had been able to get some good shots in, it ended with Biggi totally beating the shit out of him. Gaddi was taken away, unconscious, by ambulance. And, as a result, I completely stopped turning up at school, at Bústaðir, Ingaskýli, all those places. I just went down to the bus station at Hlemmur. It was the only place I could be safe. I waited continually for Mom to realize that I had stopped attending school, but it never happened. It was like there was never a complaint about attendance. I never saw Biggi again. I don't know if he ever searched for me, but I was always on guard. When I went to Bústaðir or down to Hallærisplan or anywhere kids were gathered, I always took great care. I was like a deer in a documentary on television. The deer were never safe, always looking around and ready to run away if they caught wind of any wildlife.

IN PARADISE

Just take a look around you
What do you see
Kids with feelings like you and me
Understand him he'll understand you
For you are him and he is you
If the kids are united then we'll never be divided
—SHAM 69, "If the Kids Are United"

After what happened that winter, I broke more and more away from studying and turned up less and less often. It wasn't important to me to attend school. They didn't teach me anything I wanted to learn. For me, school was nothing more than a place of humiliation and injustice where harassment and persecution steadily increased. I was surrounded on school grounds, pushed when trying to walk, chased home. The violence was gradual. First, I was only knocked over and kicked in the ass. Then kids started to punch me in the stomach and back. I feared that the day would come when I would be beaten to a pulp. I'd be kicked in the balls and punched in the face and kicked in the head. The kids, at least, seemed to hate me so much that it might happen. They clearly wanted to hurt me. It didn't much bother the teachers that I would hardly show up at all. I think some of them even didn't make a note of my absence from their class so that I would not be compelled to show up in the future. They were happy to be rid of me. When I turned up, I tried to maintain constant questioning and joking until I got thrown out. The only reason I came to school was Mom.

Because I couldn't be home during the day, there was no other option but school. I went to school because I had no other place to hang. Until, that is, I was introduced to the bus station, Hlemmur.

When I had money and didn't feel like going to, or was too afraid to go to, school I went around on the bus. I'd run about and examine Reykjavík out the window. Sometimes I met kids I knew and even made new friends on the bus. I befriended one of the drivers who drove the Eleven—Route 11. I never had to pay when he was driving. He was called Stjáni and was a young guy who had just started driving. When he was behind the wheel, I'd sometimes go on many loops with him and talk to him the whole time. We talked about everything between heaven and earth. Stjáni had a lot to say and seemed interested in what I had to contribute. He had been at sea and traveled around the world. I enjoyed listening to him talk about that. In exchange, I told him about my speculations on punk and anarchism. Stjáni had fixed political views and was a communist. There were elections coming up, and we were both in agreement about the need for revolution. We were both dog-tired of society as it was, for different reasons. Much of what Stjáni talked about I didn't understand, but I had never let on. He sometimes talked about some men and assumed that obviously I knew who he was speaking about. I had no idea but figured that they were politicians. Stjáni often complained about his salary and felt it was way too low. I asked what he got each month, and he told me. I thought it was a good salary. He got more money in one month than I'd had my whole life. But he also had a sweetheart and child to provide for. I thought Stjáni was awesome. He complained to me a lot about his girlfriend.

He called her either the crone or the missus. I couldn't help but envy him that he had a girlfriend. It was definitely a long way off before I'd get a girlfriend, if I ever managed at some future point to have a girlfriend. I didn't believe there was any girl who would think I'd make a cute and interesting boyfriend, and who I'd think was fun. Stjáni wasn't a ginger and didn't have glasses. He was cool. When it was very bright out, he put on dark sunglasses. Driving a bus, was in my mind, the most beautiful job there was. To be a bus driver was like being a pilot, in uniform, responsible, traveling. In my opinion, Stjáni had seized happiness. I was confident that if I were Stjáni I'd be the happiest person in the world, with a flashy job, a girlfriend, and lots of money. But I wasn't Stjáni, and Stjáni thought his life sucked.

Stjáni printed out transfers for me when I wanted and put times down that suited me best. That way I could travel even more. Over time, I learned his shifts, so I knew when he would be driving. The Eleven drove from Breiðholt down to Hlemmur, where it terminated. Then Stjáni went for coffee. I always enjoyed coming to Hlemmur, and I met other punks there. Hlemmur was a meeting spot where punks, bums, mental patients, and oddballs came and went around the clock. Some even hung out there all day. It really got going, though, at evenings and weekends. There were often fifteen to twenty punks at once. I don't know what happened to make Hlemmur the punk headquarters. Maybe there wasn't much else to choose from. Hlemmur was centrally located, and there were chairs to sit on and always something going on, people coming and going. When the weather was good, you could walk into town. There weren't many places that could offer such luxury.

Usually we were left in peace and weren't always being thrown out like at the shops. And maybe we all had some unconscious need to be seen and to be noticed by each other.

I made it my custom to go to Hlemmur at night, especially on Friday and Saturday. I had been there a few times with Siggi the Punk, and he introduced me to other punks. Because Siggi was the main punk, the other punks accepted me immediately.

I felt much better in Hlemmur than at school and started going there every day. Sometimes, I even got the first bus in the morning and hung out there all day, from when it opened in the morning until the evening when it closed. Day after day.

The punks were mostly the same age as me. Some, however, were older or really young. The oldest were sixteen and seventeen years old, and the youngest as low as ten or eleven. We divided into two age groups, little kids and big. Little kids were ten to fourteen and older kids fifteen to seventeen years. But the age difference did not matter because punk united us all. Older kids generally treated the younger ones with respect and consideration. We were connected by the invisible threads of punk. It was our harmony. It wasn't just outfits and music, it was the mentality. All of us had in common the fact that we were in one way or another at odds with our environment. Most had difficult home lives to wrestle with, drunken parents, or even domestic violence. Many lived with single mothers who worked away from home and had little time for them. All of us were excluded from the school system.

Icelandic punks were significantly different from their colleagues in the United Kingdom. Our clothing was set and simple and pieced together: ripped jeans that had been written on, sneakers or black military boots, preferably with loose soles and equally shabby uppers. Any jackets were allowed, but most wore either leather jackets or army coats. Other than that, coats were prohibited. Many of the older boys even had black men's jackets with logos on the lapel. The army coats were like the jeans, marked-up with black pen. Haircuts were short and messy and ideally looked like you had cut it yourself, which most people actually did. That said, there were a very few people with mohawks or dyed hair. Each individual had his logos, either a band or simply an anarchist symbol. Dog collars were popular around the neck and rings or pins in the ears. The reason for this get-up was simply that there weren't a lot of specialty shops that sold punk clothes, and what little you could get was considered expensive, so we couldn't afford it. Most of those there were boys, but there were some girls, too. They were dressed similar to the boys. Most punks came from Kópavogur. They had their own refuge at Skiptistoður in Hamraborg, but it was more fun at Hlemmur.

There were two permanently present groups who were always hanging out at Hlemmur: the punks and the winos. We were in one corner, and they were in another. The winos were adults, men, outcasts—criminals and mental patients who were homeless and slept in abandoned houses and bicycle sheds and such places. Several were sailors from the countryside on a bender in town. They were drunk and stoned from morning to evening. We had little interaction with them, except perhaps if they went to the state liquor store for us or when they gave us some pills. Otherwise we tried to leave them alone. They were deceitful and dangerous, especially if they were stoned. We weren't really into drugs.

Many of us looked down on drugs. We didn't want to turn out like the winos. I didn't think taking narcotics would be an interesting lifestyle, and I was afraid of drugs, especially heroin. It was said that if you injected yourself with heroin once, you would be addicted for life. I reckoned it was okay to use pills recreationally or for amusement but no more than that. If you became a junkie, then you were agreeing to give up and let the system win. Then people would finally stop listening to you. Eventually, you'd do something in a drug-fueled haze and end up in Klepp or Litla-Hraun.

The days at Hlemmur were all the same and marvelous. We hung out in our corner, smoked, and talked. Conversation often turned to bands and music and definitions of what was punk and what wasn't. The depth of the conversation depended on the age and background of the speakers, but we all shared a common contempt for traditional life and "provincialism," which was a synonym for "normal" and "boring" people—i.e., everyone who wasn't like us. At the bottom of our ladder, those we respected least, were the disco freaks, our main enemies. Those people wore yellow and pink sweaters, were immaculately turned out, went to the Hollywood nightclub and danced. Ken and Barbie. We were like Action Man.

Besides Hlemmur, there were two other places in the vicinity that we met up. They were the Joker arcade on Rauðarárstígur, and also Einholt. Whenever we were driven away from Hlemmur, we went and hung there until we were kicked out, and then we went back to Hlemmur. We could rarely afford to play the machines, so we hung around just watching those who were playing. In the end, we were generally thrown out for trying to cheat the machines or for messing about. It was always enough that if one of us did something that wasn't allowed, the whole group got thrown out. In our eyes, and in everyone else's, we were one mass.

The security guards at Hlemmur were generally nice to us. Some were even our friends, and we'd call them gramps or gramma. Often, they'd sit and chat with us. Whenever we were making a hullabaloo, they'd come over, speak good-naturedly to us, and ask us to stop hollering, please. Now and then one of the grandpas would come over and ask us to leave for a bit because someone had called and complained. We'd head out without a fuss, not because we were law-abiding, but out of respect and friendship for our "grandparents." We knew and understood that it was their job, and we didn't want to make things difficult for them. There were, however, some guards who objected to us. In most cases, it was the substitute guards who wanted to get rid of us. They were rude and rather cold in their manner, and when they ordered us to scram, they couldn't move us: we answered them back, twisting their words, and putting on airs. We let them chase us all around the place, and when they threw us out we snuck back in immediately. We'd break into teams and scatter ourselves all about. We teased them and let them chase us back and forth until they were out of breath with the effort; the whole time we laughed and enjoyed ourselves. It usually ended with them calling the police. Then we made ourselves scarce, popped over to Joker or Einholt, but came back as soon as the police had gone and started up the struggle all over again. We were having the best time.

In general, police interventions were usually fun, a welcome change in the everyday grayness, something happening, an excitement, a diversion. They'd show up in Black Marias and order us to sit inside. Then they'd march us across the street and into the police station. We'd wait around a while until the chief of police came and spoke to us. There was rarely a specific reason behind the police taking us in. It was more like the cops needed something to do or had been asked to seize us. They'd search us, empty our pockets, and inspect everything carefully. The chief was trying to find something he could punish, any violation of law, any drugs or substances you could sniff like gas or glue. But they never found anything; at worst, our cigarettes got confiscated.

"What were you doing in Hlemmur?"

In truth: we lived there.

"Waiting for the bus."

That was what Hlemmur was for, wasn't it?

"Shouldn't you be in school?"

"We were on our way to school when you detained us, so we missed it."

We always had answers at the ready. The police never had anything on us. More to the point, we weren't criminals. We were just kids hanging out and killing time. Ultimately, they released us and told us to go home or to school. We agreed and then walked straight back to Hlemmur. In some cases, especially on Friday and Saturday, they didn't take us in to the station but drove us a little way from downtown and left us there. It was all done most amicably. They chatted with us on the trip and dropped us off either in Heiðmörk or up at Hofda, like we were old friends. Then we walked. We walked all the way back down to Hlemmur, talking along the way.

At weekends, Hlemmur turned into something like a nightclub.

After six o'clock, other people usually stopped coming inside and instead waited outside. The winos took over because on the weekends, when they received their assistance handouts, they made up a significant crowd. New winos joined the group and also some guys who were not real winos but more like temporary winos, sailors on shore leave and guys from the country looking to have fun in town. We hung around them and bummed cigarettes and swigs of wine. There was often a lot of merriment, but Hlemmur could also be an inflammable nightclub that boiled over at the slightest provocation. Fights broke out as easily as a hand being waved. One minute everything would be just fine, then all of a sudden someone would jump forward and punch someone else in the face with a clenched fist. Sometimes some guy would go into a fit of rage and punch and kick out at anything in his reach. In an instant, quiet camaraderie turned into a bloody battlefield. Blood splashed on the windows, and broken teeth lay like bodies on the floor. Then there was the screaming. Those times, we were quick to disappear. When people are drug-crazed and confused, they don't know anything about what they're doing. Several times I'd nearly been caught up in it myself. Once, a wino I knew came up to me as I sat on a bench outside Hlemmur. He looked angrily at me for a good long time and clenched his fists. He had a brand new black eye, which was swollen shut; he stared at me with just one eye.

"Hey," I said because I recognized him.

I was terrified. He was out of his head on drugs and clearly didn't recognize me. He blinked his one healthy eye constantly, as if trying to focus, and looked at me.

"Are you a boy or a girl?" he asked in a rasping voice.

I thought about it.

"A girl," I said.

He gave me a sharp look and shook his clenched fists in my face.

"You're lucky there; I don't thump girls."

I nodded. He looked at me questioningly then gruffly said:

"You're the ugliest woman I've ever seen in my life!"

On Fridays and Saturdays the police sometimes stormed Hlemmur on a cleanup mission. They'd show up in several cars, surround the place, and drag off all those who were drunk or at all suspicious. The police, however, knew us and left us in peace. The winos were often angry and fought with the police. But it was to no avail. The cops were always stronger and got the winos face down and handcuffed them. The winos never had a chance against the cops.

The police knew that we generally never did anything. We never hurt anyone, never fought, and never broke in anywhere. Yet sometimes one of us would get hit or taunted or picked on. Then we'd stand together as one. Once, a kid in our group ran into Hlemmur as we were sitting together in a big crowd. He said that two boys had been messing with him on the Kópavogur bus. They had spit on him and hassled him because he was a punk. Among us there were some older boys who were elated at this news and wanted to know where the aggressors had gone. The kid had last seen them walking from Hlemmur in the direction of Rauðarárstígur. The whole group ran after them, ten, fifteen kids. When they saw us they took off. We chased them at a sprint and got one.

We dragged him into an alley, but when he was there, we didn't know what we should do. One of the older boys grabbed him and slammed him against the wall.

"Were you teasing my friend?"

"No," he said, struck with terror.

"Yes," said the kid who had been messed with. He was twelve years old.

Then they fell silent. Nobody said a word. The boy thought maybe we were going to kill him and began to cry.

"Oh, just let him go," someone said.

We felt sorry for him. The older boy let go of him, and he ran away. That's the way we stood together and looked after one another. It felt great to not always be alone, to be part of a group and have friends who kept an eye on you and stood alongside you.

Sometimes, I'd hang out alone in town at night. Those times, I'd generally lie to my mother that I was going to stay with some friend, or else she was away somewhere. I enjoyed staying awake at night. I always had trouble sleeping and could sometimes be awake for two nights in a row. I'd wander around and luxuriate in the tranquillity and wait for Hlemmur to open in the morning.

One night I was sitting on a bench outside Hlemmur. It was pretty warm weather. It must have been about four o'clock in the morning. There were few people up and about, but I took the chance when someone came by to bum cigarettes. Then a man I recognized came up to me. I'd seen him before. He tore tickets at a movie theater near Hlemmur. He was middle-aged, big-waisted, gray-haired. He was always in jeans with a wide, large-buckled belt and colorful shirts that were open all the way down to his belly so that his chest was clearly visible. I didn't know him, but I had often seen him. I scrounged a cigarette off him and we talked. He asked about my circumstances, what my hobbies were, and what I was doing there in the middle of the night. I really enjoyed the company and attention.

"What sort of music do you listen to?"

"I listen to punk," I said resolutely. "I'm a punk!"

"That so? I've got a lot of punk albums."

This felt strange. He didn't strike me as a man who enjoyed punk, but I had, to be fair, met a bunch of kids who were not punks and still listened to punk rock, like Alli.

"Really?" I asked, excited.

"Yes, yes."

"What bands do you listen to?"

"What bands do you enjoy?" he asked in return.

"I mainly listen to Crass."

He nodded as if he knew Crass. Then I reeled off a few other bands that I knew well and assured him that I definitely didn't like New Wave.

"Aren't you cold?"

"Yes, a little."

I was really cold; in fact, I was just wearing a T-shirt and leather jacket.

"Want to come back to mine and warm up?"

"Wow, that's not an offer you get every day."

I found it a bit odd, but I was excited at the thought that he had so many albums. Maybe he had a collection as big as Hannes's.

A real music freak.

I walked with him to Njálsgata where he lived. We went up a stairwell and into his apartment. I was a little suspicious—doubts tugged at my mind that such an old guy would own a bunch of punk albums—but the expectation of setting eyes on albums from bands I had always dreamed of, that there would be the world's best punk albums assembled all in one place, won out. There were no doors in the apartment, just hippie pearl strands hanging from the doorframes. We went into the living room, and the guy said:

"Have a seat."

Then he went into the kitchen. He didn't have many albums. I looked carefully through them. There were no punk albums, just stuff by Uriah Heep, the Beatles, the Rolling Stones, and some Icelandic crap. The old man came back with two glasses and handed me one; I could smell that it was full of wine.

"Hey, there aren't any punk albums here."

"Aren't there? I was quite sure that I had a lot of punk albums."

"No, there's no punk."

I sat on the couch, the wine glass untouched on the table, and he stood next to me. Suddenly he stroked my hair and said in a low voice:

"You have such beautiful hair."

I found that really awkward, but I didn't know how I was meant to react. I'd never experienced an old guy running his hands through my hair. Was he just tremendously nice or a little insane?

"The most beautiful hair," he said again.

"Uhhh," I mumbled awkwardly.

Was he a hairdresser, perhaps? Maybe he was just a nice hairdresser who thought that the Rolling Stones were punk? Maybe he was just such a nice guy that he went around at night and helped kids, like the old women from Ananda Marga who were sometimes down at Hallærisplan giving out soup. I had often got hot soup from them. But mainly I wanted to get out of there. The old man looked at me very strangely, and the atmosphere had become significantly uncomfortable. I wondered if I should run out. What exactly did he want? I pointed at the bottle and said:

"What's this?"

"Just have a drink. Take a sip."

"But what is it?"

"Just relax and drink. Just drink it."

"Uhhh," I said and picked up the glass.

The old man smiled encouragingly at me and went to fetch something. I seized my opportunity and poured the wine into a large plant pot that stood next to me. Maybe he wanted to poison me? Maybe there were sleeping pills in it? This was some mental shit.

I was getting seriously scared. Where had he gone? When would he come back? I got to my feet and wondered what my course of action should be. What was he going to do? Suddenly he came back: he'd stripped off all his clothes and was just in a dressing gown. What the fuck was going on here? Why was this man standing there in a gown and no clothes? This had gotten really silly. I had come there to listen to punk albums but was suddenly standing in an apartment with an old guy in a dressing gown who thought I had beautiful hair. He smiled at me in a friendly way. It was majorly uncomfortable and embarrassing. I was terrified and said:

"Well, I'm going to go."

"No, you're not going. You've only just arrived!"

"Yes, I'm just getting so tired, really."

He stared strangely at me and smiled.

"You can sleep in my bed. Just sleep here."

He pointed towards the corridor. I didn't find it an appealing prospect.

"Well, no, I don't, I—," I said and edged closer to the front door.

"Come on. Why don't we just get into a hot shower together and see what happens?"

I was filled with terror. Then it suddenly hit me: he was a pervert! A disgusting old man who thought I had beautiful hair and wanted me to go take a shower with him. I still had the glass in my hand as I took a few steps toward the front door, and he moved as if he was going to approach me. Without thinking, I raised the glass and threw it hard at him. Then I ran fast as I could to the front door, ripped the door open, and rushed out to the stairwell. I heard him call after me:

"What are you doing? What's happening? Where are you going?"

I took off as quick as my feet could carry me and never looked back. My heart thrashed in my breast as I ran down to Hlemmur. When the kids showed up in the morning, I told them about my night's adventure. Some of them recognized the guy and said he was a pervert. A few days later we went together to his house. The older punks had joined us and were at the forefront. I hid myself behind them. They rang the apartment doorbell, but I was afraid to be near the head, afraid to even see the place. The door opened shortly with a low whine. I feared for my life a little. The kids, however, took charge and went into the corridor. The old man came out onto the landing, and I heard them call:

"Are you a pervert? Are you a pervert?"

"Go away or I'll call the police," he cried.

"Then we'll tell the police that you're nothing but a pervert. You're just a fucking pervert who perverts children!"

"That's not true!"

I saw him through the door. The boy who was standing in the doorway pointed at him and asked me:

"Is this the pervert who was hitting on you?"

I couldn't speak but nodded and looked away. The old man made like he had never seen me before.

"Get lost or I'll call the police!"

"Demonic pervert! Leave kids alone!"

Other folk in the apartments around the stairwell came onto the landing, but the guy rushed back inside and slammed the door behind him.

"What is going on here?" asked an old woman.

"This pervert was trying to molest a small boy."

I saw the guy peep out of the kitchen window. I made myself safe across the street and waited for the older kids, who came out shortly after screaming abusive language and banging on the front door. "Demonic pervert," someone said, just to say it one more time. We dawdled about in front of his house, which I felt tremendously uncomfortable about having returned to. I wished wholeheartedly that I hadn't come with them, and I felt miserable and half-witted. Why had I gone home with him? How could I be so stupid? I blamed myself for everything. It was my fault.

I should not have gone home with him. I felt almost more of an idiot than he was. What on earth led me to think some old, gray-haired guy owned any punk albums?

"Let's just go," I said, downcast.

The kids continued to curse the guy. I don't know who picked up a stone. The kitchen windowpane splintered with a loud crack. We took to our feet and ran away.

We often went to the shops and asked for stuff on credit or chased after someone and begged them for money. Many people seemed to think that we were on drugs, but that was way off base since none of us were regularly using anything hard. Many of us huffed but usually not in Hlemmur. The most common substance used was glue from puncture repair kits: UHU. We would go together into an alley or a trash shed around the back of a house, empty the UHU tube into a plastic bag, and inhale. The rush was brief—dizzy head, blurred vision, giggling. The giggling, however, was perhaps more from nervousness and the tension than the effects of the substance. Sometimes, someone had crumbs of cannabis and was even willing to share. Usually this was true of the older kids, who were working and could afford to buy cannabis, unlike us younger kids, who couldn't and anyway had no connections with any dealers. Cannabis was usually smoked at home inside your room with someone. You'd only have one or two people smoking, but you always got a good buzz. It broke the malaise, created a nice tension and a diversion and, in the best cases, some feelings of joy. Contentment. Besides huffing, wine, and the occasional hit of cannabis, we also sometimes had pills. Usually it was something that someone had stolen from their parents or someone else. The winos would also sometimes slip us pills. They were usually sedatives like Diazepam and Valium but occasionally stimulants like Ritalin. However, there was one drug that could get us high that we could get in pharmacies: seasickness tablets. If you took enough of them, it left you in a strange state and you could even have hallucinations, see weird sights and hear voices.

If the weather was good, we'd go walking around town, down Laugavegur and Lækjartorg. It was possible to hang out and meet people there. Sometimes, there was an outdoor market at Lækjartorg where people were selling homemade jewelry and all kinds of stuff. But we weren't allowed inside anywhere. The traders didn't want to see us in their booths. We couldn't even get served in cafes. It wasn't much of a hardship since we never had any money anyway. We weren't allowed inside the shops, either, and frequently heard:

"Get out, kids! Out if you aren't going to buy anything. Out with you, or I'll call the police!"

People in the streets gave us a wide berth, and we noticed that they were afraid of us. It was fun to be so notorious. It was exciting.

Life at Hlemmur was all about hanging out. Some kids could sit on the same bench for hours without doing anything, though not me. I always had to be on the move or at least talking to someone. And though I could find camaraderie among the kids in Reykjavík, in many ways there was always something lacking. There was something that separated me from them. For example, they had no interest in books. I had a burning interest in reading and sometimes even brought books to read on the bus or at Hlemmur. Most of the kids knew who Þórbergur Þórðarson was.

But none of them seemed to have any particular interest in anarchism, and my ideas for an Anarchist Land didn't entice them. I didn't go to Hlemmur just to hang. I was on a quest for knowledge. I was looking for solidarity, for mutual interests, for others like me. The kids at Hlemmur had surrendered to the system. I wanted to change the system and wanted to meet someone who had ideas and who could tell me something that would help me improve things for myself, see things from a new perspective. But the kids at Hlemmur were not interested in anything and were indifferent about most everything. For them, that was punk. But not for me. I saw punk as life and creativity, not stagnation and loss of feeling. It was about becoming able to refuse to participate in the nonsense that was everywhere imposed upon us. It was a powerful uprising. Punk screamed at the system and demanded change. It was revolutionary anarchism. The two things were an integral part of each other. Punk was the body, but the soul was anarchism. I refused to give up and wanted to be more aware and better informed. I wanted people to recover their senses, to understand injustice, and then everything would change. But I did not know how you achieved that. How do you change people? I knew, at least, that it had something to do with mindset. If people changed their mindsets, their actions would change, too. You act as you think. But how to change others' mindsets? With words? Adaptation? Acting as a model?

"You have to break down in order to build up," Siggi the Punk sometimes said.

I thought about it. Was that right? And what was it you had to break down? And how? Was violence the only way? Rebellions and revolutions were usually violent. Screaming people with guns and flags, on a rampage, smashing in windows and setting fire to cars. That couldn't be the only way. The system is like the Morons: it's always stronger, and if it uses force on you and you respond with violence, then it simply applies yet more violence.

The cops were the biggest enemy for my peers. They saw everything about the police as bad. To them, the police were fascists, malicious people who enjoyed power and picking fights with others and so became cops. But I knew better. I was brought up around cops. Cops were just people like everyone else. Most of Dad's friends were all right. Dad had joined the cops because at the time it was the only job he could get. For me, the police was only an extension of the mentality of society. What the police did was not their issue but the whole community's. It was pointless to fight the cops. It was only fighting windmills. Most people are good and wish others well, but in all groups there are morons, and unfortunately they often seem to draw more attention than others, and so people judge whole groups based on the Morons. This also applies to us kids. If some punk broke in somewhere or did something wrong, then there would be news about it in the papers and even a picture. People who read the news would then condemn all punks based on that. But we were not all alike, and most of us never did anything wrong. Most punks were good kids. I think that's true everywhere, in politics, religion, the workplace, everywhere where people are grouped together. It's not advisable to take only those who draw attention because they're troublesome or evil and then judge the entire group from those people. That's akin to trying to cure cancer by killing all cancer patients.

To eliminate the problem, you have to go to the root, and the root lies deep in the mysterious minds of people. That was where I wanted to get to, I wanted to reach them. I wanted more openness and tolerance. I wanted people to be more varied and less alike. I wanted people to be nicer to each other, too. But not like hippies. They were just jerks and losers who beat their kids but protected flies.

I really felt for my friends at Hlemmur. Some were poor or had parents who treated them badly. Others were mentally handicapped or disabled in some way that affects people: dyslexia, autism, neurosis, crippling anxiety. Everywhere they were treated harshly. Everyone was ready to give up on them without ever having given them a chance. They'd been judged. The children of their parents. Future winos, junkies, and criminals. The community was like a military force that didn't want the wretched in its ranks. It had washed its hands and looked away, but these kids were still sitting there, wounded. Many of them were utterly disconsolate.

I remember one boy who hung out with me at Hlemmur around that time. His father was mentally ill, his mother was an invalid, and his sister was mentally handicapped. His home situation was so bad that he didn't want to stay there, he was treated so badly. He did poorly in school and was treated horribly there, too. He had difficulty concentrating and was teased because he stuttered. So he came to Hlemmur. No one ever came looking for him, no one was concerned about him or wondered how he felt. It seemed no one loved him, that everyone didn't care. But he found refuge among us. He wasn't teased at Hlemmur. There, it was cool to stutter. At Hlemmur he had a unique standing and was treated with a respect he had never experienced before. He came to Hlemmur to take a rest from the world. He never did anything to anyone. He was an amusing kid with friendly brown eyes, a sparkling glance, and great curiosity. He was looking for love, friendship, and acceptance.

During the winter, his sister died. He came to Hlemmur. It was the only place where he could grieve. He cried in front of us. One girl went over to him and hugged him. They sat on the bus bench outside Hlemmur, and he wept in her arms, and tears fell down her black leather jacket. I didn't really know what I was supposed to do, so I just stood at a distance and watched them. No one was interested in them; in general, people just walked past without paying attention to punks, even when they were crying. One day he stopped coming to Hlemmur. I didn't know why. I saw him sometimes on the bus and we talked. Then the social welfare agencies sent him out to the country somewhere, and I lost contact with him. I heard nothing more until a year later, when I heard he was dead. I don't know how he died. Maybe it was an accident. There was nothing about it in the papers. None of us went to the funeral. We didn't imagine we'd be welcome.

The punks at Hlemmur have now mostly become grown adults. Some have done all right and even found happiness in life, like myself. But many of these kids are dead. One good friend of mine died from drug abuse in a foreign city. Another leapt into the sea and drowned in a drug-fueled haze. Another was killed. In my memory, they are still only thirteen years old, small and confused, baby-faced and in leather jackets.

That love exists at all in this world is a miracle because if everything had gone according to plan, the brutal world would have long since killed it off.

ANARCHIST LAND

I would like to live in a country where no one has permission to rule over anyone else.

The Icelandic word for anarchism, *stjórnleysi*, really means leaderlessness. It's a poor translation. Leaderlessness is basically chaos. Leaderlessness is freedom without responsibility. Anarchism is freedom with responsibility. Anarchism is not leaderlessness. It's not chaos. Anarchism is perfection. There are schools in Anarchist Land. Not just a single school based on a system everyone must undergo. No, in Anarchist Land there are many different schools. And no one needs to attend more often than he wants to. People can learn what they want and can do what they want. If people want to learn at night and sleep during the day, that's okay.

In Anarchist Land everyone is equal and considerate and understands that not everyone is alike. But people are not utterly selfish. There are some selfish people who think anarchism is selfish. For example, it does not formally appoint people to help others. But there are people who think that's fun. People who understand that when you help others you are mostly helping yourself—not everyone understands that.

Anarchism is as varied as people are. In Anarchist Land, people can be the way they are without someone always telling them they're wrong. In Anarchist Land you can be gay or punk or a lawyer. Male lawyers can wear nail varnish if they want. You might have three wives or four. You can do whatever you want as long as you don't hurt others. You can dress how you like. You can show up naked for work, and there's no one who can forbid that. The only thing that's prohibited is being evil towards others. Everyone has something to give. Everyone needs to find out what they have to give and give it as much as they can.

In Anarchist Land I'm allowed to build my own house and make it the way I want. I can have lizards in my room and go to school on a horse. I can light a campfire in the garden. I can speak the language I want and say what I want but always without being annoying to others.

In Anarchist Land there's no money and no bank. All time is equally important. People exchange time. The doctor's time is just as important as the cleaning lady's. Women and men are equal.

I hate the system. The system discriminates against its citizens. Those who diligently learn the system do well, but those who aren't so good at that are cast out to the cold. There's only one education that's considered right, and it is the system's education. Pushy people control things. And pushy people are not especially good. They aren't even especially brilliant. For instance, understanding emotions is also an important talent. Imagination matters more than knowledge. But the system doesn't understand that. A psychologist in school can be tremendously intelligent and very educated but still cannot do anything for anyone. Someone who knows feelings well and cares about people can do more good and can help others. But the system doesn't think in those ways. It instead wants everyone to know math. Other people seem to only want to accept those who are already like themselves. They underestimate the imagination. But the imagination is equally as important as math. Neanderthal man was strong. He might also have been smart at math. But he died out because he had no imagination. The pushy and the strong oppress everyone else. Educated people stand together and set rules that hinder uneducated but good people from doing what they want. They don't want uneducated people to be equal but to be slaves. Pushy people get more opportunities than good people. Pushy people get good jobs even though they're not especially worthy or interesting. They get the job just because they have a particular education.

That's wrong and unfair. I'm nervous and scared. But I'm not stupid. I went for an intelligence test at Dalbraut. I'm quite intelligent. But imagination was not tested. They don't know how to do that. Maybe you can't measure it. Sometimes I imagine so much that I feel bad. I imagine horrible things sometimes. I think so much that I get a headache. There is no one to guide me and teach me. It's like no one understands me. People think I'm either being funny or awkward.

I could just learn in school. I just think it's so pointless. Either things are so simple that I cannot be bothered to learn them or so complex that I don't know how to learn them. I find it wrong that I have to do things I don't want to do, things that are contrary to my convictions. I don't do what the system wants. The system doesn't want me to be the way I am—but somehow different. I don't want the system to dictate what I want. I feel fine about how things are, but I just want to be left alone by the system and be the way I am. Yet there's no place for me. I'm imprisoned by rules. I'll never be a professor of anything. I'll never get any important work. The teachers have told me so. I'm going to be a trash collector. I know for sure I don't want to do that. I want to be an actor and act in movies. I want to invent something new and fun. If there was ever a school I could be a part of, it would be an Enjoyment school where the enjoyable parts are the feelings. But no such school exists. The system does not see the purpose of an Enjoyment school. The system finds all enjoyment inferior. And then it creates rules. I cannot go to drama school because I have to have a college degree. I know that's something I'll never be able to get. I have to know Danish and mathematics, although I will never use them anywhere. And though I am entertaining and imaginative, it doesn't matter. Nobody cares about that if I don't know my multiplication tables. The system believes it important to know your seven times table but not to know how to make jokes. The system's method is to get rid of people like me. Anything I do will be treated with great caution. I've become an outsider. No one is going to take me seriously. My teachers have often told me so. It amounts to an attempt to belittle me and to make things difficult for me. The system wants me to do nothing. If I learned Danish and long division, something inside me would simply die. I'd be letting the system break me down; I'd be giving up. I'd be betraying what I believe in. What I'll do in future is fail the exam. Later, I'll fail the standardized tests. Then I won't be able to go college. I wouldn't find anything there. I don't think there's anything taught there that I'm interested in learning. There's just the system with its crap and bother. I'm a dunce. All the others get seven-point-something, but I always get three-point-something. In future, I'll work as a laborer or in a factory.

The anxiety inside me keeps amplifying. I'm afraid of that vision of my future. That's not the life I want. When I start feeling so bad that I think I'll explode, I'll go to the doctor. And then he'll give me pills so I can relax and sleep. And I'll eat these pills for years until I fall asleep inside myself and my life becomes miserable. And when I'm getting really tired of all the work and the pills, I'll have a nervous breakdown. Then I'll get invited to go to a mental ward and stay there. Where there are people like me. Weird people who feel terrible inside. People who can't do anything at school, who aren't absorbed in work, who are nothing but a problem. And somewhere in all this confusion, I might even do something to myself. I would never hurt anyone. But I could very likely begin to use drugs. I could very easily get to know people who use drugs. Maybe some people like me. Maybe it would start when I first got pills from the doctor, and it would follow from that. And then maybe I would start breaking and entering in order to get money. And then I could easily end up in prison at Litla-Hraun. After that, the rules would multiply, and it would get harder and harder and harder to turn back. So I might finally give up, begin to cry in front of people, and ask them to forgive me for the way I am. Perhaps I would become exhausted of myself and ready to change. Perhaps then I'd finally be ready to learn long division and Danish and become like Pills or the politicians on TV. But maybe it would be too late. And perhaps I cannot be changed. And perhaps I'll meet with an accident. It's dangerous to be an outsider.

Pippi Longstocking was an anarchist. If everyone thought like Pippi Longstocking, the world would be a much better place than it is today. Anarchist Land does not exist. Maybe it's a country some place in the future. Perhaps, though, it's nowhere except deep down inside me.

ON HEAVENLY KINGDOM STREET

Mom wanted me to get confirmed. It wasn't up for debate. Kids getting confirmed always went on a journey, a school trip to Vatnaskóg with the Christian Studies teacher. Well, the boys went to Vatnaskóg, and the girls went to some girl place. I thought that everything about this trip was really awkward and uncomfortable, and I was apprehensive about it. I took a dim view of it all. During our preparation for Confirmation, I hung out with Eiki the Druggie, who was being confirmed with us even though he was several years older. Eiki was simple and didn't go to school. I was pretty much alone in the boat on the trip, since Eiki didn't go. I was a weird problem child, someone you needed to keep an eye on. The plan was to stay in Vatnaskóg for a few days. I took my markers with me so I could write some punk slogans someplace should the opportunity arise. We went by bus. When we arrived in Vatnaskóg we got assigned our rooms, sharing in twos. I had my stuff in a gym bag: some books, a toothbrush, and a change of top.

The first day, we played soccer. I had no interest in soccer; I struggled to run and think at the same time. Every time I tried to kick the ball, I got all twisted up, and so I never scored any goals, of course. Moreover, I was totally unable to understand the rules.

JÓN GNARR

Crucially, the soccer game at Vatnaskóg had a rule that if you swore then you were sent from the pitch AND the opponent's team got a goal. That created a loophole by which I could kill two birds with one stone: I could affect the game and get to take a break on the mountain slope. I said "hell" and "devil" every chance I got.

"Damn damn damn the devil's hell."

The Christian Studies teacher angrily blew the whistle, and I was banished from the pitch. My teammates looked at me hatefully and silently swore at me. The other team celebrated.

After the soccer game, it was snack time: sponge cake and milk. Then free time where we could stay inside our rooms or go for a walk. I went to my room, got a whiteboard pen, drew a big A in a circle on a piece of paper, then hung it on the door with sticky putty. I'd marked my room and was relieved and filled with pride. I couldn't imagine that this was going to trouble anyone since I hadn't scrawled directly on anything; it was just a piece of paper, and I hadn't ruined anything. I never imagined that anyone could get angry about it. But only a micro-speck of time had passed when the Christian Studies teacher came into my room, wearing an absolutely furious expression of anger. He looked at my anarchist sign, suddenly tore it down from the door, and crumpled it up. I sat alone, frozen on my bed, and had no clue what was up. Why was this man so terribly angry? This was odd. Was he opposed to anarchism? Did he know what anarchism was and hate it? Why? I would have understood at once if he had gotten a little irritated, perhaps thought it was untidy or something similar. But he was much more than frustrated. He was totally berserk. His eyes shot sparks, and he shook with anger.

There must be some misunderstanding. Because I thought he was too angry for the situation, I smiled awkwardly at him, as if to show him it was okay and that he had no reason to be angry—and also to let him know that I wasn't a bit angry, even though he'd torn down my sign. He rushed over to me, seized me as I sat on the bed, shook me, and yelled at me:

"And you smirk right to my face!"

I wasn't smirking. I was just surprised and scared.

"Are you completely brain-addled, child?" he said and shook me some more.

Some people came running, and my peers who had heard the hullabaloo retreated, crouching down outside the door to watch this strange scenario.

"You won't stay here a minute longer!"

An employee came and took my hand.

"Get away from this place!" the Christian Studies teacher yelled at me.

I hated this man. Psycho. We gathered my stuff into my bag, and the employee led me along the corridor and out to a car. The kids watched with surprise. I got in and set off to town. I looked out the window and saw that the boys were standing petrified, watching me. What had happened? I couldn't understand it. All kinds of thoughts rushed through my mind.

What had I done? Why was this lame-o idiot so angry? Why didn't he tell me? The employee who drove the car was angry, too, and I dared not ask him. I just stayed silent and racked my brains. How could I explain this to my mom? Why had I been sent home?

"What are you doing back?" Mom asked as I walked into the house.

"I don't know. I was just sent home."

"What did you do now?"

"Uhh, I don't know. We were in the middle of football, and I swore. I didn't know it was forbidden."

It was the only explanation that came to mind. Of course I knew it was forbidden, but not that it was quite so forbidden. Mom sighed and lit a cigarette.

It was not until the week after, when I met my classmates again, that I understood why the man had become so angry. After I had gone, all the boys on the Vatnaskóg confirmation trip were called to a meeting. The meeting was about me. After the boys had settled down, the Christian Studies teacher smoothed out a crumpled piece of paper and showed them what I had written. The A with a ring around it: anarchism.

"Do you know what this means?" he asked in a loud voice.

"Isn't that the anarchism symbol?" someone said.

"No! This symbol stands for the Antichrist. The boy drew a sign of the devil, and hung it on the door."

Everyone knew he was mistaken. Maybe he'd never listened to the Sex Pistols and "Anarchy in the UK," like Johnny Rotten sings:

> *I am an anarchist*
> *I am an Antichrist*

Maybe he thought that anarchists and the Antichrist were the same? Maybe he'd mixed them up? It made no difference to me.

He was stupid and annoying. No good.

After I was sent back to town and the meeting at Vatnaskóg was over, the good boys were able to have peaceful, curse-free days with the Christian Studies teacher. They didn't have to worry about anything because the Antichrist had been sent back to town and his mother had been notified.

There was an odd atmosphere about the management of Réttarholt School, Bústaðir Church, and Bústaðir. The guys who ran these places struck me as peculiar and almost alarming. I felt like they were connected in some mysterious way. Maybe they were just friends. I had my suspicions that they were all in some secret clique that held meetings late at night. At the meetings, they decided who was important and who wasn't, who mattered and who should be left out, and—what was most frightening— who ought to be hounded out. Kids who were beautiful and well-behaved at school and played sports were the best. They were deemed important. Kids who knew how to dance were also important. I wasn't good at any of that stuff. Me and my kind were unwelcome. I was unimportant. These guys were in charge, and the kids obeyed. I felt their power everywhere: at school, in preparation for Confirmation, in the community. And I felt that these guys were somehow disagreeable. Hitlers. There was something about them and their presence that was so uncomfortable: how they moved, how they talked and watched. I could feel no warmth in their eyes, just hardness and arrogance. And I was not the only one who felt this because it was widely talked about. Even the beautiful and the well-behaved kids objected to them.

But none of us really understood why. You couldn't talk about it too loudly; you needed to be careful who might hear you. No one wanted to say something that somebody would then rat out to the guys. It all happened in whispers. You'd hear claims of strange goings-on and didn't always know what was true and what was an exaggeration or a fabrication. It was whispered that the priest was a pervert. Was he? The girls said he was a creep. I didn't quite know what it meant to be a creep, but it was obviously not a good thing. It was said that he sometimes fondled the girls, their breasts, and said lousy things to them, that they were beautiful or something like that. All this was reported in greatest confidence. I dared not ask anything more about it. I found sexual intercourse awkward enough a topic. I didn't quite know what to make of having your breasts fondled. But I thought it was weird that some old guy would do it—especially a priest. Don't priests have to be good? And he didn't ask for permission. I would never fondle someone's breasts without permission. But it was almost a source of embarrassment. Awkward. You just got a sense that things were not as they should be. Disgusting guys. I thought the guy at Bústaðir was a creep. An old man who liked to dance. These men didn't like me, and I didn't like them. They looked at me askance, and I was wary of them. But they were careful to leave me alone and had few direct dealings with me; they just allowed the other kids to do it for them. They probably sat for hours with those kids behind closed doors and talked about how much of a loser I was, saying they should make fun of me and drive me off. They knew full well the bullying and violence that took place. They had seen it time and again with their own eyes, but they didn't care.

It was what they wanted, and I knew they were hiding something.

When I was a kid, I believed in God. Grandma taught me. She taught me the Lord's Prayer and talked a lot about God. She also told me that God watched over me, thought about me, and loved me and that I should diligently pray to him. I had absolutely tried to pray to God on several occasions but felt he didn't concern himself with me. I didn't exactly doubt his existence but reckoned he had more important matters to consider than me. It meant nothing to ask for protection from God. Once, for example, I had a really terrible toothache the day before my birthday, and I lay praying, asking God to stop me having the toothache on my birthday. I prayed and hoped, but he saw no reason to grant my wish. He felt it was okay if I had a toothache on my birthday. I didn't really think much about God; he was just somehow there with Grandma. And when Grandma died, he left my life. Punks weren't impressed by God. They were outright against him and even claimed that God didn't exist up there above our heads. Punk was partly about challenging Christian and civic values.

What, however, had the greatest impact on me were God's representatives on earth. These people I found all had one thing in common: they were no fun. I thought these people humorless and odd in equal measure. No one who listened to God listened to punk. But Confirmation is Confirmation. And Confirmation meant a party. And a party meant gifts. It felt very tempting. I was always willing to do anything for money. Anything to avoid being dependent on my father. I reasoned that by getting confirmed I might make some money to buy some albums and even possibly a tape recorder. I didn't have one. The only music player at home was the combination Crown record player inside the living room. And Mom insisted I get confirmed. I tried to talk to her but she wasn't prepared to discuss it any further. She had made her decision. That was that.

"I'm not sure I want to get confirmed."

"No! For shame!" Mom said.

"No, I'm not sure I believe in God."

She snorted at that. For her, it had nothing to do with God.

"Confirmation is just Confirmation and you will get confirmed!"

"But why should I get confirmed if I don't believe in God?"

"That doesn't matter. You will get confirmed. It isn't up for debate. All your siblings have been confirmed and you will be confirmed too."

It was impossible to draw Mom into any religious discussion or a back-and-forth about higher powers. It simply didn't concern her. I didn't want to discuss it with my dad. I knew he was an atheist and bore a grudge against priests because I had often heard him talk about it. Þórbergur Þórðarson also had a significant influence on my religious beliefs. I had read *Letter to Lara* and *The Prodigy* and knew that Þórbergur had serious doubts about the existence of God or any higher power. It was odd, though, that he nevertheless seemed quite open to supernatural creatures like elves and to energies beyond death. He believed in ghosts but not God. I didn't really know if I believed in ghosts, but I was afraid of the dark. I didn't know exactly what I feared in the darkness, whether a ghost or something else. I often reflected on Þórbergur's spiritual mentality. My father was a committed communist. For him, God was nothing but an opiate for people. A tool capitalism used to soothe the masses and keep them quiet so they would rather pray to God than insist on wage increases and better working conditions. God also wanted people to be happy just being poor and not living in decent housing. Believers had nothing to worry about, even though their lives were miserable, because the more dreariness in this life, the better they would have it in the afterlife. For Mom, belief was just part of normal life and Confirmation a formality. It was a custom, like birthdays.

I agreed to be confirmed and started going to the priest. I hung out with Eiki the Druggie there. I enjoyed messing about in church and took my chance when the kids were all there but before the priest showed up. I talked about God and the nature of divinity.

"Do you believe God is real?"

"I absolutely believe in God," said one of the girls.

"So we're in a church. What do you think God would say if I said 'damn devil hell' here in the church?"

The kids were completely shocked by me. The church had great acoustics, so everything I said echoed.

"Hell...Devil," I cried happily.

Eiki the Druggie thought it was funny, so he lustily joined in. The girls either giggled or shushed, and our goal was achieved. I thought it was tremendous fun. But Ólaf the priest didn't agree, and he took Eiki and me aside after the first Confirmation preparation session and told us that if we were quiet and good during the lessons, he would invite us to a hot dog party after Confirmation was done. The party would have hot dogs, Coke, and Prince Polo candy bars in large numbers, and we could enjoy ourselves.

We were both so simple and naïve that we swallowed this hook, line, and sinker. Eiki had the excuse that he was a bit simple, but I believed the priest and thought it was a good deal. I was really careful in class and stopped myself from getting up to any nonsense, from jabbering and teasing. I was even, shocking to say, silent and calm. I learned everything I was supposed to learn and made color pictures of some of the icons in church. Later, I got assigned a Biblical passage to memorize. I did it really conscientiously. Anything for the hot dog party and as much Coke and Prince Polo as I could manage. Soon it wasn't long until the ceremony. We kids discussed how much money we might get as Confirmation gifts. I asked older kids who'd already received Confirmation how much money they'd been given and tried to draw some conclusions. It would definitely be a damn big amount.

As Confirmation day approached, Mom started talking about Confirmation clothes. She opened some brochures she'd brought home from Hagkaup. The brochures were filled with lame guys in repulsively ugly kid-size suits and ties. I flat out refused to wear those sorts of clothes. Mom, however, was no more prepared to debate this than anything else about Confirmation and said simply:

"Jón, you will wear these clothes!"

"But I'll never wear them again."

"You'll be dressed like this at Confirmation and for your Confirmation party."

"No."

"You do what I tell you, Jón!"

"Why can't I just wear normal clothes?"

"Because you'll do as I tell you."

"But it's lame."

"You're going to get confirmed and when you get confirmed you wear Confirmation clothes. Anything else isn't an option."

Mom took me with her wandering from store to store to try on Confirmation clothes. I was morose and unhappy and didn't care what clothes she bought. Eventually, she bought a brown wool suit that was in vogue at the time. With the suit she bought a tan shirt and brown wool tie.

"You look so smart."

"It's snot-and-vomit!"

Mom ignored me.

"Can't I wear a clown outfit instead?"

Mom didn't answer that. Then she bought some brown dress shoes on top of everything else. It was decided.

Confirmation day dawned. The ceremony was in church, and I turned up there in my suit, and then I also had to have some tunic put over me. It was designed to unpunk me. Mom couldn't imagine standing up with me, as was usual with parents of children getting confirmed, because she was ashamed of how old she was. So it was down to my brother and sister to pretend they were my parents and stand up when my name was mentioned. The ceremony went pretty well. I'd managed to learn everything I had to and muttered something about how I intended to always believe in God and then rattled off the Bible passage I had memorized. Then it was done.

The Confirmation party started. It was a typical party and took place at home. A table had been covered with decorated cookies.

There were schnapps and cigarettes for people, neatly spread in bowls throughout the house. Soda and coffee were also set out. I tried keeping as much as possible inside my room alone. Mom had ordered me to wear my confirmation clothes at the party, but I soon took them off. I started with my jacket.

"Why have you taken off your jacket, Jón?"

"Oh, I was just so very hot."

Then I took off my waistcoat and then my tie, using the same excuse. Towards the middle of the party after Mom had had a glass or two and was starting to slacken off, I switched my shirt for a Sid Vicious T-shirt. The adults were drinking home-brewed wine. Then they all started playing bridge. That's how all Mom and Dad's parties ended. Drinking wine and playing bridge.

I was particularly excited about the money I would get as gifts and eagerly received each envelope I was handed; I counted the money and placed it very carefully in a drawer. I also got some interesting things. From Mom and Dad, I got a bass. It was pre-arranged. An excellent, red secondhand HOFFNER. The letters H and O had broken off the bass so it just said FFNER. Since I had a limited sense of musical instruments, I believed the bass was called FFNER, as bizarre as it sounds now. And then I somehow confused this with the legendary instrument label Fender and thought somehow they were the same, Ffner and Fender—not so different. I was extremely pleased with the bass and was totally obsessed with it the whole Confirmation party. In addition, I got Icelandic–English and English–Icelandic dictionaries. In my eyes, these were great treasures because they meant I had been brought the cipher for the code of English, and now I would be better able to solve the mysteries of punk songs. I would be able to pore over lyrics for hours at a time, and when words came along that I did not know, then I could look them up in the treasure chest of the dictionary to find out their meanings. It was a wonderful breakthrough. From my brother I got the *Tao Te Ching* by Lao Tzu. It felt like a silly, inconsequential gift. Although I didn't know my brother very well, and although he was some twenty-five years older than me, I still felt he should have given me a more significant gift than some silly hippie book. I smiled at him and thanked him for the book and made like I was awfully pleased. All the while, I was planning to take it straight down to the bookstore, return it, and get money instead. But I never did return it because when I started to look at it and read it, I found that it was really pretty interesting. Halldór Laxness wrote the foreword to the book. In it, he said it was the most important book in the world. I decided to keep it and read it. *Tao Te Ching*: the book of the path. A path it isn't possible to pave. The reality is that this one book has had more impact on my life than anything; I have it to this day. I've read it more than any other book and have tried to adopt the things it suggests.

I wanted to take the Confirmation money and buy something, but my mother wouldn't discuss it.

"No, Jón. This money all goes into a bank account."

A bank account? Fuck! Why did she always need to create these inconveniences? Why couldn't I do what I wanted? Wasn't this my money? Why had I gone through this crappy Confirmation party if I couldn't even have my own money? In the end, I got part of the money and was allowed go shopping at Grammið and buy some punk albums. Mom also drove me to the store where she'd bought the bass. The store was called The Sport Market, and sold music players, skis, and other stuff. There I proudly bought, with my own money, an excellent Sharp tape player. That meant I'd have a means of listening to music inside my own room. It would allow me to buy LPs, play them on the sound system in the living room with Mom, record them onto cassettes, and play them in peace inside my room, where I'd also have the lyrics and all the basic information about the songs, like their names and so on. I took this tape player with me everywhere I went. It had a handle so it was easy to carry around, and it took batteries. I often lay inside my room for hours listening to the tape player. I also enjoyed taking it with me into the bathroom, lying in the bath for hours listening to cassettes, and more often than not, I sang along enthusiastically.

It was a huge weight off me when Confirmation and all that related nuisance was over. My Confirmation clothes went into the closet. To my great disappointment, there was no hot dog party. No hot dogs, no Coke, and no Prince Polo candy. Ólaf Skúlason had flat out lied to Eiki the Druggie and me to make us behave. How could I have been so stupid? Like all confirmers, I got the New Testament as a gift. I only read the Book of Revelation. All about the end of the world and the devil. I had amassed all kinds of information about the Book of Revelation from various punk songs. They included, for example, lots of information about the number 666, The Number of the Beast, as the title of the Iron Maiden song goes. You can say that it was thanks to punk rock that I read the Book of Revelation. It was discomforting and thrilling.

But after reading it, I did the same thing I did with my school-books I didn't like and had an aversion to. I set fire to it. Publicly. I went outside with the New Testament, poured gasoline over it, and lit it. I felt it was a definite statement and neatly made clear that I didn't give a damn about this bullshit.

A few days later my mom announced that I had to put my Confirmation clothes on again because she was going to take me to a Confirmation photo shoot. I resisted, but she was no more willing to budge than on all the other occasions.

"I have Confirmation photos of all my children and you won't be the exception."

Mom didn't listen to my objections, and I went, wearing my Confirmation clothes, to the PhotoStore on Kópavogur with her. To mess up things, however, I'd altered myself. I'd gotten some scissors, gone into the bathroom, and cut my hair into a mess of tufts. I was thinking that all the trouble caused by the Confirmation photo shoot would be called off. But it didn't change a thing. Mom neatened my hair with hairspray and a comb so that the visible tufts in my new haircut could hardly be seen. My final hope in all this, the little I could do in the circumstances, was to take a firm stand by not letting them take a picture of me smiling like a fool, at least. I would lock my mouth so hard that it wouldn't show a smile. I was going to be cool, looking on deadpan and appearing really tough in front of the camera. Angry. Cool, tough, not an idiot. I positioned myself with a serious and mean expression in front of the photographer.

"Well, Jón. How are you? You play soccer?"

"No."

"Are you into sports?"

"No."

"Well, Jón. Do you like school?"

"No."

He adjusted the camera and looked through the lens.

"What's your favorite subject in school?"

"Nothing."

"Okay."

He turned away from me and went behind the camera. "What do you want to do when you're older?"

"Nothing."

I tried to answer everything with short, terse words. The photographer didn't react, just walked away from the camera and suddenly brought out this doll he put on his hand, then said really loudly and clearly, in a weird voice, "Hello, Jón!"

I burst out laughing. It was unexpected and funny. And then came the flashes, one after another. I was so damned frustrated. I'd been tricked yet again. In all the images I wouldn't look tough but like an idiot laughing in a suit. What crap! The proof was when Mom came home with a print of the picture. There was the punk himself, Jónsi Punk, in a brown suit and tan shirt with dorky glasses like the politician Þorstein Pálsson and, on top of it all, grinning like a loon! An embarrassment. I was embarrassed right down to my toes by the picture and hoped it would go straight into a drawer. Mom had another idea, though, and put it up neatly in the living room in front of everyone's eyes. I fiercely protested this injustice.

"I'm going to throw away this damn picture!"

"I want the picture, so you'll leave it alone," she commanded.

I hated my Confirmation picture. Every time I walked into the room, I put the picture down. Mom put it back up again immediately, and the two of us did this several times a day for weeks without talking about it.

"I'm going to destroy this image."

"You can just destroy it if you like. I have the negatives and I'll just make more pictures."

It was a losing battle. Injustice had won out once again.

SORRY, NOT A WINNER

We were always trying to get ourselves money. I was constantly struggling to get money from my parents to go to the movies or just to do anything. Mom usually didn't have any money. Dad was in charge of the money at home, and he sat on wealth like a dragon on a heap of gold, giving out really limited amounts to me and Mom. Mom absolutely refused to be an intermediary between Dad and me when it came to money—she wasn't going to do it. Money had great "sentimental value" for Dad. Maybe it was because he was brought up in such poverty and wanted to be responsible for monetary policy. When a situation came up where I badly wanted something that mattered to me and I didn't have money to buy it, I always tried to talk to Mom first.

"Mom, can I have money to buy punk cards?"

"Punk cards? Why do you need them?"

"Oh, well, there's some pictures of bands I want. They're cool."

I knew I would get the same answer as always.

"Talk to your father."

Often, I gave up there. Sometimes, however, I wanted to have something badly enough that it was worth talking to Dad.

"Dad, can I get some money from you?"

It was like I had hit him in the face with a wet rag. Silence. Whenever it came to discussions about money, Dad changed, became sad, maudlin, emotional, and worried. It was as if he wanted awfully badly to say something terribly important about money. Something that would be the ultimate truth about money—but he couldn't find the right words or didn't know quite what he was meant to say. He just got a weird look on his face, blinked his eyes continuously as though he were about to cry, then reached out for my hand. So began the same predictable play we had rehearsed so often. He held his hand outstretched in the air, and I put my palm in it. He squeezed my hand, rolled back his eyes with a thoughtful expression, and racked his brains. Sometimes he was even watching TV, and he'd squeeze my hand tight as he stared fixedly at the TV. For ages. I felt like the situation sometimes lasted an eternity. Maybe it was no more than a few minutes. But the minutes passed in a tense, absolute silence. The situation always continued until I repeated the question in an even more wretched tone. Beseechingly.

"Can I have some money?"

Then he'd move his head slightly like it was almost too much for him and he was overcome by grief, and he would say without looking at me:

"Money."

Then he thought in silence a while.

"What will you do with the money?"

I felt the tension build up in my chest, and I swallowed repeatedly.

"Buy punk cards."

"Huh?"

It was so alien to him that he could hardly repeat it.

"Punk cards?"

The question implied that he thought it completely unintelligible and, moreover, entirely unnecessary. The words didn't have any real meaning for him. I might as well have spoken gibberish: "Ramalala."

"Huh, didn't I give you money yesterday?"

"Uhh, no."

"Come now, when did I last give you some money?"

"On Saturday."

"On Saturday?" he asked, skeptical.

"Sure, you gave me money for the movies."

"And you need more money?"

We ended up in this scene over and over again. He looked at the television and squeezed my hand, and I stood embarrassed by his side. Sometimes he squeezed so hard that it hurt. How hard he squeezed bore some correlation with how difficult it was to discuss. For example, depending on how high the amount in question was, the harder he squeezed my hand. Several times he even cried for real. Money just had so much "sentimental value."

I soon became aware that I had to get a job in order to have a source of income. I couldn't keep on with this drama with my dad. I had to have some income to be able to buy punk cards and cigarettes and the like. Maybe also to be able to go into a store and buy a Coke and hang out. But there weren't many opportunities for young adults. At first, I tried selling newspapers and decided to try *The Daily Scene.* I went up to Þverholt and got a blue bag with newspapers in it. Then I walked into town and tried to sell them to people. I soon found out that I was a pretty bad salesman. It didn't help that I was both shy and withdrawn. People also maybe felt it was weird that a punk was selling the *Scene.* The kids who were selling papers seemed well-behaved, resourceful salesmen. When they were finished selling all their papers, they went back up to Þverholt and refilled their bags. But I was not resourceful. I found sales pitches uncomfortable and awkward. I tried to bump into people and ask whether they wanted to buy the *Scene* but got nothing. They had no interest in buying off me. Some said they had already bought a newspaper from someone else. I then walked downtown, where there were more people but also the most severe competition. There were many other newspaper sellers, most of them older than me, who either stood up on the steps or just on the street with one, and sometimes two, newspaper bags on their shoulders, hollering:

"*Day-ily Sce-ene! The Day-ily Sce-ene.*"

There were enterprising, witty sellers who shouted things from the front page:

"Government toppled!"

"Read all about it in *The Day-ily Sce-ene.*"

I didn't have the confidence to cry out like that, so I just doddled about and muttered to people who walked past:

"Will you buy the *Scene*?"

The older boys were quick to spot me and said:

"Piss off. You shouldn't be here."

I muttered a protest, saying:

"I'm allowed to be here, I'm selling here."

"No, this is a private area. Piss off!"

Someone grabbed me by the neck and pushed me away.

"Piss off, idiot!"

I tried to find somewhere the older kids weren't at, but then it would turn out there weren't many people there. I strolled about like this and did my utmost not to get in the way of other sellers, especially Óli. Óli was mentally disabled, a notorious newspaper seller who could be a really mean character. I had often seen Óli and witnessed firsthand how if someone was trying to sell papers near him, then he simply attacked the person. Even the punks were afraid of Óli the Newspaper Seller. When I was done walking around with the pile of newspapers, I just gave up and walked back up to Þverholt with a full bag. I didn't sell a single paper. I clearly had no future in newspapers sales and decided never to do it again. It was miserable.

Then I met a kid who was selling Red Cross lottery tickets. It seemed a profitable business. It was the first generation of Red Cross lottery tickets, the ancestor of the scratch card. It was just a strip of paper folded several times and fastened together at one end. You bought the ticket, tore the strips at the ends, and flipped the paper apart. Then it usually said inside: "Sorry, Not a Winner. Thank you for supporting the Red Cross." I immediately saw an opportunity in this. My acquaintance who was selling tickets said there would be much more money in it than in newspapers. And it would also be easier: for instance, the tickets were much lighter than the newspapers, and in addition, one could sell lottery tickets, which you would otherwise be prohibited from selling, because it was for a good cause. You weren't just making money but were supporting a good cause. I immediately felt I would be a much better Red Cross salesman than a newspaper guy, so I got an address off my friend and went and talked to some woman in Fossvogs who was in charge of it all, and she gave me 100 tickets to start with. I went with the tickets to a house, knocked, and said: "Can I offer you a chance to buy lottery tickets for the Red Cross?"

Unlike with the newspapers, I managed to sell them! People really bought tickets from me. I tried as far as possible to be pitiful and wretched and get people to feel sorry for me. I was a little, odd, ginger kid with glasses who was somewhat weird. People opened their doors with a questioning, surprised expression.

"Can I offer you a chance to buy lottery tickets for the Red Cross?" I muttered, miserably.

Then people would get an expression of pity, especially women. People thought maybe I was with the Red Cross somehow or supported by the Red Cross, even a bit special, and so they obviously had difficulty saying no, unlike with the *Scene*.

I did well and earned a percentage of every ticket sold and felt that I had found a good line of work. For the first time in my life, I had money in my hands and felt I'd begun to make a little bit of a living. After my first sales, I went up to the shop on the corner of Osland and Bústaðavegur which was called Ingaskýli. I bought a Coke and some licorice and gumballs and punk cards and even a packet of fizzy drink powder. Dad would definitely have started weeping profusely if he had seen me spend this much money on such stuff. But I didn't give a damn. It was my money that I'd worked for, and I was in charge of how I got rid of it.

My advancement as a Red Cross salesman was unexpected: I swiftly became one of the most successful sales representatives. It didn't take long before I became a kind of wholesaler and started taking a box of one thousand tickets, which I shovelled out without delay. I found the Red Cross tickets a fascinating idea and became quite excited about it, so now and then I bought a ticket myself. The tickets were arranged vertically in a cardboard box with the edges facing up. When I ran my hand over them, I'd feel like I must have found the winning ticket, as if it was somehow different than the losing ones. But I never got any prizes, and it didn't matter how strong the feeling was or how much the tickets shouted at me "buy me, buy me." When I ripped them open, I always found inside "Sorry, Not a Winner." I scrutinized the tickets carefully to see if there was any possible difference between winning tickets and the rest. They were, of course, rather primitive scratch tickets which were actually—it's true—open at one end, but you couldn't see anything even when you peeked in the opening. Then it occurred to me to wonder if it would be possible to see through them. I went into the storage closet where the light bulbs were kept and found a seventy-five-watt candle bulb that I put in a lamp and took with me into my room. I held the bulb up to the opening and turned it on. The font was faint, but I could discern the winning tickets by where the graphics of the lettering was different from the non-winning tickets. There was a clear difference between "Sorry, Not a Winner" and "Congratulations! You have won a Box of Chocolates from Nóa Síríus." After this, I dutifully illuminated all the tickets I had to sell and found a few that were winners.

They weren't remarkable prizes, mostly gift baskets and boxes of candy, though mostly just candy. But over time I got several strange prizes, such as a tow hitch, which was some kind of rope system for pulling cars. It was an orange plastic tube, and out of each end you could pull iron hooks on ropes, and if you let go of them they ran back inside the tube. It was a really handy and neat tool to have in the trunk of a car. I went and got the prizes regularly from the Red Cross headquarters. They didn't know I was a sales guy and just thought I was some amazingly lucky Red Cross supporter. I became the number one salesman—selling lottery tickets had played into my hands, an unprecedented opportunity. I got to have a sales table in Glæsibæ at Christmas. My own sales table! I sat snugly next to a large sign with the logo of the Red Cross and doled out winless tickets that I'd already shone through.

"Can I offer you a chance to buy lottery tickets for the Red Cross?"

"Yes, yes," people said and thought it was exciting.

Most folk opened their ticket in front of me. There were no winners, not a single ticket; no one ever won anything. I didn't have any morals, so this was fine. I felt like I wasn't doing anything bad because the tickets were not that expensive, and no one was angry when they didn't win. People seemed to just find it fun and exciting.

"Aha, Red Cross lottery tickets, listen, I'm going to get three tickets—and I'm going to get a prize!"

We both laughed. Of course, there was no prize.

"Listen, that was just really bad luck, I'm going to get another three tickets. Now I'll definitely win."

I smiled encouragingly.

That Christmas my parents, along with everyone in the family, got awesome Christmas presents from me for the first time. I said I'd purchased gifts with the money I had earned from being a salesman, but of course these were all prizes I had picked up from the Red Cross. Mom got a box of Norwegian chocolates, and Dad got the tow hitch. Aunt Gunna and Aunt Salla each got a box of chocolates. Everyone was happy and surprised because no one had ever received a Christmas gift from me before.

When a man hits on a masterstroke that enables him to cheat, it's vital to keep quiet about it; at the same time, it's tempting to boast about having found loopholes in the system. It is not just tempting for selfish reasons: you also want to give others a share in the discovery, and I wanted to reveal how crafty I had been in illuminating the tickets. I showed a couple of other sales guys this trick and taught them how to identify winning tickets from the rest. Two knew, then everyone knew. Next time I went to the supervisor in Fossvogur to get more tickets, I noticed she wasn't as cheerful and high-spirited as usual. Instead of handing me a box, she asked me to sit down with her in the kitchen. I was immediately suspicious that she had found out about my trick. I was sure that somebody must have talked to her. She crossed her arms and looked hard at me.

"Is it true you've been looking through the tickets?"

I put on my surprised face and appeared as though I didn't know what she meant.

"Hmmm?"

I seemed to be gaping with surprise at the very thought that someone could have such a thought in their head.

"Nahhh, who said that?"

"I was told you'd looked through the tickets and could somehow see the prizes."

I continued looking totally amazed. How could such a crazy thought occur to someone! And who could be so obnoxious as to blame me? The most hardworking salesperson! This was nothing more than a petty swindle. I shook my head.

"Nah, I don't think that's even possible."

"No, I thought not."

She clearly thought it wasn't credible. Maybe she didn't believe whoever had told her? I thought it would be best to persuade her to believe that the person who told her was jealous of me because I was so hardworking and, on top of everything else, had the most sales of all.

"Who said it was possible?"

"It doesn't matter."

"Yes. No, I've never done it," I said innocently, smiled and then added:

"I don't think it's even possible."

She looked at me thoughtfully.

"No, well, it doesn't matter."

"No, so I just want to get some more tickets," I said, in a livelier tone.

She was hesitant.

"The thing is, I just have so many people now who are selling and I simply don't have any tickets for you. But thank you, and do come talk to me next winter."

Huh? Next winter? Was she firing me? That's how I was fired from my first job, something I would go on to experience many, many times, over and over again. This was only the first of numerous jobs I would be fired from. I was once again unemployed and could no longer fund my shopping trips and cigarettes. Good advice had become costly.

GIRLS & TRAVEL SICKNESS TABLETS

The rumor was that all us kids at Hlemmur were on drugs. That was a gross exaggeration given how limited the supply of drugs was. There was just normal stuff: sniffing glue, markers, and gas. Occasionally maybe you'd get a hit from a hash pipe, but that was rare. One drug we used quite a lot, though, was travel sickness tablets. The tablets were sold in pharmacies, but they wouldn't sell you more than ten tablets at once. So you'd just go into a pharmacy, say you were really carsick, and ask if it was possible to get something for motion sickness. You'd get sickness tablets. Then you just played the game again, went to the next pharmacy, and got more sickness tablets.

"Hi. I'm going on a trip...with my dad...to Patreksfjörður. And...I get so carsick, and this kid I know said it was possible to get some kind of motion sickness pills."

"Yes, yes, there are tablets for that. Here: sea- and carsickness tablets."

"Ahh, okay."

And so you immediately had twenty tablets, enough to get a good high. You'd swallow some ten to fifteen of them. The effect: hallucinations. Enormously large visual and auditory hallucinations, a strange and alien state.

Like most boys, I was interested in girls, but it was just that I was so timid and afraid of them. Girls were exotic and mysterious beings who thought and behaved according to strange and incomprehensible laws. Moreover, I found that girls did not have any particular interest in me. I had had some conversations with girls, but they were such weird conversations. Sometimes some girl sat with me at Bústaðir and began to ask me about something connected with me, what I was up to and what I was interested in. My mind went flying. Why was she asking me this? Had anyone put her up to it? Or was she just curious? Then it happened one time that a guy who was with me at Rétto spoke to me and told me that these two girls we went to school with had asked him to invite me over while they were babysitting; they would like that. I was astonished. This guy was not an idiot. We weren't especially friends, but he was a good, decent guy who had helped me sometimes when I was being teased.

"Why do they want me to come?" I asked, cynical.

"I think one of them has a crush on you," he said.

Crush on me? How could someone have a crush on me? Who could have a crush on me? That was exciting. Some girl had a crush on me. The thought of going and meeting them was exciting but frightening at the same time. What should you do? What did they want you to do? Would we make popcorn and play a game? Or perhaps we'd listen to music and kiss? I'd never kissed a girl but still had seen quite a few kids kissing, even with tongues. I was totally up for it if that was what she wanted. But maybe we were just going to make popcorn. But what were you supposed to talk to girls about? I rarely had any interest in talking to girls and thought they usually just talked about uninteresting and boring things. I had never heard of a girl with knowledge of or interest in anarchism. But I would be so happy to talk about anything if I could kiss her. The more I thought about it, the more nervous I became. This would totally fail, for sure. I would be so nervous and awkward and definitely say something that they found silly. Maybe they would all start laughing at me. In movies, kids are always just doing something and then suddenly they kiss. I did not quite know how this contagion of kissing happened. Wouldn't it be reasonable to ask people if you could kiss them? But "Can I kiss you?" sounded lame. "Can I make out with you and fondle your breasts?" was even worse.

As the days passed and the evening approached, I became increasingly confused and nervous. I decided to go to the pharmacy and buy some sickness tablets so I could be relaxed on the evening in question. That night, I took a low dose, just right for some small visual and auditory hallucinations. When I was in that frame, I generally found people fun and relaxed. They, of course, didn't know I'd taken tablets, and just found me interesting and amusingly bewildered. Sickness tablets also allowed me to be free from cares and full of courage. There would be no problem kissing on travel sickness tablets! It would happen by itself, and it would just be fun. I met my friend up at the shops after taking a few more tablets, and I also brought some more with me, just in case. Maybe the other kids would want to do tablets, and also maybe I'd need to take a few more.

After we got to the house, the girls invited us in; they'd already got the children to sleep. We were inside the living room, just chatting. I only knew these girls from Rétto. They weren't disco freaks, just your typical girls. We talked about the teachers and how stupid they were. The travel sickness tablets didn't seem to be working. Strangely, the girl who had a crush on me was looking at me, which was both comfortable and uncomfortable at the same time, her eyes searching. She asked me about one thing and another, and I tried to answer as best as I could. Did she want to kiss me? Should I take the initiative? Do guys always take the initiative? I wondered if I should try to kiss her. But she was talking. What would she do if I tried to kiss her? Would she get mad? I was getting so nervous and didn't know what I was supposed to do, so I excused myself, went into the bathroom, and thought about things. I decided to take some more sickness tablets and get going with it. I saw the other boy and girl were kissing on the other couch. The girl with a crush on me was sitting on the couch and looked at me questioningly. I sat next to her.

"Everything okay?" she asked.

"Sure," I replied, awkwardly.

The excitement increased. Were we about to kiss? I peeped sideways at the pair on the couch, who were clasped in an embrace, their tongues up inside one another. How had it started? I shouldn't have gone off to the bathroom. Suddenly a hallucination poured over me. Someone was behind the curtains and whispering to me, but I could hardly make out the words. "Jón," whispered the voice. I giggled nervously.

"What?" asked the girl and smiled.

"Nothing," I replied.

"Just Siggi the Punk," I muttered and laughed.

"Huh?" she asked, surprised.

Siggi the Punk was hiding behind the curtains and whispering to me. The room was moving, and the furniture waddled back and forth. The girl looked questioningly and surprisedly at me. I was clearly about to fuck this up. Then everything went black.

All of a sudden I'm inside the kitchen at home, sitting at the kitchen table, and Adam Ant is lying on top of the kitchen cabinet with his hand under his cheek, gawping at me. I glance at Mom, who clearly can't see Adam Ant.

"Adam Ant?" I ask, taken aback.

Adam Ant begins to laugh. "Stand and deliver," he shouts at me. I'm starting to laugh, but my mom doesn't think it's funny.

"What tablets have you been taking?"

"What? I've not taken any tablets."

Adam Ant disappears, and someone else comes and whispers to me. Mom tries to talk to me, but I cannot hear what she says because of the whispering. My mom has a worried expression. The floor rocks back and forth. Mom stands up, walks into the telephone room, and says something into the phone. There are three people inside the room. Definitely some friend of Mom. I call out to them:

"Hello."

No answer. Adam Ant is nowhere in sight. The Sex Pistols are standing outside the kitchen window and looking inside. How great that they've turned up.

"Hey," I tell them and wink.

I'm going to bed. I'm tired. I've definitely acted fully composed and tricked Mom so she doesn't realize a thing. I just need to watch my step with the waving and rocking, to take care not to fall on my face when the floor tilts. When Mom comes back, I say firmly:

"Good night, Mom, I'm going to sleep now."

Did she hear what I said? What did I say again? Did I tell her I was going to go to bed, or did I tell her I was asleep? I repeated the words to be on the safe side.

"Well, Mom, I'm going to sleep. Good night, Mom."

I was all set to leave and had deliberated it in my mind, calculating the angle of the floor and how I could walk to my room as normally as possible. I set off, except I forgot to stand up and fell over right there and hit the floor. Damn sloping floor. I had miscalculated and couldn't stand up by any means. It was so ridiculous that I started laughing again. Before I knew it, I was sitting in the back, seat of a car and my dad was behind the wheel. The next thing I remember was that some people were running beside the car. Maybe some kids were trying to get the car. Still, it was strange because it was nighttime. It was all incredibly funny and amusing, and I laughed.

The next day I woke up in intensive care at City Hospital. Someone was sneaking about inside the hospital room. Whispers. I didn't follow what was being said. Sneaky demons shot back and forth. Whispers.

"Huh? What are you saying? I can't hear."

The room rocked back and forth and turned in circles. I was dizzy. A doctor came walking towards me, and I poked him to see if he was real—he was—but I didn't understand what he was saying and struggled to distinguish his voice from all the other voices.

"What's your name?"

"Jón. Jónsi Punk."

He took my hand.

"Do you know what year it is, Jón?"

I knew that.

"Nine hundred and eighty…" I couldn't remember. "…something," I added and giggled.

When I woke up next it was evening. The hallucinations were gone. What had happened? What was I doing here? I thought about Tintin. Did they have any Tintin here? The nurse came and asked how I felt.

"All right," I replied. "Do you have any Tintin comics here?"

She didn't answer, and I let my eyelids droop. Endless pictures of Tintin flicked past my mind's eye. I vaguely heard the nurses who came and went, taking blood pressure, saying things to me, then going ahead. I tried to open my eyes but couldn't. My eyelids were as heavy as lead shutters.

"Do you know where you are, Jón?"

"In the hospital?"

"You're here in intensive care at City Hospital, you came here with your Dad last night—don't you remember?"

"Sure," I said, but didn't.

"You'd taken a lot of pills and had them pumped out of you."

Pumped out of me? I didn't remember it. How were they pumped out of me?

"We gave you some drugs which should counteract the poison you ingested."

"Okay."

"What pills did you take?"

"Travel sickness tablets?" I asked, with eyes closed.

"Travel sickness tablets, okay."

"Do you think there's someone here with Tintin?"

The effects of the sickness tablets persisted through the course of the evening. I received a sedative, and that felt good. Tintin continued to haunt me. I tried to get the nurses who came and talked to me to talk about Tintin and read me Tintin books. I told them about my favorite book about the adventures of Tintin and then asked them what their favorite Tintin book was and so on. When I changed the subject to Tintin's friends Thomson and Thompson, I couldn't keep from laughing. The bed I was lying in was on wheels. Someone came and said something to me, and I was moved into another room. There was a closet, like inside all hospital rooms. When I was alone I crawled out of bed over to the closet, curled myself into a ball, squeezed myself into the closet, and closed the door on myself. The closet was a rocket. I was in the hospital, but it was still a rocket. But maybe this was just my own nonsense? Maybe I was just an idiot inside a closet? I heard the voice of Captain Haddock: "A hundred thousand blistering barnacles." The closet took off and shot into space. I felt the whole cubby shaking. I slept. Outer space was infinite. Someone came and opened the closet. I took a breath. Then I was back in bed where someone gave me medicine.

When I woke up the next day, I was in yet another room. I staggered out of bed, opened the door and went into the hall. I only vaguely remembered what had happened. I was filled with terror. What had taken place? A doctor or nurse came walking towards me.

"How are you feeling? "

"All right. Is this a hospital?"

"Go back to bed."

"Where am I? "

"You were brought here last night. You are in Department A2, which is in the psychiatric ward in City Hospital."

The woman followed me back into the room. The psychiatric ward of City Hospital? Was that true? Was I going to be sent to Klepp? When the woman was gone, I snuck back down and found the person on duty.

"Can I make a phone call?"

They gave me a phone. I called Alli, who I knew had some Tintin books.

"Hi, this is Jón."

"Hi."

"Would you bring me your Tintin books?"

"Tintin books? Why?"

"I'm in a mental ward."

"You're in a mental ward?"

"Yes. Would you bring your Tintin books to me in the psychiatric ward at City Hospital?"

I said goodbye to Alli and went back into my room. He came later that day with the Tintin books.

"What happened to you?"

"I don't know? I took travel sickness tablets."

"But why are you here?"

"I don't know. I just really want to read Tintin."

"Okay."

I chose *The Black Island* and began to read it. Alli sat with me for a few moments, then stood up and said goodbye.

"Bye."

"Bye," I said and did not look up from the book.

Later that day my mom came. It surprised me that she wasn't angry. She was just happy and said:

"I'm simply glad you're okay. You must never do that again, my darling boy."

"No."

We didn't have to discuss it further. I'd never do that again.

"I'm just going to read Tintin."

Mom stroked my hair and sat silently while I read Tintin. Several days went by, and I regained my equilibrium. I occasionally went out and sat in the lounge and chatted with other patients. A few days later, Mom and Dad came to get me. I learned later what had happened. I had run out of the babysitting party all of a sudden. I had probably gotten very weird, but they did not know what was affecting me. Mom was then woken up in the night and summoned outside by a kid who knew me and had found me lying under some car. It was freezing cold out, and he realized that I wasn't okay and decided to take me home. Neither Mom nor Dad discussed it ever again. We never ever discussed it.

STUDIO MEAT

When I was working selling lottery tickets for the Red Cross, I got to know a few shopkeepers from the time I had a sales table at Glæsibæ. Since I was very polite and did pretty well and was a pretty likeable youth, I decided that spring to talk to Guðmundur, the store manager in the shop at Glæsibæ. I had chatted with him a few times when I was selling tickets. I had gotten his advice about where to set up my table, and as a result we'd ended up chatting. I decided to talk to Guðmundur and see if I couldn't get some work from him in order to get some money. Guðmundur was receptive and asked if I had any knowledge of salted meat and that sort of food. I couldn't believe it! I replied without hesitation that I was brought up on Icelandic food and my dad was from Breiðafirði, that he had a sour-barrel out on the balcony full of liver and blood pudding, salted meat and seal flippers and rams' testicles and all kinds of stuff. I knew it all by name. And so I ended up with a job at the meat counter in Glæsibæ. The work consisted mainly of cutting and carving meat, carrying carcasses, and being generally of use to people as a meat-fetching-person, but also jumping in and assisting with serving when needed. This I did with great success. I served sausage meat, slices of leg of lamb, and other such things with courtesy and professionalism. Customers reckoned that I was some kind of meat specialist and were constantly asking me about this and that to do with meat. What did I recommend, would this be better than the other, and questions like that. I had no idea about any of it and just said whatever.

"Which do you recommend, lamb or pork chops?"

"Lamb," I replied, boastfully.

I of course had no idea, but people listened to my advice and seemed contented. It was no problem. It was not like I was being tested on something. People never asked whether I recommended lamb or pork chops then bought both, went home, compared them, and came back the next day and complained. So it was all very easy. When people asked what was the best sausage meat, I just pointed at something and said:

"This is tasty and delicious."

I spoke to people. I really liked this job. There was a big barrel of salted meat, and there were many women every day who came to buy salted meat. I handled it with the same professionalism as everything else.

"Can I get a cut from the spine?"

"Sure," I replied cheerfully.

I stuck the fork down so it was submerged in the barrel, stabbed something and raised it up in the air.

"That's not a cut from the spine."

"No, hahaha, I just got a bit confused."

Then I just stuck the fork on the next piece and raised it up the same way, and so it went until they saw the bit they liked. Guðmundur was extremely pleased with me. I worked hard, and I thought it was all very exciting. I even began to wonder if this wasn't something I could see myself working at in future; I thought the men who carried the meat around were pretty cool. They were tough guys with aprons that were always bloody. Maybe I could have some future with meat. I could definitely learn it. I admired the way the meat industry men took whole carcasses and sawed them into separate pieces, like chops and cuts of lamb leg and thighs and spine. But despite the fact that I dreamed of being a meat industry worker, I was mainly a punk and an anarchist. There lay my real vocation and ambition.

I had long been considering getting a mohawk. I had repeatedly seen this hairstyle in *Melody Maker* and *Bravo*. There were real punks with mohawks. The singer in The Exploited had one. There was one punk in Reykjavík with a mohawk, and that was Bjarni from Masturbation, who was also my friend. He had gotten the nickname Bjarni the Mohawk because he made a big deal about his hair. He had a wide stripe, but I wanted to have a narrow one like the singer in The Exploited. Getting a mohawk was a statement, and as a result one became more punk. It said something about a person: that the person was brave, that he didn't listen to his parents, that he was independent and had his own ways. A very specific statement. I knew that if I discussed it with my mother, she would never allow it. I decided to get myself a mohawk without asking anyone, neither king nor priest, nor even Mom. I discussed the matter with Fat Dóri. He immediately offered to cut my hair. His father owned electric hair clippers along with several combs and some shaving things. Dóri trusted himself entirely to cut my hair and found it exciting, so I just decided to strike while the iron was hot and get him to shave off my all my hair with the exception of a stripe down the middle of my head. He shaved me with the clippers and crowned his work by smearing shaving cream on my head and shaving the rest off with a cutthroat razor. I was extremely pleased with the results. This was very much a next step towards independence, as I saw it; it would arouse the admiration and envy of other punks. Together with a plastic leather jacket that I had bought at the Kattavinafélag flea market and the punk signs and dog collar, I was finally starting to resemble the punks in *Bravo*. I'd also amassed quite a collection of ripped jeans that were all thoroughly marked-up with a series of band names and slogans. Moreover, I also had some well-worn military boots with which I was extremely pleased. The army boots were an integral element of punk style—you wore your pants over the boots, of course, because if you tucked the pants down into boots, that was like Nazi style. I also had a green military coat my mother had bought at the secondhand clothing store, and I had naturally scrawled anarchist signs and slogans all over it. My mohawk totally crowned my punk creation. I was finally complete. I selected the date of my shearing for when Mom was in London with her friends and I was home alone with Dad.

The next day I went as usual to the meat counter in Glæsibæ. Of course, I took off my punk outfit before I arrived at the meat counter; I wore my rubber boots and put on my white apron. My hairstyle immediately attracted great attention and curiosity from the meat workers. People were surprised and asked why I had gotten my hair cut like this; many thought it was out of order while others laughed and thought it was funny. Before I knew it,

Guðmundur, the store manager, turned up anxiously at the door. He stood in the doorway, and it was like he had totally lost any expression. I smiled happily at him.

"I got myself a mohawk."

Guðmundur was clearly not as happy with my mohawk. He asked me to come back and talk to him.

"Why have you done this with your hair, Jón?"

I tried to explain to him that I was a punk, and it was a normal part of being a punk, that it was the fashion overseas; I tried to explain my case by saying that there was also a punk in Reykjavík who had a mohawk and that he was called Bjarni the Mohawk. I tried to point out that there wasn't anything unusual about the situation. It was just fashion, and he was an old guy who didn't get fashion. I was confident that I could explain it to him, but he just didn't get it. I brought up various examples, told him about the singer from The Exploited and Wendy O. Williams, the Plasmatics' singer. Guðmundur was silent and just listened indifferently to me. I finally fell silent. The silence became embarrassing. Guðmundur looked at me almost as if he felt sorry for me.

"Isn't it okay?"

"Isn't it okay?" he groaned. "Jón, Jón. What do you think the old ladies who have been shopping here for years, for decades, will say when they see you at the meat counter?"

I hadn't thought about that. Would they care?

"Uhh, I don't know."

Guðmundur shook his head with a sorry expression and then went away. After that, I was taken off the meat counter and put behind helping the meat industry men. After lunch, I was moved down to the warehouse, where I was put moving boxes of bananas around. At the end of the day, Guðmundur asked me to come and talk to him in his office. There he sorrowfully announced that he could not have me at work anymore because of my hairstyle and so he was forced to get some other person to take over my job. He said he was sad about all this, but he made it very clear that he could not justify having me there anymore. This totally flattened me. I didn't expect it. I always thought Guðmundur was a cool guy and so had thought he would just understand. But he did not understand in the slightest.

"You don't need to come back, Jón."

This was a huge disappointment. I'd been fired once again. And I had enjoyed it so much there and felt so good. I had even started to ponder whether maybe my path lay in the meat industry. It was a huge shock. I went away sobbing, got changed into my punk clothes and walked home, stooped down. I was totally devastated. I regretted having shaved my mohawk, and I knew full well that Mom would get angry. But then I also felt that Guðmundur was being unfair and annoying. I was extremely sad and depressed by it all. When I got home, my dad was sitting inside the kitchen listening to the radio and drinking tea. He was in high spirits and said:

"Well, well, how are you?"

After all the disappointment and tension, I broke down and began to cry. My dad was quite taken aback.

"My dear child! What is the matter?"

"They fired me from the meat counter at Glæsibæ," I sighed between sorrowful sobs.

"Now, now, why?" he asked, surprised.

"Because of my haircut."

Dad looked at my haircut but didn't seem to notice anything wrong with it.

"Because of your haircut? What is it about your haircut?"

"They feel that it just isn't okay," I answered and wept.

My father had often said and done things that seemed strange to me and was probably the strangest man I've ever met in my life. But what he did next, I have always felt was the weirdest thing he ever did. He stood up and said:

"Clean yourself up and come with me."

He got his coat on, and we went out in the car and he drove me out to the Suðurver mall. He had clearly already decided on a plan but didn't tell me what it was. He killed the engine right outside, opened the door, and told me to come with him. He went straight into the hair salon. The hairdresser came over to us with a curious expression.

"Good morning."

"Good morning. Don't you have a wig for a kid like this?"

The hairdresser looked at me.

"Yes. What happened to your hair?"

I explained mohawks to her and punk and everything. She had me sit in a chair and brought over a few wigs on plastic heads. Dad chose a thick, reddish brown wig with heavy and large curls.

"This is exactly what his hair was like!"

The wig was nothing like my hair. The hairdresser put the wig on my head and combed it. My father was delighted, but I was skeptical. He was so happy on the way back he hummed the whole way. He felt he had apparently solved the problem very well.

Maybe this wasn't such a stupid idea, after all? Maybe this was absolute genius? This way, I could continue to work at the meat counter, but also be a punk. I would definitely reconsider things; Dad had grown in my opinion. The next day I turned up at Glæsibæ undeterred and revitalized; I went right into Guðmundur's office with the wig in place, excited and full of expectation. Guðmundur was sitting at his desk and looked up when I walked through the door:

"Hi, isn't this good?"

Guðmundur looked at me with amazement and sadness in his eyes. After a while, he said:

"Poor Jón. And I had such high hopes for you."

So ended my career as a meat industry person.

In the spring it came out that I hadn't been going to the school and hadn't learned a thing. Mom had talked to the principal.

"Why don't you attend school, Jón?"

I hated that damn school. I hated the building and everyone inside it. I hated the whole damn group. The principal was hateful and the teachers all idiots. I was apprehensive about going there. When I walked onto the school grounds, I got a knot in my stomach. I felt like I was suffocating. Most of all, though, I despised the Morons who always hit me and bullied me. I'd rather die than go to school. I feared school more than anything else. I felt like there was nothing for me at school. It wasn't there to teach me anything I was interested in learning, and what I was interested in wasn't taught there.

"They're always teasing me," I muttered. It meant nothing to my mom. She didn't get it.

"Just stop talking to those kids."

Stop talking to them? I never spoke to them. They just followed me upstairs. I intended to never go there again.

"I'll never go back to that damn school," I said, resolutely.

"What do you plan to do, then?"

I wanted to go away—anywhere at all, far away from everything—to start over where no one knew me.

"Can't I go to some boarding school?"

"A boarding school? What boarding school?"

I had met a few kids who went to Laugarvatn. It seemed like an extremely enjoyable school.

"I always wanted to go to Laugarvatn."

Mom shook her head.

"You can't go to Laugarvatn. It's too close to Reykjavík."

I didn't know anything about it. I had no idea where Laugarvatn was, whether it was near the city or not. It could very well be out west or far east. But the kids who went there were happy, and no one beat you up.

"Whatever, I'll never go back to this crappy Réttarholt School. I hate it. Can't I just skip school?"

Later that summer, Mom and Dad called me down and asked me to sit with them at the kitchen table.

"I've found a school for you, Jón," said Mom. "We are going to enroll you there this fall."

"What school is that?" I asked.

"Hérað School at Núpur in Dyrafirð."

Núpur in Dyrafirð? I had never heard of it before. What was it? And, what's more, where was it? This sounded exciting. I was happy and looking forward to getting away from everything.

JÓN GNARR was born in 1967 in Reykjavík. As a child, Gnarr was diagnosed with severe mental retardation due to his emotional and learning differences, including dyslexia and ADHD. He nevertheless overcame his hardships and went on to become one of Iceland's most popular actors and comedians.

In the wake of the global economic crisis that devastated Iceland's economy, Gnarr formed the joke Best Party with a number of friends with no background in politics, which parodied Icelandic politics and aimed to make the life of the citizens more fun. Gnarr's Best Party managed a plurality win in the 2010 municipal elections in Reykjavík, and Gnarr became major of Reykjavík.

His term as mayor ended in June 2014, whereupon he served as artist-in-residence at Rice University's Center for Energy and Environmental Research in the Human Sciences in Houston, where he finished work on the final book in his trilogy of childhood memoir-novels: *The Outlaw*.

He plans to use his post-mayor years to continue writing and speaking on the issues that are most important to him: freedom of speech, human rights, protecting the environment, tolerance, compassion, the importance of philosophy, and achieving world peace.

Gnarr currently writes weekly columns for the newspaper *Fréttablaðið* and serves as the head of domestic content for 365 Media in Iceland, overseeing the production of original entertainment in the Icelandic language. His first big project is to produce a television show about a man who runs for mayor of Reykjavík as a joke—and wins. Gnarr, of course, will star as the mayor.

LYTTON SMITH is the author of two collections of poetry, both from Nightboat Books, and several translations from the Icelandic for both Deep Vellum and Open Letter, including Jón Gnarr's *The Indian* (Deep Vellum, 2015), *The Ambassador*, by Bragi Ólafsson (Open Letter, 2010), and *Childreen in Reindeer Woods* by Kristín Ómarsdóttir (Open Letter, 2012). He has received awards from the Poetry Society of America and the Icelandic Literature Fund. He is Assistant Professor of English at SUNY Geneseo in upstate New York.

ALSO AVAILABLE BY JÓN GNARR

The Indian

Gnarr! How I Became the Mayor of a Large City in Iceland and Changed the World

Thank you all for your support. We do this for you, and could not do it without you.

DEEP
VELLUM

DEAR READERS,

Deep Vellum Publishing is a 501c3 nonprofit literary arts organization founded in 2013 with the threefold mission to publish international literature in English translation; to foster the art and craft of translation; and to build a more vibrant book culture in Dallas and beyond. We seek out literary works of lasting cultural value that both build bridges with foreign cultures and expand our understanding of what literature is and what meaningful impact literature can have in our lives.

Operating as a nonprofit means that we rely on the generosity of tax-deductible donations from individual donors, cultural organizations, government institutions, and foundations to provide a of our operational budget in addition to book sales. Deep Vellum offers multiple donor levels, including the LIGA DE ORO and the LIGA DEL SIGLO. The generosity of donors at every level allows us to pursue an ambitious growth strategy to connect readers with the best works of literature and increase our understanding of the world. Donors at various levels receive customized benefits for their donations, including books and Deep Vellum merchandise, invitations to special events, and named recognition in each book and on our website.

We also rely on subscriptions from readers like you to provide an invaluable ongoing investment in Deep Vellum that demonstrates a commitment to our editorial vision and mission. Subscribers are the bedrock of our support as we grow the readership for these amazing works of literature from every corner of the world. The more subscribers we have, the more we can demonstrate to potential donors and bookstores alike the diverse support we receive and how we use it to grow our mission in ever-new, ever-innovative ways.

From our offices and event space in the historic cultural district of Deep Ellum in central Dallas, we organize and host literary programming such as author readings, translator workshops, creative writing classes, spoken word performances, and interdisciplinary arts events for writers, translators, and artists from across the world. Our goal is to enrich and connect the world through the power of the written and spoken word, and we have been recognized for our efforts by being named one of the "Five Small Presses Changing the Face of the Industry" by Flavorwire and honored as Dallas's Best Publisher by *D Magazine*.

If you would like to get involved with Deep Vellum as a donor, subscriber, or volunteer, please contact us at deepvellum.org. We would love to hear from you.

Thank you all. Enjoy reading.

Will Evans
Founder & Publisher
Deep Vellum Publishing

LIGA DE ORO ($5,000+)

Anonymous (2)

LIGA DEL SIGLO ($1,000+)

Allred Capital Management
Ben Fountain
Judy Pollock
Life in Deep Ellum
Loretta Siciliano
Lori Feathers
Mary Ann Thompson-Frenk
   & Joshua Frenk
Matthew Rittmayer
Meriwether Evans
Pixel and Texel
Nick Storch
Stephen Bullock

DONORS

Adam Rekerdres
Alan Shockley
Amrit Dhir
Anonymous
Andrew Yorke
Anthony Messenger
Bob Appel
Bob & Katherine Penn
Brandon Childress
Brandon Kennedy
Caroline Casey
Charles Dee Mitchell
Charley Mitcherson
Cheryl Thompson
Christie Tull
Daniel J. Hale

Ed Nawotka
Rev. Elizabeth
   & Neil Moseley
Ester & Matt Harrison
Grace Kenney
Greg McConeghy
Jeff Waxman
JJ Italiano
Justin Childress
Kay Cattarulla
Kelly Falconer
Linda Nell Evans
Lissa Dunlay
Marian Schwartz
   & Reid Minot
Mark Haber

Mary Cline
Maynard Thomson
Michael Reklis
Mike Kaminsky
Mokhtar Ramadan
Nikki & Dennis Gibson
Patrick Kukucka
Richard Meyer
Steve Bullock
Suejean Kim
Susan Carp
Susan Ernst
Theater Jones
Tim Perttula
Tony Thomson

SUBSCRIBERS

Andrew Strickland
Adam Rekerdres
Aimee Kramer
Amber Appel
Andrew Lemon
Antonia Lloyd-Jones
Ben & Sharon Fountain
Ben Nichols
Bill Fisher
Bob Appel
Bradford Pearson
Caroline West
Charles Dee Mitchell
Cheryl Thompson
Chris Sweet
Ciara McHaney
David Weinberger
Ed Tallent
Elizabeth Caplice
Erin Kubatzky
Frank Merlino
Horatiu Matei
Jeanne Milazzo
Jill Kelly
Joe Milazzo
Joel Garza
John Schmerein
Joshua Edwin
Julie Janicke
Kaleigh Emerson
Kenneth McClain
Lisa Pon

Lissa Dunlay
Lori Feathers
Marcia Lynx Qualey
Margaret Terwey
Martha Gifford
Mary Costello
Meaghan Corwin
Michael Holtmann
Mike Kaminsky
Naomi Firestone-Teeter
Neal Chuang
Nick Oxford
Nikki & Dennis Gibson
Owen Rowe
Patrick Brown
Scot Roberts
Stacey Bristow
Steven Norton
Susan Ernst
Theater Jones
Tim Kindseth
Tom Bowden
Will Pepple
Will Vanderhyden